finding grace

by Allison Green Martin

ISBN-13: 978-0692624944
ISBN-10: 0692624945

Published by Cedar Branch Press
P.O. Box 1094, Conover, NC 28613

Edited by Rachel C. Brown
Cover design by Elizabeth and Cameron Proctor
Original cover concept by Phinthone Senesombath
Cover model: Ava Catherine Pariano

Printed in the United States of America

DEDICATION

For Jane H. Green,
for too many reasons to list.

"But unto every one of us is given grace according to the measure of the gift of Christ."

Ephesians 4:7 King James Version

~1~

Janna Petersen glanced at the clock on the wall of her supervisor's office while she chewed at a hangnail on her index finger. It was unusual for her boss to want to speak with her in private, so she could only assume it had something to do with the Brenner case. Even though everyone kept telling Janna the incident wasn't her fault, her coworkers' pity-filled stares were beginning to feel like accusations.

The creak of the old office door startled Janna as her boss Maxine strode to her desk, coffee mug in one hand and a stack of thick manila folders under the opposite arm. Janna sat up straighter in her chair and adjusted the collar of her blouse while Maxine struggled to set the folders onto her desk without spilling her coffee. Janna's fear of the conversation she felt sure was about to take place kept her from rising to help Maxine with the shuffle of folders.

"Janna," Maxine started, smiling the way all of Janna's coworkers had been smiling at her for the past two months. A smile that effortlessly combined pity, judgment, and thankfulness that it wasn't them going through her situation. "We need to talk."

The understatement of the year. Janna had needed to talk to someone for months now, but no one seemed to be in a hurry to address that until she blew up at the monthly staff meeting yesterday and embarrassed her supervisor.

Maxine opened a file from her stack and adjusted her thick designer knockoff glasses, looking over the file with a sympathetic purse of her lips. "Janna, when you started here seven years ago, you had so much passion for this kind of work. You said you were ready to make a real difference in the world. To really help people. Who are you helping these days?" Maxine laced her fingers together and sighed. "You come to work late at least a few times a week, you're missing important deadlines, and your counselor told me you stopped attending your sessions a month ago."

"They weren't helping," Janna interjected. "All the psychologist wanted to talk about was how the incident made me feel. Why would I want to rehash that over and over? It's done, and there's nothing I can—"

"This is exactly the kind of behavior I'm referring to, Janna." Maxine shook her head. "You're still defensive about what happened when no one even blames you. You're taking it personally when we all know we can't take cases personally. Work is work, and sometimes this kind of work gets messy. If you can't deal with that—"

"I can deal with it." Janna willed the hot tears forming behind her eyes to stay put. "I *am* dealing with it."

Maxine shook her head again. "I think your outburst yesterday proves just the opposite. You're just surviving, Janna. That's not good. For you or your job."

Janna stared at the plaque above Maxine's head. She glared at the words COMMITTED TO EXCELLENCE emblazoned across the award her boss had been presented at the Child Welfare benefit last year. That's all Maxine and Janna's other coworkers cared about—winning awards. For what? Removing a few kids from abusive situations? They weren't making a real difference, and judging from their lack of reaction to the Brenner case, they weren't exactly interested in justice either.

"Janna," Maxine continued, "I say all this, not to condemn you, but to let you know that I understand what you're going through. What happened with the Brenner girl was devastating to us all, but life goes on. There are other children who need our help. In your current state of mind, I feel that you are no longer capable of effectively supporting the continuity of family relationships for the minors within your case load."

Janna leaned forward, expecting to see a copy of the DSS Standards of Practice on top of Maxine's desk. Her boss's little speech could've been ripped straight from its pages. Janna had always thought of Maxine as a friend, but today she definitely exerted her position as Janna's superior. If Maxine was going to fire her, Janna wished she'd just get it over with. She couldn't stomach much more of her boss's policy rhetoric.

Maxine smoothed a dark, tight curl back into her low ponytail. "Janna, we think it'd be in everyone's best interest if you took a leave of absence until September. It'd really give you time to process everything. Away from distractions." She closed the file and looked up at Janna. "A leave of absence *with pay.* It'd be like a vacation really. Give you time to gain a new perspective before you come back to work."

A new perspective was what she needed? Hmph. Maxine meant they all hoped Janna could get over everything that happened with the Brenner case in a neat sixty days and return to work as if it never occurred. *Well, nice try, Maxine.*

Janna responded with a weak, "If that's what you all think is best." She smiled professionally as she stood to leave. At least she'd have what little was left of her dignity after yesterday's meltdown. "If it's okay with you, I'll just gather a few things from my desk before I go."

"Of course."

Janna swallowed the hard lump in her throat. "Thanks." If they were forcing her to leave, at least they couldn't say she'd made it hard for them.

She turned and headed toward the door to Maxine's office. As Janna's hand reached for the doorknob, Maxine cleared her throat. Janna stiffened her back.

"And Janna, I really hope you'll take this time to reflect and let go of the guilt you've been carrying around. I'd love to see the idealistic, exuberant woman I met seven years ago make a return. Only this time you should tell her to remove her cape first."

Janna thought it'd be in poor taste to pretend to gag on her own finger, so she settled for rolling her eyes while her back was to Maxine as she strode out the door.

As she walked back to the work area she shared with her coworker, Nate, Janna wiggled her head and mimicked Maxine in a nasal voice. "Tell her to remove her cape first."

She huffed, plopping down into her desk chair. "Sheesh. Where does she get that stuff?"

Nate looked up from his computer. "Who? Maxine?"

"Yes." Janna shook her head. "The woman has more one-liners than a bad afterschool special." She pulled an empty file box out from underneath her desk and began packing up the few personal items she kept on top of her desk.

"She just cares about you, Janna. We all do." Nate smiled warmly at her, exposing the dimple in his left cheek. "I'm assuming she told you to take a leave of absence. Like I've been begging you to."

Janna blew out a long breath. "Well, I guess you got your wish." She rolled out the large file cabinet drawer on the bottom of her desk and retrieved the stack of files related to the Brenner case, stealthily sliding them into the file box as well. No one would miss them for now.

Nate left his desk and walked around to Janna, propping his backside against the top rim of her desk. "You act like I want you to leave and never come back."

He placed his hand gently on her shoulder, but she jerked away and stood up, slipping her purse strap over her head and across one shoulder. She put the lid on the file box and held it in front of her body, creating some space. "Listen,

Nate. We tried to make this work, but I think we've both realized that dating a coworker, especially in this line of work, is a bad idea. It might be better if you didn't call me for a while, at least until I figure out what I'm going to do. I'm sorry."

Nate stared at her dumbfounded. They'd been dating for a couple of months. The truth was Janna had needed a good-looking distraction from all the emotions she was dealing with during the Brenner case, and Nate's tall, dark, and handsome looks had fit the bill. He had tried to be there for her—she'd always be grateful to him for that—but Janna had given up on the idea of a lasting relationship years ago.

"Okay," was all Nate said as he walked back to his desk like a scolded child. "Suit yourself, Janna. But you might discover the one thing you need right now is a friend. If you change your mind, let me know."

Although Nate had never been the target of her passive aggression in the past, she'd definitely seen the crushed look in his eyes before. *Why would she even think of that?* It was a lifetime ago, but she was pretty sure her flight response was the same as it'd always been.

Janna walked to the elevator and pressed the button. Where could she run now? She'd been avoiding home for a long time, always creating some excuse for why she couldn't

11

visit her parents. She knew how much it hurt them, especially her mom, but it had been too hard to go back after what happened. Every year that passed made it even easier for Janna to pretend the life she once had there was just a distant dream.

As she stepped into the elevator and pressed the first floor button, she shifted the cardboard box of belongings onto her hip and thought about the girl Maxine had described. At 22, Janna *had* believed in things, in people's ability to change with the right motivation and education, and had thought she could make a difference. At 29, her perspective had become jaded by too many cases like the Brenners'. Too many circumstances out of her capacity to help; too many situations out of her control.

A warm coastal breeze tousled her hair and the salt in the air stung her contacts as she exited the building and walked to her car. After she slid the box of files onto her passenger seat and closed the door beside her, Janna stared out the window of her Acura. She reached up and twirled the glass butterfly suncatcher hanging from her rearview mirror. Where else could she go? She'd just burned the only bridge she had left.

Flipping on the switch to her internal autopilot, Janna started the car and drove back to her apartment complex. Her body felt heavy as she climbed the stairs to 2B, the weight of her situation finally catching up to her as she unlocked her front door. Instead of hanging her keys and purse up on the hooks in the entryway, she dropped them on the floor by the file box before walking back to her bedroom and flopping down onto the bed. She stared up at the white popcorn ceiling. *What now, Lord?*

Since Janna and God hadn't exactly been on speaking terms the past few months, she knew it was a pretty weak cry for help, but it couldn't hurt.

A few minutes later, she sat up and glanced around her bedroom. The clean lines of her furniture and the stark white of the walls and bedding had always been relaxing to Janna, but today it looked more like a high-class padded room. If she had to stay there for sixty days, she'd go nuts.

Jerking herself from the bed, she walked to the closet and flung open the doors. Moving quickly so she wouldn't have time to think, she grabbed an armful of her favorite outfits and a couple pairs of high heels and laid them in a neat pile on her bed. Where she was going no one would care what she was wearing, but it was important to Janna that she looked put together.

She flew to the bathroom, filled a makeup bag with all the essentials, and shoved some other toiletries into a Ziploc bag. After throwing both bags on the bed next to her clothes, she dropped to her knees and retrieved her rolling suitcase from underneath the bed. She folded the clothes—hangers and all—in half and pressed them into the suitcase. Tossing the shoes and toiletries on top, she zipped up the suitcase and rolled it to the front door.

It was probably rude to show up unannounced on her parents' doorstep, but if she called her mother, her return to town would be on the evening news. Besides, they'd probably be so glad to see her, they'd forgive her for surprising them.

Janna made sure to grab the box of case files on the way out the door and loaded everything into the hatchback of her car. She pealed out of her driveway and headed toward Highway 17. Telling herself she had five hours to change her mind, she rolled down her windows, cranked up her radio, and set her cruise control to five over the speed limit. It was time to face what she'd been avoiding the past seven years. It was time to go home.

~2~

Night had begun to remove its indigo bruise from the sky as Deputy Sheriff Cade Thompson stared through the slats of his bedroom mini blinds. He rubbed the sleep from his eyes and reminded himself that taking an early morning phone call from a lonely old widow was part of his duty.

"I heard this loud racket coming from the pantry. Sounded like someone looking through things." Mrs. Keever's voice trembled. "You think someone would break into my house to steal food?"

Cade walked to his dresser, pulled out a dark grey t-shirt from the top drawer, and slipped it on over his head. "Mrs. Keever, are you sure it couldn't have been your cat chasing after something?"

"You're right. It's probably nothing. If that's all it is, I hate to ask you to drive all the way over here for somethin' so silly. But, you know, since I'm a woman, and I live alone—" She paused for effect. "I might be a prime target for hoodlums."

Oh, great. She's been watching America's Most Wanted again.

"I just haven't felt safe in this big 'ole house since Check died." Her voice cracked at the mention of her late husband.

Man, she knew how to make a guy feel like a bum. Cade thought losing an extra hour of sleep to go over to Mrs. Keever's now might save him from the nagging of a guilty conscience all day.

"I'll tell you what, Mrs. Keever. I'm getting dressed right now, and I'll be over in about fifteen minutes." Cade held the phone between his ear and his shoulder as he pulled on a pair of jeans. "Do you think you can hold off the . . . uh . . . 'perp' until then?"

Ignoring Cade's rude comment, Mrs. Keever transformed her tone from that of a distraught widow to excited hostess. "Oh, good. I'll have some homemade banana bread waiting for you when you get here. You like your coffee black, don't you?"

Once she discovered she'd be having company, Mrs. Keever seemed to forget a psychotic killer waited to assault her in the pantry.

"Yes, ma'am, black coffee is fine. I'll see you in a little bit, okay?" He hung up the phone and cursed himself for being such a pushover.

Cade's stomach growled its frustration as he headed downstairs to make a quick breakfast. As tasty as Mrs. Keever's banana bread was, it certainly wasn't as hearty as his usual morning meal. He pulled down a cast-iron skillet from the cabinet and grabbed a carton of eggs from the door of the refrigerator. The crack of the eggs over the pan broke the silence in the still house, and the scrape of the wooden spoon across the skillet brought him some strange comfort. After scooping the scrambled eggs onto one of his mother's ivy-covered dishes, he sat down at the table and shoveled each forkful into his mouth like someone might take it.

When he was finished, he walked over to the big farmhouse sink to wash his plate and fork before placing them into the empty dish rack. He made a mental note to stop by the grocery store sometime this weekend before he grabbed his keys from the counter and locked the back door behind him.

The gravel popped under the tires of his Jeep Wrangler as he backed out of the driveway and eased onto the road. The morning sun lit its flame above the horizon while he drove the short mile to Mrs. Keever's house.

It took little time to discover the strange noises had originated from Mrs. Keever's new kitten, Muffin. Her first attempt at shrubbery propulsion had gone awry—evidenced by the decorative ficus tree in the corner, now laying on its side, and several cans of cat food scattered across the pantry floor. A feat witnessed firsthand when the kitten attempted another jump from the tree's overturned container once Cade made his way into Mrs. Keever's pantry.

He massaged a kink from the back of his neck. "You didn't tell me Mitzi had a litter, Mrs. Keever."

The fluffy grey-blue kitten wandered away from her launching pad and pranced over to her owner. Mrs. Keever's knees popped as she bent down to stroke the small cat's head. Cade offered his hand to steady her as she wobbled trying to stand back up.

Mrs. Keever shook her head and cinched in the belt on her flower-covered housecoat. "Well, she was the only one that survived. Born too early, the poor things. But look . . ." Her face brightened as she fixed her gaze upon the newest addition to her feline family. "She's a feisty little thing, isn't she?"

They watched as the kitten shifted her predilection from houseplants to footwear, throwing her body down at Cade's feet and playing with his shoelaces.

"Maybe you should keep the pantry door closed from now on, Mrs. Keever." Cade scooped the kitten up and placed it in her arms. "I guess I'll be heading out now. Do you need anything else?"

"Oh. You have to go already? You just got here."

"Yeah, well, with all the 4th of July festivities going on this weekend, I should head to the station soon."

Mrs. Keever looked past Cade at the solitary steaming mug of coffee sitting on the kitchen table. "But you haven't even touched your coffee yet, and I still owe you a slice of banana bread for your trouble."

Would it kill him to humor the poor woman? He walked to the table, picked up the mug, and gulped down a big mouthful of the dark liquid. It took every shred of manners within him not to wince when he realized it was a little stronger brew than he'd been expecting. Mrs. Keever must've still been getting used to making coffee for one.

Cade pounded his chest with his fist, choking back a cough. A bitter aftertaste lingered in his throat. "Whew, nothing like a strong cup of Joe to get you going in the morning." He tried to look pleased. "I really appreciate your hospitality, Mrs. Keever, but I need to be going."

"Well, if I can't persuade you to stay and have a piece of my famous banana bread, I can at least wrap up the loaf and send it with you for the other boys at the station." She winked at Cade and pulled a roll of pink saran wrap from one of the cabinets, properly packaging up the banana bread for her guest.

Cade didn't know how he'd be able to leave if he didn't accept her gift. Last week, when the mysterious noises were coming from the guest bedroom, it took him nearly an hour to explain he would never be able to eat a whole German chocolate cake by himself. He eventually gave in and put it in the break room at work. The week before that, a batch of warm cinnamon rolls rewarded him for his hard-hitting detective work. It'd be best to save himself the trouble and just thank Mrs. Keever for her kindness.

"Boy, the guys at the station are going to be awfully glad to see me stroll in there with this delicious banana bread. Thank you." He eased backward in the direction of the front door. "Officer Myers told me last week your German chocolate cake was the best he'd ever tasted."

"Oh, well, I try." Mrs. Keever followed Cade out to his car. "Thank you for stopping by. I feel much safer now that you've checked everything out."

"No problem, Mrs. Keever. You just let me know if you have any other issues arise, and I'll send someone out here to look in on you."

Mrs. Keever returned to her porch and waved goodbye until Cade backed out of the driveway and her line of sight. Even though it was a hassle, he felt good about checking on Mrs. Keever. It occurred to him he was probably the only person who ever came to see her on a regular basis. Her husband died two years ago of a sudden heart attack. Their only daughter ran away from home sixteen years before that. Cade imagined the loneliness she must be feeling. He was becoming an expert in that himself.

Driving past a few of his neighbors' homes, Cade dialed his friend Brian's number. "Hey man, you and Stacy need me to bring anything tonight?"

"Nah, we've got it covered." Brian paused and cleared his throat. "So . . . I guess you know she's back in town."

"Yeah, I heard she was home for awhile." Cade cradled the phone on his shoulder, putting both hands on the steering wheel. "Tell Stacy not to get any crazy ideas about inviting her, though."

Brian laughed. "I always try to make sure no crazy ideas ever enter her lovely little head."

"Okay man, see you tonight." Cade pressed the END button on his cell phone and slowed the vehicle, turning right beside Dellinger's Farm and Dairy.

He noticed the Dellingers' corn crop had been affected by the tremendous drought the town had been experiencing. Although the tops were still dark green, the bottoms of the stalks were a dry mustard color, and striations of yellow and brown streaked the leaves.

Many of the stalks were bent over in the middle, some laying flat to the ground like they'd been wounded in a battle with the sun. A bad sign for the summer harvest. He continued to drive by several acres of dying corn stalks. Since all the mills around Shady Grove had closed, the town had learned to thrive on agribusiness alone, but if the crops didn't produce, the farmers wouldn't make any money.

Cade glanced back into the rearview mirror, stealing one last look at the Dellingers' fields. Something strange caught his eye. He slammed his foot hard on the brakes, causing his vehicle to swerve to one side. The smell of burnt rubber filled the air, while Cade's mind ran wild for a moment. *Were his eyes were playing tricks on him?* Shifting to reverse, he backed up to get a better look.

A little girl walked alongside the road by the cornfield, running her fingers over the middle of the dry stalks as she took each step. Cade put the car in park and studied the girl as she continued to walk close to the road, still touching each stalk like she was counting them in her head. What would a little girl be doing out here at this hour of the morning? He turned off the engine and pulled the key out of the ignition.

Switching on his emergency blinkers, Cade climbed out of the vehicle and called to the little girl. "Hey, what are you doin' out here?"

The little girl turned around and stuck her chin out, squinting to see who had called to her. Maybe she didn't hear him.

"What are you doing out here?" Cade repeated as he crossed the road and walked toward the little girl.

He guessed she was five or six years old. The stains on her flower-speckled sundress and the dirt on her tiny feet made it obvious she had not been wearing shoes during her early morning trek through Mr. Dellinger's cornfields. She stood motionless, staring intensely at Cade. She still hadn't answered his question.

He squatted beside her, trying a more friendly approach. "Hey there, I'm Cade. What's your name?"

She silently studied Cade's face, keeping a solemn expression on her own.

Maybe she couldn't speak. Maybe she was deaf. Maybe men made her nervous. A hundred other scenarios cycled through Cade's mind while he tried to think of a reason to explain why she was out here and why she wouldn't answer him.

"Uh, can you talk? Can you tell me your name? It's okay. I just want to help you."

Another silent stare.

Cade stood and looked around, checking both sides of the road for any vehicles pulled off on the shoulder. Her family may have been driving and stopped for a stretch break out there or something.

He pulled his cell phone from his pocket and dialed the number to the police station. No one answered. After the eighth ring, Cade gave up. He figured only a few rookies would be working today. It would be "all hands on deck" tomorrow, so most of the senior officers had taken part of the day off for the 4th of July weekend.

Cade had intended to make a lazy day of it as well, but his boss had asked him to drop by the station for a few hours to make sure things were going okay. He figured he might as well do what he could to find the little girl's family until he could pass off the case to someone on duty. He wanted to stop in town and visit his dad later, anyway.

"I guess I could check the county's missing persons reports to see if anyone is looking for you, huh?" Cade scanned the little girl once more to see if he could come up with something distinguishing about her appearance.

Her long, light blonde hair fell well past her shoulders—the ends tangled, like she'd been running around in the wind. Her violet eyes matched the flowers on her dirt-smudged sundress. They looked deep into Cade's like they knew him.

The sunlight bounced off something on her wrist, making it flash. Cade bent down again, gently taking her hand to get a closer look. A small charm bracelet dangled from her wrist. A heart with the word *Grace* etched into its silver center hung from the clasp.

"Is that your name? You're Grace?" Cade stood up and squinted down into the girl's petite face.

She looked up and smiled, revealing a slight gap between her two front teeth. She placed her small hand into Cade's palm and squeezed it.

"I'll take that as a yes then, Grace. Come on, I'm taking you to the station to see if we can find out where you came from. Unless you can tell me." He hoped one last effort on his part would make her communicate.

Grace smiled again but said nothing.

***

Cade pulled up outside the police station and looked at Grace, who had ridden in silence the entire way there. Not so much as a sniff. He walked around the other side of the car, opened the door, and unbuckled her seatbelt.

"C'mon." He lifted Grace out of the seat and carried her through the station entrance. "Let's see if we can find out a little more about you."

"Mornin' Cade," chirped the station's receptionist Pam. She sounded out of breath and was too busy trying to shove an oversized purse into her bottom desk drawer to look up.

Cade leaned forward and placed Grace on top of the counter above Pam's desk. Pam took a second look at the merchandise in Cade's arms. The look on her face said he'd better explain himself.

"Pam, this is Grace. I found her wandering the cornfield at the Dellingers' this morning. I tried calling here first to let you know, but no one answered." He smirked, hoping she caught onto the implication that she fell short of her responsibilities.

"It's been a rough morning." Pam looked like she wanted to add more clever banter, but Cade didn't want to waste any time finding Grace's family.

He spoke again before she could come back at him with a retort. "Hey, do you think you could watch her for a few minutes while I try to find out where she came from? She needs some shoes, too."

"Sure." Pam stood up and walked around her desk. Cade could always count on her to be helpful, especially if it meant she didn't have to sit there waiting for the phone to ring. The bracelets on Pam's wrist clinked together as she offered her hand to Grace. "I don't know what I can do about shoes, little miss, but I'm sure I can find you a morning snack in the break room. Are ya hungry?"

Grace looked at Pam and smiled but then raised her eyebrows and bit her lower lip. It seemed she wanted Cade's permission before accepting completely.

"It's alright, Grace. Pam will take real good care of you, okay? I'll just go see if anyone has missed you yet. I'll be right back."

Cade looked around as he walked back to his desk through the unusually quiet station and suddenly felt resentful.

Just once, he'd like to have a whole day off without having to do anything for anyone else. He listened to Pam chatter at Grace as they walked to the station break room and tried to snap out of his mood.

Selfish thinking would only make him bitter. The one deputy at the station without a family, he seemed a natural candidate for the expectation of handling more than the other officers. He consoled himself with the thought he'd avoided street patrol downtown today, where he figured most of the newbies were.

Plus, he had Brian and Stacy's barbeque that night, which promised to be an interesting time. Stacy was always trying to fix him up with one of her flaky, superficial friends. Although Cade never acted on her promptings, there was something extremely entertaining about watching grown women fawn all over someone like a pack of middle school girls. It was a mindless sort of fun and a nice distraction from the burden of his day-to-day.

Cade plopped down in his desk chair and logged into his computer, then into the county's missing persons database. He typed "Grace" into the search box next to "First

Name." *No matches found* blinked at him from the screen. Not too surprising for a county as small as theirs.

He clicked on "File a Report" and began filling out a description of the little girl before an awful thought occurred to him. Experience had taught him things weren't always as clear-cut as they initially seemed. Her family may have dumped her off in the cornfield. If that were the case, advertising her discovery wouldn't be the most effective way to locate them.

Cade stretched his arms and exhaled through clenched teeth, considering how someone could just abandon a little girl on the side of the road. Before he could decide how this would affect finding out whom she belonged to, Pam returned with Grace in tow.

"Any luck?" She leaned over to catch a glimpse of the computer screen. Cade looked at Grace, her dirt-smeared face now covered in powdered donut crumbs as well.

Cade gave Pam a crooked smile. "I see you found her something healthy for breakfast."

"Hey. That's all we have back there, except for coffee. I brought a cup for you." Pam placed a steaming styrofoam cup on his desk. A warm, rich aroma emanated from its mouth filling the air around Cade's desk.

"It's fine." Cade laughed. "Thanks for watching her."

"Sure thing, hon. What'd you find out?"

Cade shook his head. "Nothing. Either no one knows she's missing yet, or they were the ones who helped her disappear."

"I should call Social Services and see if we can find somewhere for her to stay while you keep looking for whomever it is she belongs to." Pam turned to walk back to her desk.

"Wait a minute, Pam. I'd like to speak with them myself and see if they know who Grace is. Those social workers deal with the same families over and over again, so if they recognize her description, they may know who Grace's parents are."

"Why don't you call over to the health department and see if Teresa is there?" Pam called out the telephone number.

Cade dialed and waited for an answer.

A droll voice provided his greeting, "Chatfield County Social Services."

"Yes, is Teresa Williams in?"

"She's on a call, sir."

He let out a breath. "Any idea when she'll be back?"

"No, sir. I just answer the phones here. I don't keep tabs on the employees." She made no effort to disguise the

30

irritation in her voice. "If it's an emergency, you can try the hospital."

"Alright, I'll try over there. Could you have Teresa call me when she gets in please?"

"Yeah, sure."

"Thank you."

He clicked the receiver with his index finger and punched some numbers into the phone again. "I'll try the hospital's social worker," he said.

Pam looked down at Grace and stroked the hair back from the little girl's forehead. Cade watched as Grace looked up at her momentarily but then became distracted by a piece of loose string on her dress. He could feel the tension forming between his brows as he listened to the hospital receptionist explain that the social worker was on vacation.

"Uh huh." He fiddled with the extension cord. "Do you know who I could call since she took the day off for the holiday?"

He felt Pam staring at him. Her curiosity was rarely tempered with patience, so he expected it killed her he didn't put the call on speaker.

"Thank you anyway." Cade rubbed his forehead in frustration and hung up the phone.

Teresa might not be back in the office for a few hours and by then Grace's family may have already left town. He needed someone trained to deal with this sort of thing.

Pam seemed to read his mind. "You know who you *could* call, don't you?" The kind-hearted receptionist was stepping into dangerous territory. "She's a social worker."

"Yeah, in Wilmington. Not here." Cade avoided looking at Pam's face.

Even though the person Pam referred to could probably help, Cade wasn't sure he felt ready to make that call.

"I'm just saying, she could probably help you. Besides, you two can't avoid each other forever, Cade."

Pam had been looking out for Cade since his days as a rookie. But when it came to this area of his life, he preferred it when she kept her opinions to herself.

"Don't you have some phones to answer?" he said.

Pam raised an eyebrow. "Mm, hmm." Not one to be outdone, she added, "You're exactly right. You need a little privacy to make this call. I'll be at my desk."

Cade put his hands behind his head and huffed out a sigh. Pam sauntered to the other side of the station, while Grace climbed up to sit on top of his desk, swinging her dirt-covered legs over the edge.

Cade stared at the phone. What if he couldn't reach Teresa Williams at Social Services? How big of a deal would it be if he put off the search for Grace's parents until next week? She could just stay with him at the farmhouse this weekend. Although he didn't know how to take care of a child.

There was Brian's wife, Stacy. She loved kids. Maybe Grace could stay at Brian's house.

Cade battled with his conscience. He didn't have to call *her*. He could just send Grace to stay with Stacy and Brian. The rest could wait until Monday. Or better yet, he could turn the case over to someone else.

Don't be a coward, Thompson. It happened seven years ago. Let it go, be a man, and deal with it. His conscience should have been a lawyer.

He reminded himself this wasn't about some personal wound to his ego; it was about Grace. A little girl who needed to find her family—the helpless victim depending on Cade to prevail in his mission.

His pulse quickened as he dialed a number he'd memorized long ago. "Why do I have the feeling I'm going to regret this?" He looked over at Grace.

She smiled.

~3~

Janna was drowning. Deep under water, her lungs felt as though they may burst. Her air supply diminished with each passing second. Every time she swam toward the light above her, waves pounded over her head and slammed her back into the place with no air. Over and over she tried to make her way to the surface, but the water churned around her, making it impossible to escape. She wanted to cry out, but her lungs would fill with water. Making one final attempt to get to the light, she could see someone's hands above her. She reached out to grab them, but instead of taking her hands and pulling her out of the water, the hands shoved her down and held her there. The water grew darker around her. Struggle as she might, she could not free herself from those lead-filled hands. Hands pushing her away from life and into unconsciousness.

The phone rang, startling Janna awake and saving her from the same nightmare she'd been having for weeks. She slid into an upright position and gasped in fresh air. The phone rang again.

She grappled for her cell phone on the bedside table. "H . . . huh . . . llo?"

No answer.

She cleared her throat. "Hello?"

Silence.

She jerked the cell phone from her face and studied the screen. A third ring—but this time she could tell the sound came from downstairs. She reclined against her pillow and took another deep breath, remembering where she was. *Mom and Dad's phone.*

She'd gotten in so late the night before, she'd barely had time to say hello to her parents and drag her suitcase upstairs before she collapsed onto her old bed and pulled the soft Chenille bedspread over her head.

Despite the fact she could have used a few more hours of sleep, she laid still, her eyes closed, listening to her mother's slightly muffled voice on the phone. The walls in this house had always been paper-thin.

"Oh, hello." Her mother sounded surprised. "I'm fine. How are you? Janna? Yes, hang on a moment. I'll see if she's up yet."

Oh, great. Maxine had called, and her mother told her what a lazy slob she was, sleeping in until ten. Janna thought "vacation" meant she wouldn't have to hear from anyone at work. They hadn't even given her a day.

A soft knock on the door interrupted her thoughts.

Her mother Julia cracked the door open. "Honey, someone is on the phone for you."

"Who is it, Mom?" Janna ran her fingers through her hair and tried to shake the grogginess from her mind.

"I asked him to hold until you came downstairs." Her mother's voice trailed off down the stairs.

Him? She didn't remember giving Nate her parents' number, but maybe he'd asked Maxine for it. She rarely mentioned her parents when they spent time together, but he'd probably assumed she'd go there for a while before she'd sit moping in her apartment.

Janna pushed back the bedspread and sat up to collect herself before she headed downstairs. She glanced down at her right arm. Small, red marks dotted the circumference of her bicep. She pulled her arm closer for a better look and ran her hand across the smooth, rounded marks. They looked like her fingerprints. She must have been gripping her arm in her sleep. Or maybe the hands holding her underwater in the dream belonged to her.

"Janna, honey, he's waiting," her mother called from the foot of the stairs.

Dissecting her nightmare would have to wait. Janna padded softly down the stairs to the kitchen. Her mom stood chatting with the caller on the other end of the line.

"Here she is," her mother said, putting her hand over the mouthpiece as she passed the phone to Janna.

Who is it? Janna mouthed. She took the receiver and pulled the phone to her ear.

Instead of answering, her mother led Janna's father away from the island in the kitchen, where he sat reading the newspaper, and into the other room. From the television on the counter, Janna could hear Dr. Phil blasting some poor loser for his life choices and reached over to click it off before she offered her greeting to the person on the phone.

"Hello?" Janna held her breath waiting for the mystery to be revealed.

"Janna? Hi, it's uh . . ." The caller heaved a small sigh. "Uh, it's Cade, Janna. I realize this may be a bad time, with you visiting your parents and it being a holiday tomorrow and everything, but I could really use your help with a situation

37

here at the police station." His words poured out like he was in a race to empty them from his mouth.

Janna listened as he switched over to officer mode and filled her in on the circumstances of a little girl's arrival at the station.

"You're a social worker, right?"

He already knew the answer to that question or he wouldn't have called her. And how had he known she was home?

"You handle cases like this all the time, I'll bet."

Janna responded with silence, so Cade continued to plead his case.

"Listen, Janna, I think maybe Grace would talk to you. You've always been good with kids. I . . . well . . . I think if she could tell you how she ended up at the Dellingers' and we could find her family, she wouldn't have to stay in some stranger's house for the night."

Janna could hear the compassion in Cade's voice but hesitated to get involved in another child neglect case.

"Um, Cade, I don't know." She ran the edge of her thumbnail across her bottom teeth. "I don't . . . I mean, I'm kind of out of that line of work, at least while I'm here I guess."

Janna grimaced, aware her statement contained too many holes, but she didn't feel like explaining and hoped Cade wouldn't notice.

"Please Janna." The familiar resonance of his voice softened her reserve. "I need your help."

This was the first time she and Cade had spoken in the past seven years. Seeing him again, after all this time, was a completely different proposition. After all that happened between them, she knew it would be difficult to carry on a normal conversation with him, but maybe if there was something to work on, someone to help, it might be a little more comfortable. If nothing else, it would give them common ground.

"Uh, hello? Janna?"

"Can you give me half an hour to get ready?" Janna slapped her forehead. "I arrived last night, so I'm not even unpacked or anything."

She confirmed the exact time she would be arriving at the station and looked up in time to observe her mother's attempt to reenter the kitchen without being noticed. She watched with amused indignation as her mother glided over to a stack of cookbooks on the counter and pretended to flip through a couple of them. She would want a full report of her daughter's conversation with Cade the second it ended.

"I appreciate your willingness to help me out. I know you didn't come home to work." His tone carried a hint of conflict.

"I'm not promising I'll be able to help at all, but I'll see what I can do."

"I'll see you in a few minutes, Janna. Thanks."

"Okay. Bye." Janna placed the phone back into its cradle with a soft click.

Her mother abandoned her pretend recipe hunt and turned around, studying Janna's face with an annoying exuberance. "What did he say, Jan? Does he want to see you?"

"Mom," Janna dragged out the word slowly and pointedly. "Did you tell anyone I was back in town?"

Her mother shrugged, avoiding Janna's eyes. "I may have mentioned it to a few of my friends, and your girlfriend Stacy."

Janna huffed and rolled her eyes. "Mom."

Her mother continued, undeterred. "This is a good chance for you and Cade to talk. Seven years is too long to avoid someone you were so close to, Janna. As much as we've loved visiting you at the beach, your father and I have been praying for God to find a way to bring you back home where you belong. God's giving you both a second chance so you can make things right again."

Here it comes. Janna put her face in her hands, trying to keep her thoughts from slipping out of her mouth. "Mom, you know the only reason I haven't been back before now is because things have been so crazy at work, and I've had . . . I've . . ."

"Been *busy*. I know." Her mother put her hands on Janna's shoulders.

Janna looked up and met her mother's eyes.

"I know your job demands a lot, but we both know that's not the reason you haven't been back here before now. From what little I've been able to coax out of you the past few years, I know you and Cade hit some sort of rough patch before you left. Your father and I always tried to give you space because we knew things were tough on you when that happened. We knew it would be difficult for you to return home for a while. All I'm trying to say is maybe there's a reason you're here now. Don't try so hard to control everything. You might be pleasantly surprised with what God hands you."

Janna shook her head and pushed her hair behind her ears. "Okaaay, Mom . . . I can't talk about this right now. I have to go down to the police station. They found a little girl out in the Dellingers' field. Cade needs me to help them find out what happened to her. I've got to shower, get dressed, and be over there in thirty minutes."

"A little girl? Is she okay? Who would leave a child at the Dellingers'?"

Janna shot her mother a withering look. Her message translated loud and clear.

"Towels are in the closet in the hallway." Janna's mother leaned forward and kissed her on the forehead. "Tell Cade we said 'Hello.'"

Her mother began humming as Janna left the kitchen and climbed the stairs to the hall closet. She grabbed a couple of towels and headed for the shower, hoping the steamy water could refresh her weary spirit and clear her mind.

***

Janna drove down Main Street, passing rows of dilapidated storefronts and going-out-of-business signs. The stores that were still going strong sported red, white, and blue banners from every available window. However, so few people trafficked the sidewalks, no one would have known it was a holiday weekend.

As the Shady Grove Police Department came into sight, Janna switched on the radio to get her mind off the gnawing in her stomach.

A country star with a deep twang offered her some advice about why you can't go home again. Janna punched the power button. Maybe silence would be better.

A parking spot farthest from the police station entrance would be her best choice. She didn't want to run into Cade any earlier than she felt prepared to handle, nor did she want him to see her coming.

Why did she agree to do this? She was probably the last person Cade wanted to see. Why did he call then, if he didn't want to see her? A few other thoughts ping-ponged through Janna's mind.

She gripped the steering wheel with both hands, bracing herself for emotional impact, and pushed all the air out of her lungs. She needed a release from the mounting pressure in her chest.

"Janna, you can do this." She pulled down the visor and checked her appearance in the mirror. No smudged mascara. *Check.* No wacky hairs standing up on end. *Check.* She smoothed down her imaginary flyaways once more and popped the visor back into its original position. She climbed out of the car and pressed the keyless locking device on her key chain. The alarm sensor on her Acura beeped its "good luck" as she walked to the front door of the station.

Janna's heart began to race. She resisted the urge to turn around and run back to her car like a frightened child. Taking one last cleansing breath of courage, Janna pulled the door open and walked into the station. It had been a long time since she had been there, but everything still looked like a bigger version of the police station on *The Andy Griffith Show*.

She jumped as the heavy door slammed behind her.

Pam McClain's face peeked around the side of the counter encircling the receptionist's desk. Janna's amused expression must have let Pam know she'd been discovered because she jerked herself out of sight.

Janna swallowed a nervous laugh. She had always liked Pam.

Her heels clicked loudly on the old tile floor as she walked to the front desk. She wished she'd had something more casual to wear, but she'd packed in such a hurry. Anyway, work attire would help her stay in professional mode once she saw Cade.

Janna reached the counter and felt relieved to see Pam's back facing her. The receptionist appeared to be checking emails. Janna adjusted her handbag on her shoulder and cleared her throat, trying to remember her manners as she stood facing the front desk.

"Excuse me, Mrs. McClain?"

"Oh, my!" Pam turned around a little too dramatically and placed a hand over her heart. "You can't be little Janna Petersen. Look at you! You were a child when I saw you last. My, what a lovely young woman you grew up to be."

"Thank you." Janna laughed at Pam's less than subtle theatrics, feeling more at ease. Janna knew the warm-hearted receptionist must have been aware of her impending visit, but she thought it was sweet of her to make a fuss.

Pam rose from her seat and walked around her desk. "Give me a hug, honey. I haven't seen you in ages."

Her motherly show of affection calmed Janna's nerves even more. "I'll bet your mama is tickled pink you're back home where you belong."

"Oh . . . well." Janna pulled away politely from Pam's embrace. "I'm sure she is glad to have me home for a *visit*."

"We're all glad, aren't we Cade?" Pam glanced around Janna, giving her little warning of his arrival.

"Hey, Janna." Cade's voice sounded steady and sure.

Janna hesitated to turn around. A sense of dread crept over her, but she put a pleasant smile on her face and turned around to confront the biggest part of her history in this town.

Thick, sandy brown hair. Blue eyes. A smattering of freckles across his nose that gave him a boyish look, despite his 30 years of age. There was something comforting about the fact his appearance hadn't changed much. He was a little more muscular now, but his face remained the same.

Judging from the way he seemed to be taking her in right now, she realized how different she must look to him after all this time. Luckily, through a strict diet and running regimen, she'd been able to maintain her slim figure, but she knew the sharp contrast to her former self was evident in the short, straight hair that replaced the soft blonde ringlets of her youth.

She allowed her eyes to pierce Cade's for a moment and wondered what he was thinking.

Pam's voice splintered the awkward silence hanging thick in the air between them. "I guess you should probably meet Grace. Sweetest little thing. Won't say a word to anyone. Although, she has taken quite a shine to Cade. You know, it seems like children always recognize a kind person when they meet one."

Cade's hand appeared to jerk back on its own. A petite girl emerged from behind his leg, holding onto his thumb.

Cade scooped the child up, bringing her eye level with Janna. It was almost uncomfortable the way she stared into Janna's eyes.

"Grace, this is Janna. She's going to try to help us find out what happened to you."

Grace smiled. She reminded Janna of the Brenner girl.

"Hello, Grace. Can you tell us why you, er . . . how you, uh . . ." Janna's mind went blank. Something unnerved her about the way the girl looked so intensely at her. Cade didn't seem to be bothered by it, so why should she?

She took a deep breath and sorted through her thoughts. "Were you playing out in Mr. Dellinger's field this morning?"

Grace nodded, her tiny face perking with a smile before she wriggled down from Cade's arms to the floor. Janna exchanged confused looks with Cade and Pam. Grace walked over to the window behind Cade's desk and pointed outside. They all followed her.

"I found you outside?" Cade shrugged his shoulders. "Is that what you're trying to tell us?"

47

Grace shoved her finger at the windowpane again, indicating an error in Cade's guess. This time she pointed toward the clouds and peered back at Janna.

"Are you pointing to the sun? Did someone leave you to play in the cornfield this morning?" Janna snapped her fingers. "Or, do you mean it wasn't daytime? Someone left you last night?"

Janna bit her lower lip. She had a theory behind Grace's sudden interest outside the window. She lowered her voice so only Cade and Pam would hear. "You know, sometimes when children have been through something traumatic, they go into shock, and because it's too difficult for them to talk about, they find other ways to communicate. If someone did leave her out there to fend for herself, she may be repressing some feelings of fear or abandonment. It's possible she is able to speak, but she can't articulate what happened to her yet."

She motioned for Cade to step away from the window. "You know what I think?" She brought her voice down to a low whisper. "I think someone dropped her off in the cornfield last night. Maybe she slept out there somewhere, or she found her way to the Dellingers' house from the road and slept on their porch or something. Look at her. Covered in dirt and no shoes. It's evident no one has been taking care of her."

Cade rubbed his chin. "We should go back out to the Dellingers'. See if they noticed anything strange last night, like an engine idling or car doors slamming."

"Well, I . . ." Janna picked at the strap of her handbag. "I don't think I'll be able to. I have a very busy day planned."

Cade seemed to sense what her reservations centered around. "Look, Janna. All our history aside, it's clear you have the expertise to communicate with Grace. It's likely she will eventually open up to you if she gets to know you a little better. Besides, if she has been through some sort of trauma, I'm the last person who could help her through it. All I'm asking for is your help. Nothing else."

Janna heard the earnestness in his voice and a wave of nauseous guilt hit her. She, of all people, knew Cade had been through some trauma of his own in the last few years, partly due to her. Her presence here had to be as difficult for him as it was for her. She peeked over his shoulder, back at Grace. The little girl returned her gaze, affirming how Janna should answer Cade's request.

"I guess we're going to the Dellingers' then." Janna pulled her keys from her purse. "I'll drive."

~4~

"Absolutely not," Cade said, as he carried Grace to his red Jeep Wrangler, parked outside the police station entrance. "I'm the one who dragged you all the way out here during your vacation. Driving is the least I could do since you're doing me such a huge favor." He opened the passenger side door for Janna before walking around the back of the vehicle and buckling Grace in behind the driver seat.

"I don't mind. I actually like driving," Janna lied, as she and Cade both climbed into their seats simultaneously. She adjusted her purse in her lap. "It helps me think."

"I insist," Cade said with a firm smile.

As he backed out of his parking spot, Janna racked her brain for something to say. It was always safe to talk about the weather. "Mom said Shady Grove hasn't gotten much rain in the past few months."

ALLISON GREEN MARTIN

"Yeah, it's been kind of a rough summer." Cade's gaze remained fixed on the road as it unfolded before the car. "The Dellingers' corn crop caught my attention this morning and forced me to slow down for a second look. That's actually how I spotted Grace. Based on the lack of rain we've experienced and the damage on the stalks, I would assume Mr. Dellinger won't be able to produce much of a crop this season. Most of the stalks look dead already."

"What will they do for income?" Janna studied Cade's face, wondering if he was as uncomfortable with them being thrust back together as she was.

He squinted as the sun increased its intensity on the windshield. "I'm not sure. I think his wife still works at the library."

"Yeah, but that's not much of a salary to live on and run a business. What will happen if they can't keep up with demand?"

Before he could answer her, the vehicle arrived in front of the Dellingers' small white farmhouse. Janna remembered coming here with her class from school in the fifth grade. The paint on their siding showed more wear and tear since then, but she could still smell the familiar, overpowering scent of the cows in the field adjacent to the Dellingers' front yard.

Faye Dellinger stood on her front porch watering the bright pink petunias suspended in pots from the roof's eave. She waved at Cade but cocked her head sideways at Janna, as if trying to place her.

Suddenly, Janna thought it might be best to remain in the vehicle. "Uh . . . I think I'll stay in the car with Grace while you talk to Mrs. Dellinger."

"Alright." Cade shrugged and rolled down the driver's side window. "I'll leave this down so you two don't get too hot."

Janna watched through the windshield while Cade asked Mrs. Dellinger some questions. She rolled the passenger window down a few inches hoping to hear what they said but was disappointed as their words drifted away on the slight breeze in the air. Cade turned back to the car and motioned toward the cornfields. Mrs. Dellinger nodded a few times, but Janna couldn't quite figure out what the gesture meant. If only she could read lips. She glanced in the rearview mirror at Grace, who seemed to be studying her closely.

"Are you hungry or anything? I might have some cheese crackers in my purse."

Janna's offer received a smile, but Grace seemed too preoccupied to respond further. She pointed her little finger at the front windshield as Cade walked back to the car. If

Mrs. Dellinger had shed some light on Grace's situation, it didn't show in his face.

Cade remained silent as he climbed into the driver's seat, closed the door, and put on his seatbelt. Janna raised her eyebrows, silently begging him to recap his conversation with Mrs. Dellinger.

"Well . . ." Cade huffed out a breath. Janna hoped it meant he'd found a lead. "She said they didn't hear anything strange last night, car doors or otherwise. She said I could wait for Mr. Dellinger to get back from the hardware store and ask him, but counting on Harold's auditory skills seems like a lousy bet. Even if his hearing aids were in all the time, he wouldn't hear an alien spacecraft come down and abduct his cows."

Janna laughed. Cade grinned. He looked pleased. Although his corny joke provided a nice break from the tension in the air, Janna wanted to avoid getting too comfortable. She erased her smile and cleared her throat. This was a job, not their high school reunion.

Cade cranked the engine and turned around in the Dellingers' paved driveway. "Anyway, she said we could head out to the cornfields to take a look if we thought it would help, so I figured we'd head out there now, unless you've got somewhere else you need to be."

Janna wished she'd made plans before coming down to stay with her parents. It would have made it so much easier for her to bow out of the situation if she had a legitimate excuse.

She peered back at Grace in the rearview mirror, letting the girl's solemn expression make the decision for her. "No, it's fine. We can check the cornfields."

***

Cade eased the Wrangler off the side of the road, directly across from where he'd originally spotted Grace. He exited the car and stepped back to retrieve Grace from the backseat. Shifting the little girl onto his hip, he checked either side of the road, hoping to spot anything he might have missed earlier that morning. He took long strides, crossing to the other side of the road. A glance over his shoulder at Janna revealed she was struggling to keep up in heels.

Cade retraced the same path he had seen Grace take beside the stalks. Tiny footprints littered the ground, so he knew he was headed in the right direction.

He heard Janna stumbling behind him but pretended not to notice. Maybe those fancy shoes she wore were a little harder to navigate through the dry, dusty dirt than she'd bargained for. Although, he imagined her line of work rarely required a field trip through stalks of corn and clumps of dirt.

"You doing okay back there? I probably should have told you to bring different shoes," he called back.

Janna kept her eyes on the ground, watching each step, but glanced up in time to catch the bemused grin on Cade's face as he watched her.

"Ugh. This is ridiculous, isn't it?" She rolled up the legs of her pants, slipped off her shoes, and dropped them inside her large handbag. "There. That's better."

Cade turned around before she could catch him smiling again. He didn't want to be disrespectful while she tried so hard to keep up her professional facade.

He stopped to survey the area. "This is the spot where I found her, I think."

Janna lifted her hand to shield the sun from her eyes and nodded.

"There's no way to tell how long she'd been walking or from which direction, so we may need to scan the whole area by car later. This is probably the best place to start until we have more information. I'll take her through some of the rows with me. Who knows? Maybe it'll spark a memory for her."

Janna shooed a fly away from her face. "So . . . should

I just wait here?"

Cade nodded. "If I find anything, I'll call out to you."

***

Janna scanned across the acres and acres of fields the Dellingers owned on either side of the road while she waited for Cade and Grace to return from their inspection. In her opinion, the corn crop seemed to be holding its own, despite the recent drought Cade had mentioned. She turned around and scrutinized the row of stalks behind her.

They looked fine. She pulled down one of the leaves for closer study, then stepped to another stalk to compare its appearance. Both were shiny and green. From what little knowledge Janna had gleaned from her time in 4-H, it looked like these stalks had been perfectly nourished in the past few months. Although normal for this time of year, no pest damage appeared on the stalks either. Whatever caught Cade's attention earlier that morning seemed a mystery to Janna now.

The stalks behind her rustled, announcing Cade's return from his trek through the field.

"I didn't see *anything* out there." He shifted Grace to his other arm and kicked at a clump of dirt. "What about you?"

"I wish I could say I found something, but no." Janna pursed her lips, deciding if she should bring up what she noticed while he and Grace were gone. *What could it hurt?* "Cade, I thought you said the Dellingers' corn crop was struggling."

"Yeah. Everyone's crops have been hit hard this year." Cade tilted his head. "Why?"

"No reason, I guess." Janna shrugged. "But judging from the few stalks I've seen around here, it actually seems to be thriving."

"What do you mean?" Cade's forehead wrinkled.

Janna swept her hand across the air. "See for yourself."

"Here, could you take her for a minute?" Cade stepped toward Janna as Grace leaned into Janna's body to make the transfer.

Janna's purse strap slid off her shoulder, and her bag hit the ground as she shuffled to adjust the girl in her arms. Grace felt lighter than she'd expected.

"It's so strange." Cade ran his fingers across the waxy leaves. "This morning, this same section of corn was yellow and dry. Most of the stalks were even laying on the ground. I mean, they were *dying*, Janna," Cade said, his voice tinged with defense.

"I'm not saying they weren't in bad shape when you saw them this morning, but something definitely changed between then and now. What shape were the stalks in where you came from a minute ago?"

Cade looked back toward the field behind him and let out a sigh. "I . . . I'm not sure. I wasn't really looking at the stalks very well I guess."

"Maybe Mr. Dellinger came out this morning and gave them some kind of fertilizer or something," Janna offered, raising her eyebrows.

Cade shot her a doubtful look. "There's no fertilizer powerful enough to bring those stalks back to health after the shape they were in this morning."

"How do you explain this then?" Janna yanked off a full ear of corn from the stalk beside them and held it up. "I mean, how can they be producing these if we haven't had any rain?"

***

Cade wondered if Janna meant to use the term "we" when she described the town drought. Maybe she still considered herself part of the town after all.

He noticed she remained barefoot, even after they walked back and loaded up into the car. She definitely *looked* like a different person, but he wondered if it was just a costume she wore to disassociate herself from a small town persona. He wished they'd had a moment or two to talk before she met Grace, but now it looked like that conversation would take place much later than he would like.

Janna's voice brought Cade back down to earth. "Well, what should we do now? Head back to the station?"

"Yeah, we can head in that direction. Maybe grab some lunch? The last thing Grace ate wasn't exactly the breakfast of champions, so it might not be a bad idea to stop at Mac's Diner before we go back to the station."

"Sure, lunch would be good." Janna's nonchalant tone made it hard to tell if she'd be glad to have more time for them to talk before continuing the investigation or if hunger made her so quick to comply.

Cade started the engine and headed toward town. The cornfields became smaller and smaller in the rearview mirror.

"Okay, so we'll stop for lunch. I can call Pam and see if she's heard anything yet. Although with the holiday, I doubt anyone will be in a hurry to return my call. Then—" Cade stopped mid-sentence as something clicked in his memory.

"And then?" Janna repeated.

Cade ignored her, his mind too full to explain the link he'd just discovered between the events of the morning.

"Um, Cade? Hello?" Janna waved her hand in front of his face. "And then what?"

He disregarded her again, applied strong pressure to the vehicle's brakes, and swerved to the right before forcing the steering wheel back to the left. He accelerated to complete the 180-degree turn in the opposite direction of town. Janna clawed at the top of her seatbelt.

Cade steadied the Wrangler on the road and looked to verify everyone made the turn in one piece. Janna let out a breath, readjusting herself in the passenger seat.

"Um, you wanna tell me why we went for the little ride back there, Bo Duke?" Janna swirled her finger around in the air, simulating Cade's maneuver.

Cade's preoccupation with his new hypothesis overrode his desire to care what she thought right now. He studied Grace's reflection in the rearview mirror. "We're gonna make a quick stop before lunch. I *knew* she looked familiar."

"Who looked familiar? Grace? Does she look like someone you know?"

Cade wasn't sure he wanted to share his entire theory

with Janna right now. If it proved incorrect, it would just sound crazy anyway. He needed to check something first.

"Cade, do you know where Grace came from?" Janna spoke slowly, her tone one typically reserved for small children. She must have thought he'd lost his good sense.

"Uh, I . . . I'm not completely sure, but I got an early morning call from Mrs. Keever today. She said she heard a noise coming from her pantry. I thought it was just one of her cats or an overactive imagination at the time, but maybe Grace tried to find someone to help her and stopped at Mrs. Keever's before she went to the Dellingers. By the time I arrived at Mrs. Keever's house and checked everything out, Grace would have had plenty of time to make it over there to the cornfields. Maybe that's why the Dellingers didn't hear anything last night. Grace never went to their house at all."

**

Janna remained silent as they continued to Mrs. Keever's house. She wanted to laugh at Cade's exuberance for his newest hunch but refrained, thankful for an opportunity to see him the way she'd remembered him. Excited, passionate, full of determination.

Since Cade's thoughts seemed to have more of his

61

attention than her, Janna soundlessly rehearsed what she'd wanted to say to him since the police station.

So, Cade, have you forgiven me for leaving you to deal with my own selfish needs right before one of the worst times in your life? wouldn't flow off the tongue with as much delicacy as she'd hoped. *Do you wish I'd stayed, or do you even care—*

Cade's voice broke through her inner monologue. "You said you're not doing social work anymore. Are you considering a career change?"

Janna kept her eyes focused straight ahead. "I guess you could say I'm taking a little hiatus from social work. My last case really drained me and required a lot of overtime, so my boss thought it would be a good idea if I took a vacation."

"What did the case involve? Or can you even tell me?"

"Actually, it's not all that exciting, it just . . . like I said, it drained me. Child neglect cases usually do."

Janna could feel Cade's stare intensify as he turned into Mrs. Keever's driveway and pulled into the front yard. No one needed to know the real reason she was home, especially Cade.

"Here we are," she announced unnecessarily, as he put the car in park. She thrust her feet back into her shoes and quickly escaped from the passenger seat before Cade asked her any more questions.

Cade unbuckled Grace, helped her climb down from the backseat, and met Janna at the front bumper.

"I hate to make her walk barefoot, but she almost seems to prefer it." Cade looked down into the little girl's face, grasped her hand, and began walking toward Mrs. Keever's front porch.

Janna was ready to follow behind them when she realized she'd forgotten her purse and turned back to grab it from the front seat. She caught up with them at the foot of the porch steps.

Cade rang the doorbell twice before calling out. "Mrs. Keever?"

He turned and shrugged his shoulders at Janna. Cupping his hands around his face, he peered into the picture window before he rang the doorbell one last time and called the elderly woman's name again.

A voice called from the backyard, "I'm back here."

Cade scooped Grace up and descended the front steps. Janna trailed closely behind them as they rounded the side of the house. Mrs. Keever looked up from her flowerbed with a smile.

As their trio walked closer to her, Cade refreshed Mrs.

Keever's memory. "Mrs. Keever, you remember Janna Petersen, don't you? She used to live in Shady Grove and has come home for a visit."

Mrs. Keever smiled again and nodded her recognition. "Oh yes, I remember you. How are you, dear?"

Before Janna could answer, Grace wriggled loose from Cade and walked over to Mrs. Keever, who still kneeled by the flowerbed. Janna exchanged a confused glance with Cade as Grace stroked Mrs. Keever's soft white hair and looked deep into her eyes the way she'd done with Janna at the police station. She threw her dirt-streaked arms around Mrs. Keever's neck and hugged her tightly.

Mrs. Keever, undeterred by the fact she didn't know the little girl, held her closely. Tears glistened in the corner of her eyes. "Who is this little angel? Does she always come up to strangers like that?"

"As long as we've known her." Cade grinned at Janna.

Grace released her grip on Mrs. Keever, and Cade helped the older woman to her feet. Mrs. Keever brushed the grass from the back of her dress and looked at Janna. "Well, she certainly is a friendly little thing, isn't she? Is she yours?"

Janna widened her eyes. "What? Oh, no. She's Cade's."

Mrs. Keever raised an eyebrow.

"Uh . . . what Janna means is I'm the one who found her," Cade clarified.

"You found her? Do you mean someone left her on her own?" Mrs. Keever gave Grace a protective squeeze. "Who would do such a thing?"

"Actually, Mrs. Keever, we thought you might have some answers that could help us find the *exact* person who would do something like that." Cade's intense stare was directed at Mrs. Keever now, as if he was trying to decide if she was hiding something from them.

Janna wondered where he could be going with this. She'd always admired his straightforward way of speaking, but she wasn't sure if the best approach in this case was being so forthcoming with the information in his head. In her experience, people shut down if they realized someone was onto whatever game they were playing, even sweet old ladies like Mrs. Keever.

Cade remained quiet for a moment. He seemed to be working up the courage to say what was on his mind.

"Mrs. Keever, I hate to ask you this question, but unfortunately, there's no way around it."

"If it'll help this little one," She stroked Grace's hair. "You can ask me anything, Cade."

"Okay then." A hard swallow progressed through Cade's throat, loud enough for Janna to hear. "Mrs. Keever, when was the last time you saw your daughter?"

~5~

A flash of pain swept across Mrs. Keever's face. She offered them a tight-lipped smile as she seemed to struggle for words. "Let's go inside. We can talk while I make us all some lunch. I just picked some really nice cucumbers from the garden. First time all summer I've had good cucumbers with this drought. Are y'all hungry?" Before they could answer, she took Grace's hand and headed toward the back of the house.

Cade glanced at Janna, whose not-so-subtle glare told him he should have run his theory by her before assaulting Mrs. Keever with such a personal question.

Shrugging his apology, he took a step back and motioned for Janna to follow Mrs. Keever into the house. "Well, you said you wanted lunch."

Janna closed her eyes and huffed before breezing past him.

Cade hooked his thumb backwards and called out to her diminishing frame. "I'm just gonna glance around for a second to see if there's evidence Grace was here. I'll be right behind you."

Without turning around, Janna threw a hand in the air and waved her acceptance, continuing briskly toward the back porch.

***

Taking long strides to escape the nagging voice inside her head, Janna lectured herself all the way up to the back door of Mrs. Keever's house. Why had she agreed to get involved with this? She could be watching TV right now, sleeping, reading—anything but sticking her nose in where it didn't belong. Cade was the one who wanted to go snooping into Mrs. Keever's personal life, yet somehow it was Janna who had ended up alone with the woman.

Janna entered through the back porch and into the kitchen where Grace sat at the table sipping a glass of milk while Mrs. Keever shuffled around the kitchen, retrieving bread, butter, and cheese from the refrigerator.

"Let me help you, Mrs. Keever." Janna collected the items from Mrs. Keever's overfilled arms and placed them on the table.

"Would you pull out, let's see, two, four, six . . . eight slices of bread for me, dear?" Janna could tell Mrs. Keever was mulling over Cade's question and trying to deal with her stress by playing hostess. Of course, her own coping mechanism for stress was to go missing in action, so who was she to judge?

"Here you go." Janna stacked the slices of bread on the plate Mrs. Keever laid out by the stove.

The older woman went to work buttering each slice and placing them onto a square cast-iron griddle. Janna knew it must be hard for her to think of her daughter. If they had to make her relive her daughter's disappearance, she hoped Cade's guess proved to be right. Where was Cade, anyway? How long could it take to "lock down" the area or whatever they called it?

The slam of the back door answered her question. Janna took a few steps back from the kitchen, watching Cade stop by the pantry to look around before he entered the kitchen. He must have been checking to see if his hunch about Grace being the noise Mrs. Keever heard in the pantry that morning was correct.

Once he stepped into the kitchen, Cade made eye contact with Janna.

Where were you? she mouthed.

Cade cleared his throat and resumed his officer's tone. "Janna, could I speak with you for a moment, please?" He gestured toward the hallway connecting the rest of the house to the kitchen. "Excuse us, Mrs. Keever. We'll be right back."

Mrs. Keever kept her focus on grilling the sandwiches. "Don't be too long. Lunch will be ready in just a few minutes."

Escaping into the privacy of the hallway, Janna could no longer restrain her curiosity. "Well?"

Cade stared back cluelessly. "Well . . . what?"

"What took you so long? Did you find something outside?"

"No. The back porch is immaculate. Nothing in the pantry either. If Grace was out there, she cleaned up before she left." He chuckled.

"I'm glad you think this is so funny." Janna's voice sharpened. "I can't believe you asked that poor woman about her daughter, and Grace wasn't even here."

"Would you hold your horses and lower your voice please?" He sounded irritated. "I didn't say she wasn't here—I said I didn't find anything. That doesn't mean I'm wrong."

He stepped behind her and pointed to a picture hanging on the wall. "Grace looks an awful lot like Mrs. Keever's daughter, don't you think?"

Janna and Cade were in middle school when Mallory Keever had run away from home, so Janna couldn't really remember what she looked like. All she could recall was how everyone talked about it at church the weeks following her departure. The women would shake their heads and say, "Poor Linda. Mallory always was a handful." Janna wondered if they said the same thing about her when she left. It was impossible to hide anything for very long in a small town, and even if someone could, the rumors created from the few facts people gathered would destroy a reputation before the truth had a chance to ring out.

The picture appeared to have been taken when Mallory was a few years older than Grace, maybe eight or nine. Janna narrowed her eyes, trying to catch any resemblance the Keever girl had to Grace. She did have a slight gap in her teeth like Grace and the same solemn expression.

"Cade, we were just kids when she left town. How did you remember what she used to look like?"

"I didn't remember. But I saw this picture this morning when I stopped by to check on Mrs. Keever. It seemed like nothing at first, but the more I kept thinking about Grace, I thought she looked like someone I'd seen before. Then I realized that picture reminded me of her."

"That's hardly conclusive evidence that she's Mrs. Keever's granddaughter." The words came out a little more condescending than she intended, but years of documenting cases for child protective services had taught Janna not to rely on circumstantial details. "This could all just be a coincidence. I mean you did just see the picture this morning. Maybe the image stuck in your head, and when you saw Grace, you instantly connected her with Mallory."

"O-kay. Well, why don't we go talk to Mrs. Keever and find out then?" He turned to head toward the kitchen. Without thinking, Janna grabbed his forearm and pulled him back.

"Wait. Do you think it's right to bring up such an obviously painful subject with this woman? It's clear from her reaction outside she doesn't want to talk about it. Maybe we should just leave it alone."

"How else are we gonna find out if Grace is related to her or not?"

"I don't know." Janna threw her hands in the air. "I just feel like if someone doesn't want to talk about something, you shouldn't force it."

Cade ran his hands over his hair and rubbed the back of his head. His patience seemed to have reached its breaking point. "Ya know, not everybody wants to keep things hidden, Janna. Sometimes people want to talk about things that've hurt them, but no one ever asks them what they're feeling. They just assume you should brush it under the rug and never bring it up again. How else will we find out the truth if we're afraid to face it?" He jerked his arm free from her grasp and headed back into the kitchen.

Janna deserved that. Clearly, Cade wasn't as comfortable with her being back in town as he originally pretended, but before Janna could process his comments, Mrs. Keever announced that lunch was ready.

***

"Would you bless the food, Cade?" Mrs. Keever placed a bowl of sliced cucumbers in the center of the table next to the sandwiches. She took hold of Grace's hand and held her other hand out to Janna. Cade grasped Grace's free hand but made no attempt to make the same offer to Janna. Janna bowed her head before she could feel insulted and listened as Cade spoke.

"God, we thank you for this food and good friends to share it with. We ask that it nourish our bodies and give us the strength to make it through the day."

Huh, friends plural? Janna peeked up from the table and studied Cade as he continued to pray. He seemed to be trying to think of the right words to say, but she couldn't tell if those comments he directed to God were about her or not.

"We continue to ask for rain to replenish the land and bring life back into the gardens and fields in Shady Grove. And finally, we ask for special help in finding Grace's family. We know we found her for a reason. We ask that you make that reason known to us soon. Amen."

As they passed the grilled cheese sandwiches around the table, Cade avoided Janna's obvious stare. She watched the muscles in his jaw clench several times while he worked up the courage to ask Mrs. Keever for more details about her daughter. *Not so brave after all.*

"Mrs. Keever, I know this may be a difficult topic to discuss . . ." He glanced at Janna from the corner of his eye,

"But we need to know about your daughter, especially if she may have a connection to Grace."

Mrs. Keever put down her sandwich and relaxed in her seat. She seemed more ready to answer him now.

Maybe Cade had been right about talking through difficult experiences. Was it possible that some people did want to share their hurts with willing listeners? The whole idea seemed as foreign to Janna as unsweetened iced tea.

"You can't hide things forever, I guess. No matter how upsetting they are." Mrs. Keever took a bite of her sandwich and chewed it slowly before continuing. "It's been so long since anyone asked about my daughter, I figured most people forgot I ever had one. I think it's time to clear the air though, once and for all." She paused again as if trying to determine how much to divulge. "Did you know Mallory wasn't my biological daughter?"

They shook their heads in unison and waited for Mrs. Keever to clarify.

"Check and I weren't able to have children, so we adopted Mallory right after her eighth birthday. Her real mother had been quite abusive to her, and the poor thing had nightmares for months after she arrived. She would wake up screaming every night. It seemed to get better as she got a little older, and we thought the nightmares had ended. But sometimes a person carries more scars on the inside than the outside. She never truly got over the abuse her mother subjected her to. We tried our best to love her and provide a good home for her. It just wasn't enough."

Mrs. Keever wiped a tear from her cheek and pressed her lips together. She rose from her seat to retrieve a tissue from the box on top of her refrigerator. Janna, struggling with emotions of her own, could feel Cade staring at her. She had let his words sink in the past few minutes, and the gravity of them weighed heavily on her.

Janna felt sorry for Mrs. Keever, she really did, but she also knew children who come from abusive situations often have problems lingering well below the surface. In the process of working so many neglect cases the past couple of years, including the Brenners', she had learned to become detached from the specific details of these types of situations. It was how she survived, just like Maxine had said. Janna carried the same detachment into her personal life, which was probably why it'd been so easy for her to break things off with Nate.

She moved her eyes to Grace, who met her gaze with a haunting stare. The same stare as the Brenner girl's. Grace had the same vulnerability, the same need for protection.

Janna felt pressure building up in her chest like it had in her drowning nightmare earlier. The heaviness of her anxieties became unbearable. She needed some air. "Mrs. Keever, I'm sorry to interrupt this conversation, but I need to step outside for just a minute." She slid her chair back from the table and grabbed her purse by the strap.

Cade rose from his seat and leaned in toward her. "You okay?" His concerned tone a vast contrast from the one he'd used in the hallway.

Janna waved her hand back and forth, trying to get air to her face. "Yeah, yeah, yeah. You two just stay here and finish talking. I'll take Grace with me."

Cade nodded in agreement.

Grace sprang up from the table at the mention of her name. She grabbed Janna's hand and pulled her through the hallway, past the living room, and through the front door to the porch like she'd been in the house before. Cade's hunch may have been right after all.

Grace ran over to the porch swing and hopped onto the seat. Janna followed her lead and sat down beside her, pushing her heels against the grey painted floor boards. The old swing's chains creaked as they swang back and forth.

After walking around that cornfield all morning, Grace probably needed a full bath. The least Janna could do

77

was to remove the tangles from her hair. She slowed the swing and pulled a brush from her handbag. "Do you want me to brush your hair?"

Grace nodded. Janna pulled her onto her lap and began working, carefully pulling the brush through the gnarls in the child's hair. She continued rocking the swing.

"I used to love for my mom to brush my hair when I was your age."

Grace didn't respond, but she seemed to enjoy the swaying salon Janna had created for her. She leaned back in Janna's lap and sighed.

Janna pulled the brush back and chuckled. "I guess you're finished with your makeover." An urge to hug the little girl overtook her. She wrapped her arms around Grace's and gave her a light squeeze.

"I wish you could tell us where you came from." Janna began braiding Grace's hair. "I can't imagine anyone just dropping you off in the cornfield. Maybe your family was traveling through and you just got lost from them. That's easy to do, you know. Get lost. I'm pretty lost myself right now."

Grace sighed again. The sound had a distinct note of frustration in it this time. Janna knew what she said made little sense to a small child and Grace was growing bored, but Janna continued anyway.

"I thought I wanted to live in Shady Grove forever. Get married, have kids, become a teacher or something. I don't really know when all that changed, but I just got to the point where I couldn't stay here. I was scared things wouldn't work out the way I'd planned. When I get scared, what do I do? I run." She finished Grace's braid and tied it off with an elastic hair band from her purse. "It's stupid, really, the reason I left. I think we all do stupid things when we're young. That's what I keep telling myself. I truly didn't mean to hurt anyone. I just thought things would turn out differently."

Janna didn't know if it was because she knew Grace wouldn't share anything she said, or if she just wanted to tell someone, but she felt a strong compulsion to tell this little girl everything she'd been holding in for the past seven years.

Before she could spill it all, Cade stepped out from the front door. The screen door closing behind him broke Janna's train of thought, and she remembered why they were at Mrs. Keever's.

A small butterfly flitted past Janna and Grace on the swing. Grace hopped down from Janna's lap and chased it out into the front yard, leaving Cade and Janna alone to talk.

Janna stood and took a step toward Cade. "What did she say? Does she think Grace might be related to Mallory somehow?"

Cade's face looked discouraged. "From what Mrs. Keever told me, it would be impossible for Mallory to have had a child."

Janna furrowed her brow. "After the way Grace led me to the porch, I think you may be onto something, though. How can she be so sure? I mean if she ran away and Mrs. Keever hasn't seen her, she could have a grandchild she doesn't know about."

"I would tend to agree with you under normal circumstances, but—" Cade's face remained solemn.

"But, what?" Janna interrupted. "I don't think we should rule out any possibilities, Cade. If there's even a chance Grace is Mallory's daughter, we'd be wise to press Mrs. Keever for more details. What did she say exactly?"

"She told me . . . well . . . she said . . ." He rubbed his hand across his forehead and stared out into Mrs. Keever's front yard where Grace chased the butterfly around some flower beds. "You know, maybe you were right when you said we shouldn't bring up Mallory. Maybe I should've just let it go."

Janna studied his pained expression. "What do you mean? Cade, what did she tell you?"

Cade heaved a long sigh and turned to look at Janna. "Mallory Keever didn't run away sixteen years ago, Janna." He shook his head. "She committed suicide."

~6~

"What?" Janna lowered herself back down to the swing. "How does she know for sure?"

"I think Mrs. Keever told me more than she's ever told anyone about Mallory, but she might not appreciate me sharing it with you on her front porch. Let's head back to town and grab some real lunch before we check in with Pam at the station. If she's heard back from Teresa Williams at Social Services, you can go home and enjoy the rest of your vacation." He tried to mask his disappointment at the thought of that possibility.

Janna nodded numbly. She seemed to be taking Mrs. Keever's revelation as hard as he was. Janna didn't know Mrs. Keever well enough to be so distraught over the news of Mallory's suicide. He watched her for further reaction, wondering if something else was on her mind.

He raised the bundle stashed beneath his arm. "Mrs. Keever gave me some of Mallory's old clothes for Grace. She still needs shoes, but maybe we can stop somewhere on the way back to the station for those."

Janna stood up and adjusted her purse on her shoulder. Her eyes held a vacant stare, one usually associated with trauma, but Cade couldn't gauge what made her so upset. They walked back to the car in silence, and once they were all buckled in, Cade navigated the vehicle toward Main Street.

***

Everyone remained quiet during the short drive to Mac's Diner. Cade pulled into a parking spot and helped Grace out of the backseat. He walked to the diner door and held it open for Janna.

The diner hadn't changed a bit. Spotless formica countertops encircled by chrome-covered stools with red cushioned tops. Oldies played from the ancient jukebox in the corner as Janna took in the familiar plush booths lining the memorabilia-laden walls. Walking into that place always felt like being transported through a time machine to the fifties. She wondered how it continued to stay in business after all these years, especially since she, Cade, and Grace were the only customers in the place. It was a little late for the regular lunch crowd she supposed.

A waitress breezed by her. "Seat yourself, hon."

Janna turned back to Cade and shrugged. "Any preference?" She caught a glimpse of the booth they used to share with Brian and Stacy after football games. Thankfully, he pointed toward the booth in front of them instead.

They slid into their seats, and the waitress who flitted by earlier returned to take their drink order. Janna scanned her menu while the waitress got their drinks, although her appetite had diminished after Cade shared Mrs. Keever's secret. She wanted to hear the details but couldn't remove thoughts about her own mother from her mind. What did her mother tell people after she left?

Janna imagined she and Mallory weren't that different in some respects. They both ran away from their problems in hopes of avoiding them altogether, but she figured Mallory's were too big to handle on her own. Janna knew firsthand the stupid things fear could make you do, so it wasn't much of a stretch to assume Mallory thought ending her life would allow her to evade her issues once and for all.

The waitress placed their beverages on the table. "She can pick a song from the jukebox if she wants," she said, motioning to Grace. "Kids love playing with that thing. I'll give you a few more minutes to decide what you want."

Janna dug a few quarters out of her wallet and held them out to Grace. "Why don't you go pick out a song and let Cade and me talk for a little while?"

Grace took the quarters with both hands and climbed over Cade's lap and out of the booth. They watched as she walked over to the jukebox on the opposite end of the diner. She seemed to be deciding which song to play. Janna wondered if she could even read.

"So," Janna took a sip of her tea. "Tell me about Mallory. Mrs. Keever just let everyone think she ran away when all the time she knew she was never coming back? I . . . I mean . . . what happened? How did Mrs. Keever find out?"

"She's the one who found her, Janna." Cade ran his finger around the rim of his glass while he talked. "Mallory had been gone for a few months when she called Mrs. Keever one night from a hotel room in Raleigh. She apologized for hurting them and said she wished she could come back home. Mrs. Keever thought this was an answer to prayer, but I guess Mallory was so lost in the painful memories of her childhood that she just couldn't escape them. The Keevers thought she was asking for help, but it sounds to me like she called to say goodbye.

85

"They tried to hurry to Raleigh, but by the time they got there, it was too late. They found her lying on the bed in the hotel room with a bottle of sleeping pills next to her. They decided to bury her in Raleigh and let everyone continue to believe she ran away."

"How horrible." Janna's voice cracked a little. "Why didn't the Keevers ever tell anyone what really happened?"

"C'mon Janna. You know how this town is. I'm sure it was hard enough to have a child run away from a good home, much less to do something as drastic as Mallory did."

Janna peered out the diner window to the parking lot, afraid to make eye contact with Cade. "It must have been hard for her to keep the secret for so long."

"Well, it's like I said earlier . . ." He picked up his menu and appeared to be deciding on lunch. "Most people want to talk things out, but someone has to be willing to listen. Like we did today."

"You mean like *you* did today." Janna rubbed between her eyebrows. "Listen, I'm sorry about leaving you alone to question Mrs. Keever, but I didn't think Grace should be listening to such an adult conversation."

"I appreciated you thinking of that." Cade smiled at her.

Janna tilted her head to the side and adjusted the salt and pepper shakers on the back edge of the table. "I guess it also upset me when she told us Mallory had been abused before they adopted her. I—"

The waitress returned with a couple of pitchers and refilled both their drinks. Janna waited for her to leave before she continued. "I should be used to that in my line of work, but—"

"What'll ya have folks?" The waitress interrupted them again, pulling a notepad from her apron pocket and hovering a pencil above it.

Cade closed his menu and motioned for Janna to order first. Janna chose something simple, hoping the waitress would leave quickly and they could finish talking about how she'd reacted at Mrs. Keever's. Cade placed his order and added chicken nuggets for Grace. The waitress jotted everything down and turned to walk back to the kitchen.

"Cade, I wanted to explain—" Janna began.

"Honey, did you want Southern style or Orchard style chicken salad?"

Janna sighed as she pointedly looked at the nametag on the waitress's apron. "Southern style is fine, *Sherri*."

"Okie dokie." Sherri said, bouncing her way back to the kitchen.

Cade looked amused as Janna tried again. "What I was saying was that I should be used to hearing stories like Mallory's, but they still always bother me."

"I'd be worried if you said they didn't bother you, Janna." Cade smiled at her again. "Just means you're human. Cut yourself some slack. I'd think a little compassion goes a long way in the type of situations you deal with. Hang onto that. I can't imagine some of the things you probably see."

The jukebox began playing some sort of honky-tonk hit behind them. Janna cleared her throat. "Actually Cade, there's something I should tell you about my job. I, uh—"

Cade's cell phone rang before she could complete her sentence.

Seriously? Janna watched him study the caller ID screen.

"Could you hold on for one second? It's Pam. She may have found out something. I'm so sorry, but I probably need to take this."

"Yeah, you're right." Janna nodded. "It's fine. We can talk about it later." A wave of relief washed over her. *This could wait, right?*

"Are you sure?" Cade scanned her face.

Janna nodded as the phone rang again.

Cade mouthed *Sorry*.

"Hello. Yeah. No luck at the Dellingers'. Have you heard anything from the social worker? That's all she can do? I guess I'm not too surprised, but what am I supposed to do with Grace in the meantime? She certainly can't stay with me."

Cade nodded a few times but didn't respond to whatever Pam suggested. Janna wished he'd put the call on speaker.

"Okay, Pam. I'll think about it. Could you do me one other favor? I hate to cut into your weekend, but I'll probably have to go back out to the cornfield tomorrow morning to double check for evidence. Do you think you could try the missing persons database in the morning and see if anything new shows up? Okay, great. I owe you one. Thanks, bye."

Janna tried to sound nonchalant as her leg bounced under the table. "What did Pam have to say?"

Cade looked over at Grace by the jukebox before meeting Janna's expectant stare. "The social worker is on her way to the beach for the Fourth, so she won't be available until Monday. Pam said she appointed me temporary legal guardian until they can find Grace's family's whereabouts."

"Okay, great. Can she do that?"

"I guess. You'd know better than I would, but I assume it's within protocol or she wouldn't have allowed it."

Janna nodded her agreement with his statement as Sherri returned with their food.

"Wow, you guys are quick. Thank you." Cade accepted his plate and unrolled his silverware from its paper napkin. "There's just one problem, though."

Janna placed her napkin on her lap and waited for Sherri to leave again. The servers here were a bit too attentive in Janna's opinion. Maybe nosy was a better word for it.

Finally, they were alone at the table again. "What's the problem?" Janna asked.

"Grace needs someone to stay with for the next couple of days. It wouldn't be appropriate for me to have a little girl staying at my house. So I thought . . ." Cade raised his eyebrows and grinned hopefully at her.

"Huh, you're funny." Janna took a bite of her sandwich, enjoying the crisp taste of celery.

Cade sobered his expression and glanced at Grace across the diner from them. He tilted his head like a puppy pleading for a treat. "C'mon, Janna."

Janna swallowed her bite and gaped at him. "No, Cade. *No.*"

***

"Hey, Mom," Janna began before explaining Grace's current situation to her mother over the phone.

The hum of the car's engine made it difficult to hear some of what her mother said as they drove back to the police department. Her mom seemed more than willing to take on another houseguest. "I would love to have her stay with us. Someone just left her out there by herself? How awful!"

It took very little to work her mother into a frenzy, so Janna dialed the situation down a bit. "Actually, we don't know if someone dropped her off there or if she just became separated from her family. I think it's best to avoid jumping to conclusions this early in the investigation."

Janna smiled at Cade, hoping he would remember how excitable her mother was and play along when he saw her.

"Make sure you invite Cade to dinner, too, honey."

Janna could feel Cade studying her as she finished up with her mom.

She gritted her teeth. "Okaay, mom. I will. Bye." She hung up and shoved her phone back into her purse before she gave Cade the official verdict.

"Mom said she has plenty of room for Grace in the spare bedroom. Oh, and I'm supposed to invite you to dinner." She thrust the last sentence from her mouth, still annoyed with her mother's meddling.

Cade laughed. "Gee, thanks."

"No, I'm sorry." Janna put her hand to her forehead and massaged under both eyebrows. "You should come for dinner. I mean, I'd like you to come to dinner, Cade," she said, finally mustering up the right tone. "It's just . . . sometimes Mom is so exasperating. You know how mothers are, always thinking they're right about everything."

Cade's face fell as he turned away from her to focus on the windshield.

Why did I say that? Janna scrunched up her face in embarrassment and tapped her hand against her forehead lightly, trying to knock the right words loose from her brain.

"I'm sorry, Cade. I don't think before I speak sometimes. I just ramble on and on and then I don't know what I'm saying until it escapes from my mouth like a verbal grenade just exploding over everyone." She motioned wildly with her hands.

Cade didn't say anything until he had turned into the police station parking lot and pulled into the spot next to Janna's car. "It's okay, Petersen." A wide grin spread across his face. "I've always known you had a *special* way with words."

"Ugh . . . it's not funny. I feel really bad, and you're making fun of me." Janna hit him playfully in the arm.

He flinched and rubbed his shoulder, pretending she'd hurt him. "Easy, Guns. I don't want to have to arrest you for assault."

They both laughed this time. A familiar feeling filled the space as they eased into being together again. Janna caught a glimpse of Grace smiling in the rearview mirror.

"Well, I guess we should head over to your parents' house, huh?" Cade said.

"Yeah, I'll clear out my backseat and Grace can ride with me."

Janna slid out of the passenger seat and unlocked her car. She grabbed the filebox from work from the backseat of the Acura. Cade held out his arms, offering his assistance in moving it to the trunk.

"You brought all this home on your vacation?" He adjusted the box in his arms with his knee.

Janna pointed the key fob toward the back of the car and remotely opened the hatch. "Well, these are just from my last case. Like I told you earlier, it was a child neglect case, so most of it is documentation from home visits and interviews with the minor."

"That's a lot of documentation." Cade raised his eyebrows. "Is it typical to have so much paperwork for one case?"

Janna could tell he was just curious, but she didn't want to get into all of it right now, not with Grace waiting to be shifted from Cade's car to hers and her mother preparing dinner for them at home. She checked her watch and changed the subject.

"Listen, we'd better get going. Mom said dinner would be ready at five thirty, and Grace needs a bath before we eat."

Cade seemed to catch on that he'd hit some kind of nerve. He followed Janna's lead and extracted Grace from the backseat of his car. "Grace, we're gonna go to Janna's house for dinner. Would you like that?"

Grace looked at Janna and smiled. She nodded to Cade, who buckled her into Janna's rear seat. He closed the door gently and looked back to Janna.

"Okay, well I guess I'll meet you at your parents?"

"Yeah, that'd be fine."

Cade grabbed the bundle of clothes Mrs. Keever had given them from the back of the Wrangler and handed them to Janna. "I need to take care of a few things myself, so tell your mom not to wait on me to serve dinner, okay?"

"I'll do my best." Janna shrugged. "But I make no promises."

They exchanged a smile before they climbed into their cars and started the engines. As she watched Cade drive away, it hit Janna how much she'd missed him. She wished things could have gone differently between them, but at the time, it seemed like leaving was the only option.

***

Before he could spend any more time with Janna, Cade needed to talk through some of the things he was feeling. He needed someone who wouldn't offer advice, just someone who could listen and give him some perspective.

Pastor Mabry might be working today. He could probably shed some light on the whole awkward situation.

Cade pulled into the parking lot of the Shady Grove Community Church and parked under an oak tree. He wasn't sure if anyone would be there today, considering the holiday weekend, but it was worth a shot.

Leaving the car unlocked, Cade headed for the side door, which was closest to Pastor Mabry's office. He pulled on the handle. It was locked. So much for the open-door policy Pastor Mabry always talked about. Cade couldn't blame him. Even pastors needed a vacation every now and then.

Cade took a seat on the cement steps. He bowed his head and prayed aloud.

"God, I know all things happen for a reason and only you know the reason sometimes. But if you want to send a couple hints my way, I'd greatly appreciate it." He chuckled even though he didn't find it very funny. "I'm supposed to show Janna grace, right? Let go of what happened, but I just—I don't know. It's not that simple."

Cade picked at the paint on the handrail beside him, trying to determine what truly bugged him about the whole situation. "I want to know why, God. Why all this happened—is happening. Everything that's gone on the last few years seems so unclear, so unfair. And now here's Janna. Did you bring me this blast from the past or is her showing up now just a coincidence? It seems she's the only one who can help me with this little girl you've entrusted to my care. What am I supposed to do with *that*?"

He sighed, reminded of the words he'd prayed a few nights ago after visiting his father. He repeated them. "God, I need you to show me the way."

Cade couldn't think of what else to say, so he closed with a quick, "Thank you, amen" and lifted his head. He stood to head back to his vehicle, glancing briefly at the graveyard by the side of the church. Something caught his eye, and he changed direction to get a closer look.

He walked over to a headstone reading *Miranda Thompson, beloved wife and mother*. His mother. Sitting on the small ledge extending from the gravestone was a mason jar, like the ones Cade's mother had used to can green beans. Bright pink peonies burst from the mouth of the jar—his mother's favorite flower.

He bent down and ran his thumb across the emblem etched into the glass. Who would have brought those?

Cade brushed bits of dead grass from the bottom of the grave marker. "You know, people have stopped asking me how I'm doing. I guess they don't want to know anymore, or they think it's too painful for me to talk about. Maybe they just don't care. Dad's no help either—" He shook his head as anger swelled up inside his chest.

He ripped a handful of weeds from around the base of the headstone. His mother couldn't hear him. He knew that. But it was nice, once in a while, to indulge the idea that she was looking down on him from heaven. At times like this, he wished she could hear him and provide him with the kind

97

of great advice she would have given him if she were still here.

It had been rough the last several years, and sharing his grief was no longer a possibility. His dad's health began deteriorating a few years after his mother's death. Early onset Alzheimer's was the diagnosis. It progressed more rapidly than doctors were expecting, which had forced Cade to move his dad into the local assisted living center to receive the care he required.

"Shoot." Cade snapped his fingers, realizing he had forgotten to stop by the Center to see his dad that afternoon. He looked at his watch. Already five o'clock. They would be serving dinner now, but they didn't encourage visitors during this time because some of the patients wouldn't eat when their loved ones came to spend time with them.

He would just have to stop by there in the morning. Besides, he would be really late to Janna's if he stopped by there now. Janna probably didn't know about his dad, unless her mother told her.

Cade stood up, looking at the peonies in the mason jar again. A guess about the bestower of his mother's favorite flowers popped into his head. Only one person he knew of in town loved peonies as much as his mother. Janna.

~7~

Janna's mother turned out to be as enthralled with Grace as Mrs. Keever.

"She is precious! I can't believe someone would just leave her out in a field by herself." Her mom's face twisted with disdain.

Janna pulled her mother away from Grace to the opposite corner of the kitchen and lowered her voice. "Listen, Mom, I hate to assume someone abandoned her, but unfortunately not everyone is fit to be a parent these days, so I'm not ruling it out. I know she doesn't say much, but Grace can still hear you, so it's important we don't jump to conclusions yet, especially in front of her."

Janna struggled to control the resentment in her voice. She had shared next to nothing about the last case she worked, but she knew her mom tended to be very intuitive

99

about her, so she must have known there were some terrible circumstances involved or else Janna would not have retreated home.

"Okay, honey, I'll keep these things zipped until you tell me otherwise." Her mom ran her fingers across her tightened lips as they walked back to Grace. "Supper won't be ready for another twenty minutes. Why don't you take Grace upstairs and get her cleaned up? Does she have any clothes to change into while I wash what she has on?"

Janna pulled the stack of clothes from her bag and laid them on the kitchen counter. "When we stopped by Mrs. Keever's place earlier, she gave us some clothes for Grace." She chose a yellow sundress from the pile and spread it out across the top of the island in the middle of the kitchen. It looked homemade.

"I thought you said Cade found her at Harold Dellinger's place."

Oh, boy. Janna didn't know how much her mom knew about what happened to Mrs. Keever's daughter, but she also couldn't guarantee her mother wouldn't get it out of her if she tried. She'd have to avoid divulging too many details so her mother wouldn't find the information very interesting.

"Oh, he did. We just thought maybe Mrs. Keever saw Grace walking earlier in the morning or something." She played with the hem of the sundress, avoiding eye contact with her mom. It seemed to work.

Her mother ran her hand across the dress, smoothing out the wrinkles. "Looks a little big for her, don't you think?"

"I guess Mallory was a little older than Grace when she wore these clothes, but I think they'll serve their purpose just fine." Janna glanced down at Grace and nodded. "Right?"

Grace smiled, taking Janna's hand.

"C'mon, let's get you cleaned up." Janna led Grace out of the kitchen before her mother could ask anything further about Mrs. Keever.

They headed up the stairs. Janna stopped in the hallway to grab a towel and a washcloth before they walked through her bedroom to the bathroom.

Pink and blue splashes on the wallpaper greeted them from the walls. Janna's mom hadn't changed anything in the bathroom or her bedroom, for that matter, since her middle school days. She figured it was her mom's way of hanging onto the memories they'd shared in these rooms.

Janna hung the towel over the side of the claw-foot tub and instructed Grace to raise her arms so she could help her out of the dirty sundress. Grace did as she was told. Janna scanned briefly over her arms and back for any signs of bruises. Abuse was often prevalent in situations like this. Nothing. Despite being outside in a field littered with sticks and rocks all morning, not so much as a scratch marred the girl's skin.

Janna turned the tub faucet on and squeezed some shampoo into the warm water for good measure. The faint smell of honeysuckle filled the room as water rose up the sides of the bathtub.

She lifted Grace and placed her in the sudsy water. The girl looked so tiny, enveloped by the size of the tub. Janna dipped the washcloth into the bathwater. Grace closed her eyes and held perfectly still as Janna wiped a few smudges of dirt from her petite face. After removing the dirt streaks from the little girl's neck, arms, and legs, Janna rubbed the dirt from Grace's feet. As Janna cleaned between her toes, Grace grinned. She must have been enjoying the foot massage. Not a scratch, blister, or scrape could be found anywhere on Grace's feet either.

Janna poured a small dollop of shampoo into her palm, grabbed a plastic cup from the tray stretching across the tub, and filled it with warm water from the faucet. Grace shivered as the water spilled over her hair and down her back and then grinned at Janna again.

Janna laughed. "You like the way the water feels?" She poured another warm cupful over Grace's hair and worked in the shampoo, creating a thick lather. "Now, you'll have to lean back so I can wash the shampoo out without getting it into your eyes. Don't worry. I'll hold you while I rinse it out, okay?"

Without hesitation, Grace leaned back into Janna's extended arm. Pouring the water over Grace's hair to remove the shampoo, Janna let her mind flood with thoughts about her last case. She wondered if that mother told her little girl she'd hold her while she rinsed the shampoo out of her hair. It took some strength to hold Grace up while she rested all her weight on Janna's forearm. How much more strength would it take to push her down under the water and hold her there? To hold her down as she struggled beneath an adult's weight—reaching out for help but being pushed farther underwater by the hands of someone who was supposed to protect her.

A single tear slipped down Janna's face and into the bathwater as her mind ran through all those terrible thoughts. She studied the sweet, contented expression on Grace's face. How could someone look at a face like that and do something so horrible to them? Janna had grappled with

103

thoughts like this for months, but she'd never put herself in the mother's position before.

A knock on the door startled Janna.

"Honey, dinner's almost ready," her mother said.

Janna wiped the tear from her face and sniffed. "Okay, Mom. We'll be right down."

She squeezed the water from Grace's hair, wrapped the fluffy towel around her small frame, and lifted her from the tub. Bending down, she placed Grace on the tile to dry her off, but the little girl clung tightly to Janna's neck as she tried to release her and stand. Janna realized the poor thing just wanted to be held. Remaining on her knees, she pulled Grace into her lap.

She held Grace snugly in her arms, stroking her wet hair. The girl's tiny arms fastened their grip around Janna's neck as the weight of everything that had happened over the past few months at work came crashing down on Janna's spirit. She had tried to bury the guilt and responsibility she felt after the case closed. But in this moment, as she rocked Grace in her arms on the cold tile floor, Janna did something she hadn't done in a long time. She let herself cry.

***

Cade pulled into the Petersens' driveway and sat in the driver's seat for a few minutes before walking up the steps of the front porch. Why had this seemed like a good idea?

Although Cade spoke to Janna's parents at church each Sunday, he had done his best to avoid long interactions with them when he could. It was just too awkward.

He grabbed a grocery bag from the front seat and climbed out of his car. Walking to the front steps, he noticed the yellow snapdragons hanging in baskets on either side of the porch. Maybe Janna's mom had put the flowers on his mother's grave. He'd have to discover the answer to that mystery later though. As apprehensive as he was about seeing Janna again and spending time with the Petersens, he actually looked forward to this dinner. Eating alone was getting old.

The front door was wide open—a white screen door the only thing between visitors and the entryway. Cade could hear the sound of plates clinking together back in the dining room. "Hello?" he called out.

Julia Petersen greeted him at the door, her left hand full of silverware. "Come in, come in. Dinner's almost ready. Janna will be down in a few minutes. She's upstairs giving Grace a bath."

Cade nodded.

Julia extended her free arm to offer Cade an awkward side hug. "How have you been?"

"Okay, I guess. Thank you for inviting me to dinner."

"I'm just glad we have an excuse to see you, not like we need one. You were practically family," she rambled like her daughter. "I feel awful we haven't had you over sooner, but you seemed to have your hands full with your job and . . . your . . . dad."

"It's okay, Mrs. Petersen. I do stay pretty busy."

"Well, I hope this won't be too uncomfortable for the two of you, but," Julia leaned toward Cade and whispered, "You and Janna need to clear the air. Seven years is too long to let things go unsaid, don't you think?"

If only her daughter felt the same way. Cade smiled at Mrs. Petersen's transparency.

"Calvin," Julia called toward the living room, past the entryway. "Cade's here."

The shuffling of a newspaper and the creak of a recliner answered for him until Janna's dad emerged from the other room to greet his company.

"I'm gonna head back into the kitchen and start putting things on the table. You two catch up for a minute," Julia suggested.

Calvin Petersen extended his hand to Cade. "Good to see you, Cade. How's your father?"

Mr. Petersen and Cade's father were old childhood friends. Cade wondered if it was as hard for Calvin to see his friend's health deteriorating as it was for him to see it as a son. *Calvin Petersen* had been signed on the visitor's log a few times when he went to visit his dad, so Cade knew he still went to visit every once in a while.

Cade tipped his head to the side. "He has good days and bad days. Thanks for asking."

Calvin put his hand on Cade's shoulder and gave it a firm squeeze. "Your father is a good man, Cade. I'll bet he's real proud of you. Your mother would be too."

Most people avoided talking about Cade's parents like the plague. It must have all seemed too tragic for them or something. His mother's death followed by his father's ailing health. Talk about a string of bad luck.

Cade realized this was probably the longest conversation he'd ever had with Janna's dad. Calvin was a man of few words, but Cade had always respected him. Not having to walk around on eggshells with him, like he did with everyone else, put Cade at ease.

Janna appeared at the top of the stairs, cutting into their conversation. Grace was in her arms, now dressed in yellow. Grace's hair was still wet on the ends. Her little face lit up when she spotted Cade.

"Hey, Grace. You look nice for dinner." He smiled at her. "Oh." Cade remembered the merchandise in his hand. "I picked up some flip-flops for her at Miller's Grocery. Pink, purple, and blue were my only choices, so I got purple to match her dress. I guess purple goes with yellow too, right?"

Janna looked amused, descending the stairs to meet her dad and Cade in the entryway. "Doesn't purple go with everything?"

Cade thought Janna's eyes looked red, like she'd been crying, but maybe she was just tired. It had been a long day.

Grace reached for Cade, and he took her from Janna. She hugged his neck tightly before pulling back to stare into his face.

"Time to eat," Janna's mother called from the other room.

***

The troop headed into the dining room and claimed their seats. Janna's father took a seat at the head of the table. Janna placed Grace in the chair to the left of him and sat down beside the little girl. This meant her mother would sit to the right of her dad, putting Cade directly across from Janna.

Her father blessed the food and placed a slice of meatloaf on his plate before passing the serving tray around. Starting with a spoonful of mashed potatoes, Janna filled Grace's plate and set it before her.

Everyone savored the food quietly. Janna could feel both Cade and her mother staring at her. She pushed a big clump of mashed potatoes back and forth on her plate like it was giving her meatloaf a high five. Seemingly oblivious to the tension Janna felt hovering over the table, Grace and Janna's dad ate their meals contentedly.

Her mother finally released them from the silence. "Cade, did I hear you say your father is doing better?"

Janna looked up at her parents and then Cade. No one else at the table seemed to think it was a strange question. "Is your dad sick or something?"

Cade shifted uncomfortably in his seat. He stared down at the food on his plate for a moment and swallowed the bite in his mouth prior to providing her with an answer.

"Several years ago, after Mom passed away, I started noticing Dad was forgetting things. Simple things, like how to get home, where I worked." Cade took a sip of his drink. "At first, I thought it was a sort of delayed grief reaction, but one

109

day he wasn't home when I got off from work. After driving around for a half hour, I found him wandering down Main Street. He had no clue who or where he was. He was diagnosed with early onset Alzheimer's disease. The doctors prescribed some medicines for him, which were supposed to help, but the disease progressed more quickly than expected, and I couldn't take care of him anymore. I eventually had to put him into the Shady Grove Senior Center."

Cade avoided eye contact with Janna, directing his words at her mother instead. "His doctors are still trying to get the right combination of medications for him. Some of them make him agitated. Some make him lethargic. You never really know what kind of day he'll end up having. I actually meant to stop by and see him today, but with everything that's been going on, it slipped my mind."

Her mother dabbed the side of her mouth with a napkin. "Maybe you can go visit him tomorrow. I'm sure he'd like to see Janna and meet Grace."

Janna shot her mother a withering look and felt an urge to duck out of the room. "Um, who needs something else to drink? Dad? Cade?" She jumped up from her seat like there was a pin sticking out of it. "Mom, why don't you help me in the kitchen with these?" Her tight lips and wide eyes should've gotten the message across.

Her mom seemed unaware she was meddling again. She rose from her seat, grabbed her husband's glass, as well as her own, and followed Janna into the kitchen.

Janna pulled the pitcher of sweet tea from the refrigerator and began filling Cade's glass. She waited until the door to the dining room closed behind her mother.

"Mom, do you think you could have mentioned to me before that Cade's dad wasn't doing well?"

Mom took the pitcher from Janna and filled up the two glasses in front of her. "I thought I did, honey."

"I think that's something I would've remembered. Now I've hurt Cade's feelings." Janna threw her hands in the air. "He's been through so much in the past few years, and I just made things worse. Someone should have told me his dad was in a home."

"It's not a home." Her mother raised her eyebrows and shook her head. "It's a senior living center."

"Mom, that's not the point. I should have known this," Janna hissed.

"Sweetie, would you stop worrying about this and just go out there and talk to him. I think it's clear to everyone at the table, except for maybe you, that Cade still cares very deeply for you."

"Listen, Mom. I know you always wanted us to get married. I'm sorry it didn't work out, but I thought you understood why I needed to leave. You've got to quit pushing this so hard." She picked up Cade's glass and headed out of the kitchen.

Just before she got to the swinging door separating the kitchen and the dining room, her mother hit her with another bombshell.

"Janna, do you think a person would wait seven years for you if he didn't love you? Tell me you know that's not something you brush off."

Janna whipped around and walked back to her mother, setting the two glasses in her hands on the counter. "He's not . . . I don't—"

"You need to stop trying to control everything, Jan. We both know stuff like this happens for a reason, and if you can't figure out the reason on your own, I feel it's my right as your mother to let you in on the secret." Her mother scooped up her refills and breezed by Janna adding, "Besides, all the hostility you carry around with you is creating a big wrinkle. Right there." Her mom motioned to the space between Janna's eyebrows with her pinky finger.

Janna scrunched up her lips and rubbed the anger line from her forehead. Her mom was right. She couldn't control anything. The Brenner case certainly proved that. No wonder she was so worn out all the time. Constantly clinging to the reins of everything was exhausting.

Taking a deep breath to collect herself, Janna reentered the dining room, placing Cade's filled glass down by his plate.

"Thanks." He took a sip.

Janna returned to her seat and cleared her throat. Her mother mouthed *Talk to him*, while everyone continued eating.

"I'm sorry about your dad, Cade. I didn't realize he was in such bad shape." The words exploded from Janna's lips like a gush of water from a burst pipe.

Cade's face filled with the same broken expression as Mrs. Keever's had earlier.

Smooth. Janna could feel the prickly heat of embarrassment crawling up her neck, and she could see her mother's horrified expression out of the corner of her eye.

"What I meant to say was I . . . I—" Everyone stared at her now, waiting for her to redeem herself. Her mind drew a blank.

Just think of *something*.

Before Janna could open her mouth, Grace's hand dropped down onto the silverware sticking out of the mashed potatoes on her plate. The force of her hand on the utensil created a lever, sending a forkful of mashed potatoes flying directly into the side of Janna's head. Fluffy white globs of potato fell to the floor and clung to Janna's hair.

Everyone stared at each other for a moment, waiting for a reaction. Janna sat motionless, stunned by the vegetable missile just launched at her. Her mother gaped at her, while her dad looked around trying to catch up with what happened. Cade's eyes were wide. His face began turning red, his lips pressed tightly together. She didn't know if what she'd said made him mad or if he was so shocked by what he'd just seen that he'd forgotten to breathe. No one had to wait long to find out which emotion he struggled with.

He let out a deep, guttural roll of laughter, one that sounded like it had been pent up for a while. He doubled over in his chair, his body shaking, and continued to laugh. Janna began to laugh too. Soon the whole table was in tears, except for Grace, who looked around at everyone else, possibly unsure if she had done something wrong.

"It's okay, Grace," Janna choked out through her continued laughter, patting the little girl on the back. "I needed someone to shut me up!"

The table roared with laughter again. Janna dipped her napkin into her water glass and ran it over her hair, a pretty ineffective measure considering the clumps of potatoes now stuck to it like glue.

Janna smiled and stood up from the table. "If you'll excuse me, I think I'm the one who needs a bath now." Bits of potato dropped from her hair. She tried to catch them in her napkin. "I'll be back down in a few minutes."

Heading up the stairs, Janna heard her mother ask, "Would anyone like some more mashed potatoes?" This sent the table into another round of laughter. Janna chuckled to herself and continued to the bathroom to shower. Never, in all her life, had she been so thankful to have food thrown at her during a meal.

~8~

Janna finished her shower and checked the clock perched on the shelf above the towel rack. Seven o'clock. It had taken so long to get the globs of mashed potatoes out of her hair that she hated to waste any more time blowing it out straight. She wiped the fog off the mirror and stared at her reflection. Though her hair was still damp, flaxen ringlets began to form around her face. She hoped by now everyone downstairs had forgotten the stupid things she'd said at dinner.

Rummaging through her suitcase for a change of clothes, Janna quickly remembered she neglected to pack any casual pieces of clothing. She sighed and looked at the closet. *Mom keeps everything,* she thought. *It's worth a shot.* Janna walked to the closet doors and pulled them both open at the same time. Several pairs of jeans from her high school days and a

116

few faded T-shirts hung from the middle of the closet rod. She reached for a light pink T-shirt with the word *Lucky* written across the front in a large cursive font. Amazingly, she still fit into the first pair of jeans she selected. She finished dressing and headed downstairs to see if Cade was still there.

As much as Janna hated to admit it, Mom had a point. She needed to talk to him. Lay everything out on the table. She overheard Cade telling her dad about discovering Grace in the cornfield. She paused briefly at the bottom of the stairs.

Lord, I know I've kinda been off your radar for a while, or well, I guess you've been off my radar. Anyway, if you could just keep me from saying the wrong things long enough to get the truth out, I'd really be grateful. Cade deserves to know the truth.

Janna rounded the corner to the living room and noticed Grace first, coloring a picture of a butterfly at Cade's feet. Grace colored perfectly within the lines, unusual for a girl her age. Grace pulled several more crayons out of an old Strawberry Shortcake lunchbox that was Janna's as a child.

As Cade's eyes finally met Janna's, a ding sounded from the kitchen.

"Oh, the cobbler." Janna's mother popped up from the rocking chair where she had been sitting and walked out of the room.

Janna took a seat in an oversized chair beside her dad's recliner. She tried to look relaxed as she propped her legs up on the ottoman. Cade smiled at her.

Good. He was still amused about the mashed potatoes and maybe had forgotten the comments she made about his dad.

"Dessert is ready," Mom said, carrying in a tray holding two small saucers, each containing a mound of blackberry cobbler with a scoop of ice cream on the side. A warm, buttery smell wafted through the air and settled under Janna's nose.

Two tall glasses of tea also sat on the tray. "Here you go." Janna's mother held out the tray to Cade. "You know, it's such a nice night, not too humid like it's been the past few weeks. Why don't you two have your cobbler on the front porch?"

Subtle. Janna rolled her eyes, noticing her mother brought only two spoons with her. No doubt all part of her master plan to get her daughter to open up to Cade.

"Thanks, Mrs. Petersen." Cade rose from his seat and accepted the tray from her. He looked at Janna. "You want to take these outside?"

So, he was in on it too.

Janna removed her feet from the ottoman and stood. "Uh, okay. Mom, are you sure you and Dad don't want to join us?" She lifted her eyebrows and tried to send a telepathic message to her mother.

Her mother placed a couple of cloth napkins next to the glasses of tea on the tray. "Oh no, it's going to be past our bedtime soon. I think I should get this little one up to bed as well." She patted Grace on the head. "Besides, I'm sure you two have lots of interesting things to discuss. Your father and I would only bore you."

Cade laughed and nodded for Janna to lead the way. He didn't seem to mind her mother's little scheme.

Janna walked through the entryway and stepped out onto the porch, taking a seat on the porch swing. Cade set the dessert tray on a wicker table by the swing and took a seat on the matching wicker love seat, across from the swing. Janna passed him a spoon. They ate in silence for a few minutes until Janna couldn't bear it anymore.

"I checked Grace for bruises, but I didn't see anything indicating she's been harmed in any way." Janna took another bite of cobbler, keeping her focus on her plate. "At least not physically."

"Well, that's one blessing, I suppose. You heard me tell Pam I was thinking about going back out to the

Dellingers' in the morning." Cade picked up a loose blackberry from his plate and popped it into his mouth. "I'll make sure to check their barns and tractor shed this time for any signs Grace may have stayed there last night. I probably need to survey the whole area surrounding those fields, so I'll call Brian and see if he can help me tomorrow. At this point, I'm still not sure where she might have come from before I found her."

"You still think someone dropped her off?" Janna swirled the slight bitterness of the blackberries around in her mouth.

"I'm not sure what I think." Cade shook his head in disgust. "It still blows my mind that anyone would leave her helpless out there, no shoes, no jacket for when it gets chilly at night, not that it's been chilly lately, but that's not the point. They didn't even leave her any food. I mean, who could do that to their own child?"

"You'd be surprised. I know they say blood is thicker than water, but in my experience, it seems like other things are more important to a lot of the people I tend to deal with." Janna took another bite of her cobbler but realized she'd lost her appetite.

***

The whirring song of the cicadas began to pick up in the trees surrounding the Petersen house. Their chorus filled up the empty air between Cade and Janna.

Cade admired the way Janna's hair fell into curls now. He preferred it to the straightened version, much softer. He also noticed she wore a very familiar T-shirt and wondered if that was a coincidence or if she was beginning to remember the Janna she used to be. He wished they'd kept in touch a little more so she would've known about his dad and been spared the embarrassment at dinner.

Contacting her after their breakup wasn't an option she'd offered. Everything had been so final, like they would never talk or see each other again. Would Janna have even come to see him at all while she was in town if it wasn't for Grace?

She seemed to struggle with something as she picked at the blackberries on her plate. He wished he could help her in some way, wished he could make it better for her, make her more comfortable. She was on edge most of the time and not much like the sweet, spunky girl he'd loved so long ago. Well, if he was being honest with himself, the girl he still loved. Maybe it wasn't important why she left before. She was here now. That had to count for something.

"You've had some rough cases, huh? People not taking care of their kids?" Cade prayed she wouldn't close him off the way she'd done so many other times that day.

Janna bit the corner of her lip and looked past Cade into the yard. "You could say that. I believe most people really do care about their kids, but every so often you get a parent who never intended to be one, and they can't see past their own needs to take proper care of their children."

Janna hesitated and pushed a lock of hair behind her ear. She was definitely holding back from him. Maybe it had something to do with the box of files in her car. He was more than willing to listen if only she'd realize it.

"Actually . . ." She took a breath. "That's why I'm taking a little break from social work for a while—maybe for good."

"Really? I'm surprised. From the way Stacy always talked, it seemed like you really enjoyed your job, helping people, I mean."

"Well, I really did like it at first. The helping people part of it, anyway. I felt like I made a difference in people's lives, like what I did mattered. But then the past few years, all these child neglect cases started to get to me."

Cade nodded, afraid to break Janna's willingness to share by speaking.

"My last case . . ." Janna sighed and Cade recognized the broken expression in her eyes. "Well, it was one of those instinct things I guess. My gut told me abuse was going on, but with all the red tape *and* paperwork *and* going through the chain of command, I felt like no one would listen to me."

Janna blinked away the water welling up in her eyes.

"There was a girl about Grace's age or maybe a little older. Molly Ann. Her mother had a habit of talking her way out of things and had most people convinced she was a good mother. They initially assigned me to the case because the neighbors reported shouting going on at night in their apartment, along with the fact that her school had referred Molly Ann to Social Services because they thought she wasn't being fed on the weekends. After a few home visits, I don't know . . . I started feeling like more was going on below the surface than her mother was letting anyone know."

Janna seemed to be replaying the whole ordeal in her mind and remained quiet for a moment. Cade leaned in, resting his elbows on his knees, and waited for more.

"I shared my findings with my supervisor—like how Molly Ann always wore long sleeves and long pants, no matter the temperature outside, or how she told one of her teachers she didn't like it when her mother's boyfriend stayed over. But Maxine—my boss—she just advised me to keep

123

good documentation of all my discoveries and maybe I could get enough evidence to remove the girl from the home eventually." Janna took a long sip of her tea.

Cade studied her carefully before working up the courage to ask her about the box from her car. "All those files in your car? They were from her case?"

She nodded soberly. "I brought them home to look over . . . you know, to see if I missed anything. To see if I could've done anything else to help Molly Ann."

"Are you still going to see if it's possible to remove her from the home?"

Janna looked into the distance beyond Cade again. "I don't have to remove her—" Her voice cracked and her chin quivered. Tears welled up again in her eyes, but this time she let them spill over and run freely down her cheeks.

Cade handed her one of the napkins from the tray.

Sniffing, Janna dabbed the cloth under her eyes. "For weeks, I tried to build up a case against Molly Ann's mother, but she had an excuse for everything. One day I decided to stop by for a surprise visit, hoping to catch her off guard and find out what really went on in that apartment." Janna folded the napkin on her lap and stared at it, playing with the edges of the hem. "When I got there, no one would answer the door. I saw it was cracked, so I pushed it open and went in, calling for Mrs. Brenner, then Molly Ann. Everything was gone. The TV, her mother's clothes, the food in the kitchen. I looked around the rest of the apartment, hoping to find something that would tell me where they went. That's when I heard the water dripping in the bathroom."

Tears raced each other down Janna's face. Cade felt a strong urge to move to the swing and hold her, but he knew it wouldn't be appropriate now. Obviously, she had gone through more in the past few months at her job than she'd let her family or Stacy know.

"I pushed the bathroom door open and stepped into several inches of water covering the floor. It was overflowing from the bathtub onto the linoleum." Janna's voice trembled again. "Molly Ann was floating face up in the tub. I rushed to her, pulled her out, and called 911. I tried to perform CPR, but I just—I got there too late." She lifted her legs up on the swing and pulled them close to her chest.

Cade tried to think of something to say. He got up from the love seat and moved to the swing. He tried not to sit too close to Janna but hoped to offer her some comfort with his presence. Clearly, she felt responsible for the girl's death.

"You know what happened to Molly Ann wasn't your fault, right?" Cade leaned down to catch Janna's eyes.

"Yeah, I know," Janna said soberly, resting her chin on her crossed arms.

"Hey," Cade said, gently bumping his shoulder to hers. "I mean it, Janna. It sounds like you did everything you were supposed to."

Janna looked at him, tears still glistening in her eyes. "What if I had made more of a big deal of things? What if Molly Ann died because I was too much of a coward to buck the system and force someone to look harder into her situation?"

Cade shook his head. "Playing 'What If' is dangerous, Janna. I'll admit I've gone a few rounds myself, but trust me when I say it will drive you crazy. It is what it is. You did all you could. It sounds like you need to release yourself from the burden of guilt in this situation."

"I'm not sure I know how to do that." Janna's red-rimmed eyes finally met Cade's.

He wanted to reach out and take her hand, but before he could decide if now would be the right time to do that, Janna's dad stepped out on the porch.

Mr. Petersen cleared his throat. "Your mother wanted me to tell you she thought the girl might not want to sleep alone in the guest bedroom, so she's putting her to bed in your room, Janna." If he noticed his daughter had been crying, he didn't let on.

Janna wiped the remaining tears away with the back of her hand. "Okay, Dad."

Calvin nodded his goodnight at both of them and turned around, heading back inside as quickly as he'd appeared on the porch.

Cade smiled at Janna. "I see where you get your way with words."

"Yeah, the Petersens have always been gifted in that area."

They both laughed, releasing the tension in the air and bringing them a much-needed break from the seriousness of their conversation.

Cade rose to his feet and offered his hand to help Janna up from the swing. "Are you okay?"

She surprised him when she took his hand for a moment. She sniffed again and nodded before letting go. "Yeah, I'll be fine."

Cade noticed it had gotten darker. Lightning bugs began to fill the dusky air with their mini flashlights. "It's getting kind of late. I suppose I'd better be going."

"Okay," Janna said. Did he detect a hint of disappointment in her voice?

127

Janna followed Cade to the edge of the porch. He shuffled quickly down the steps, but turned back to face her from the bottom of the stairs.

"You know hearing stories like that really makes me thankful for parents like the ones we have. It's good to know not every parent is like Molly Ann's. You keep that in mind, okay."

Janna nodded again. "I'll try."

"Oh." Cade snapped his fingers, remembering the next day's plans. "If it's alright, it'd probably be best if Grace stayed here with you until lunch tomorrow. That'll give me and Brian plenty of time to comb over the Dellingers' property. Unless you have other plans while you're in town." He looked down at the ground and brushed his foot across imaginary dirt on the sidewalk.

"Actually," Janna's face brightened. "I was thinking I'd like to visit your dad tomorrow."

So she did care. Cade swallowed the catch in his throat that followed her offer. "I'm sure he'd love to see you, too."

"Well, goodnight then."

"Goodnight, Janna."

He turned to leave again when Janna's voice called him back.

"Cade."

"Yeah."

She paused, seeming to struggle with what she was feeling and what she wanted to say. "Thank you for listening. I've needed to tell someone Molly Ann's story for a while."

"Anytime." He nodded.

Janna smiled at him again before walking back into her parents' house. Cade watched her disappear behind the door and turned to walk back to his car.

A cluster of lightning bugs caught his attention as he traveled down the sidewalk to his vehicle. The blinking insects formed a little procession as they flew through the air. They swirled around him for a moment and then flew back toward the Petersens' house. He turned to watch them congregate around one of the upstairs windows, Janna's room maybe. They formed a tiny promenade, swirling single file in figure eights around the window.

Cade blinked and rubbed his eyes. He looked back up to the window, but the lightning bugs must have flown off somewhere else.

It had been a long day. He unlocked the car door and started the engine before glancing back to the upstairs window. No lightning bugs now, just the soft glow of a lamp.

He shook his head and backed out of the Petersens' driveway. "You need to get some sleep, Thompson."

~9~

"Remind me again why I agreed to get out of my nice, comfortable bed on a Saturday morning to help you poke around some cornfields." Brian yawned.

"How about . . ." Cade bent down to survey the ground level and tapped his index finger on his lips. "To serve your community? To help a little girl? Most importantly . . . because it's the right thing to do." He punctuated his sentence with a firm nod.

"Oh, yeah. That." Brian slapped a cornstalk out of his way. "I guess as a firefighter it's my duty to help protect the innocent and weak, right?"

"Right." Cade turned away so Brian wouldn't catch him smirking. "Besides, with everyone gearing up for the Fourth of July parade, all the other officers are patrolling Main Street, so you were kinda my last resort."

"Gee, thanks."

Even though it was early, the humidity made it seem hotter than the actual temperature. Brian wiped away the beads of sweat glistening on his forehead. "Listen, we've been out here for an hour, Cade. Don't you think if there was anything to find, we'd have found it by now?"

They had already checked Mr. Dellinger's barn and tool shed. Much to Cade's disappointment, they hadn't found anything there. He glanced at his watch. Its digital face read *8:30*. He didn't want to burden Janna with Grace much longer. It didn't appear much of anything would turn up out here, so it might be a good time to head back to the Petersens'.

"Yeah, you're probably right. Although, there is one place we haven't checked out." He pointed to the abandoned farmhouse in the middle of Mr. Dellinger's cow pasture.

The farmhouse—the original home for the Dellingers' property—had belonged to Mr. Dellinger's great-grandfather, Moses. When Cade and Brian were in high school, people said the farmhouse was haunted. Teenage boys would dare each other to sneak onto the Dellingers' property late at night and knock on the door of the run-down structure. If you knocked three times, the legend was that Moses would knock back. Cade had always chalked it up to creaky woodwork and overactive imaginations. Brian, on the other hand, swore he tried it once and heard the knock.

Cade raised his shoulders and shot a mischievous look at Brian. "Well, Mr. Dellinger did say we could check wherever we'd like."

He walked across the road and tried his best to shimmy through the barbed wire cow fence without getting scratched. Brian, who had gained some weight after he'd married Stacy, had a little more trouble, leaving behind a piece of his light blue T-shirt.

It didn't appear Harold Dellinger had done much to keep the brush down around the farmhouse, other than allowing his cows to roam the field and eat some of the roughage back. Briars grabbed at their jeans as they walked closer to the farmhouse.

Cade stood facing the old house for a moment, examining the front porch. It didn't look like anyone had been there except some curious bovines. He climbed the steps to the front door and turned around, looking back to where Brian stood staring up at the windows of the house. He didn't seem too eager to follow Cade.

"Uh . . . are you sure this is a good idea, Cade? I mean what are the odds that little girl even knew to come inside this house?" Brian looked around nervously.

Cade rolled his eyes. "Are you seriously still afraid of this place? You put out raging fires for a living and run into burning buildings to save people you don't even know, and you're scared of an old empty house?"

"Of course not." Brian shook his head before propelling himself up the stairs to join Cade. "It's daytime, and besides, there are no such thing as ghosts, right?" He laughed, but his smile quickly faded. He seemed to be trying to convince himself more than Cade. Lowering his eyebrows and narrowing his eyes, Brian added, "Anyways, I'm a man."

Cade suppressed his laughter and gestured for Brian to take the lead. "That's right, you mighty beast, you. Now, why don't you go on in ahead of me and check out the lower level?"

He patted Brian on the back, who cautiously turned the door knob. The door creaked as Brian pushed it open to reveal the entryway. Cade playfully shoved him through the doorway, causing him to trip over its frame.

Brian's eyes went wide, and he threw his hands up, waving them wildly. "Dude! Could you not touch me right now?"

Cade laughed as they moved through what used to be the living room. They headed across the hall to the next room when a loud THUD, accompanied by the unmistakable sound of scurrying feet came from above them.

Maybe Grace wasn't out here alone.

Brian froze. "What was that?"

Cade stared at a few drooping spots in the ceiling. More scurrying sounds unsettled the dust from the spaces between the rafters. He exchanged a look with Brian and hooked his thumb toward the stairs leading to the second level. "Let's go find out."

"Uh . . ." Brian wrinkled his nose like a skunk had entered the room. "Why don't I finish looking down here, and *you* go check out the situation upstairs?"

"If that's what you want to do." Cade patted his friend on the back again. "Would you like me to tell Moses 'Hello' for you?"

Brian wiggled his head dramatically. "You're real funny. Maybe if this cop thing doesn't work out, you can take your little comedy show on the road." He turned to walk toward the kitchen. "You know, it's all fun and games until the ghost of some old farmer eats your face off. Just keep laughing, Cade."

Cade chuckled as he walked to the foot of the stairs.

"Hello? Is someone up there?" Cade leaned toward the wall to see if someone lurked by the top of the banister.

"This is the Deputy Sheriff. If someone is up there, please come downstairs. It's not safe for you here."

No answer, just more shuffling noises. Like someone trying to hide from him.

Since this person didn't plan to show himself, Cade figured it was time to discover who it was on his own. He took the steps two at a time, hoping whoever was upstairs wouldn't have enough time to sneak away. Just before reaching the top step, he felt the stair give way under his foot as he busted through the rickety old wood. He fell forward and caught himself on the top step, but not before he turned his ankle on the inside.

"Ahh!" His voice bounced off the empty walls of the upper level. He removed his foot from the hole in the stairs and tried to stand. It surprised him that Brian didn't hear him yell out and come to see what happened, although he'd probably run out of the house thinking Cade met his demise at the hands of Moses Dellinger.

Cade stretched his foot back and forth, discovering his injury was not as bad as he thought, but he'd have to take it easy on his right foot as he combed the rest of the house. He strained to hear where the shuffling noises came from. Someone was moving around in the last room at the end of the hall.

He hobbled down the hallway, trying not to put too much weight on his ankle. He slowly pushed the door of the last bedroom open and scanned the layout, looking for whomever it was making those sounds. An old bureau still sat between the windows of what Cade assumed to be the master bedroom. A small, dusty picture frame even sat on top of the bureau. He wondered when the Dellingers last cleaned out this place. Maybe the bureau had just been too heavy to move.

Cade noticed a closet in the corner of the room. It must have been added to the house as an upgrade long after initial construction because the frame was positioned into the wall at a crooked angle. This tilt in the frame caused one of the closet doors to stay cracked open. Either that or someone crawled in there to hide when he heard Cade coming and forgot to pull the door shut.

He pulled the handle of the side that was already opened. Not too much in that side, just some old shelves stacked against the wall. He heard the shuffling noises again. This time he was sure they were coming from the other side of the closet.

"It's okay. I'm here to help you." Cade pushed the other closet door open.

A pair of glittering black eyes met his as a raccoon jumped down from one of the higher shelves still attached to the closet wall and chattered at Cade as it ran out of the room. The shelves stacked against the wall tipped over like dominos and landed with a crash. Startled by the wild array of sights and sounds, Cade stumbled backward and bumped into the old bureau, knocking the picture frame to the ground. The glass shattered inside the frame.

He bent down to pick up the frame, tapping out the broken glass so he could see the picture better. It was a photo of a couple on their wedding day. It had to be really old considering the yellow tinge the photo carried. Judging from the date, Cade figured it to be a picture of Moses Dellinger himself. He squinted and looked closer at the bottom of the photo. Someone had written in loopy, cursive letters, *Moses and Eliza Dellinger*. There was something else written underneath their names, but Cade had trouble making it out. He took the corner of his shirt and wiped away the dirt underneath the Dellingers' names. It was a Bible verse. Cade read the carefully scribed words.

"But the God of all grace, who hath called us unto his eternal glory by Christ Jesus, after that ye have suffered a while, make you perfect, stablish, strengthen, settle you."

I Peter 5:10 (KJV)

Cade read it one more time, trying to gather its meaning.

"After that ye have suffered a while . . ." Cade thoughts wandered to Janna. Maybe that's why she came back to town. God brought her home to settle her after she suffered the loss of Molly Ann. Cade's mind ran through the possibility that Janna leaving the first time could have been God's will for her, for both of them. Had God brought her back to him? And if that was the case, what could he do to keep her here?

"Hey, uh, Cade," Brian called up the stairs in an anxious voice. "I think you need to come see something down here, man."

Cade slipped the faded wedding picture out of the broken frame and into his back pocket. It might be wrong to take it, but the Dellingers hadn't cared enough to grab it when they cleaned out the place, so he felt certain they wouldn't miss it.

Avoiding the second step this time, he hurried downstairs to find Brian. His best friend was bent down, looking at something on the bottom of the back door that led out of the kitchen. Upon Cade's arrival, he stood up, giving his friend a closer look at what he'd been studying.

"What do you think it means?" Brian glanced at Cade and shivered.

On the bottom of the door, scrawled in what looked like red paint, were the words *Grace we'll find you.*

***

Cade stood silent for a moment, hundreds of scenarios flying through his head. He couldn't tell if the handwriting belonged to an adult or a child. Maybe someone left the message for Grace to find, some kind of promise that they would return for her. Or maybe Grace wrote down something she'd heard someone say to her. Janna had said children who survive a trauma sometimes resort to other methods of communication. Perhaps the words on the door were Grace's way of letting someone know she was in danger.

"We should probably get back and check on Grace." Cade pulled out his phone and snapped a picture of the red writing on the door. "I want to get over there and make sure everything is okay."

"Fine by me." Brian followed Cade back through the house. "This place gives me the heebie-jeebies anyway."

As they climbed back into the car, Cade's cell phone rang. Caller ID read "Pam McClain." He pressed the answer button. "Hey, what's up?"

Brian leaned toward Cade. "Is that Janna?" The loud, obnoxious tone of his voice drowned out Pam's words on the other end of the line. "Tell her it's about time she came home and you guys made up."

Cade elbowed Brian in the side. "No, it's Pam, you goof. Would you be quiet so I can hear her?"

Pam explained the progress she'd been able to make with Grace's case.

Brian was still rubbing his side when Cade hung up the phone and shared the summary of his conversation. "Pam said nothing else has come into missing persons, so she's going home to spend the rest of the holiday with her family." He started the engine and shifted the Wrangler into drive, heading in the direction of the Petersens' house. "From the looks of that message, it seems someone is coming back for Grace. I'm not sure if that's good or bad, though. Janna may know a way to find out. We'll just have to see if she can get anything about it out of Grace."

"So . . ." Brian dragged the word out like a low musical note. "What's going on with you and Janna? I received strict orders from my very sweet but extremely nosy wife to get the scoop on you two."

"What do you mean?"

"What do you think I mean, man? You don't hear from her in like five years, and now she's back and you're hanging out again. Is there something you want to fill us in on?" Brian's eyebrows bounced expressively on his forehead.

"She's been gone *seven* years."

"But who's counting, right bud?" Brian snickered. "The point is it's plain as day to everyone in this town you never got over the girl. Now that she's back, I guess we're just wondering how this is all gonna play out."

"First of all, it's no one's business how any of this works out, and second of all, who says I never got over her?"

"No one," Brian started.

"See—"

"Wait a minute. I was going to say no one has to say it. I think the fact you still carry her picture in your wallet says it for you." Brian patted Cade on the shoulder and shook his head sympathetically.

"How did you know—you know what, never mind. It doesn't matter. It was a long time ago, Brian. She's home on vacation. I don't even know if she plans on staying much longer."

"Maybe you could change all that, Romeo." Brian bumped his elbow against Cade's shoulder.

"Would you give it a rest already? You can tell your lovely, nosy wife that Janna's helping me on a child abandonment case and that's it. Okay?"

"Whatever you say, bud." Brian smiled like he was in on a secret Cade wasn't aware of yet. "I just want to know what happened to the two of you. Despite my well-meaning wife's best efforts, you weren't exactly Mr. Share-My-Feelings after it happened. One day you two are all googly-eyed and planning a wedding. And then Bam! Next thing we know, she's skipping town and you're moping around here like someone ran over your favorite dog."

Cade scoffed. "Nice analogy."

Brian furrowed his eyebrows. "Okay, okay. All joking aside, man. What happened between you two?"

~10~

"I can't do this, Cade."

The scene had replayed in Cade's head a million times since Janna left town. They'd been sitting on the same porch swing where Janna shared the tragic story of her last case, and that's what she had said before she handed the engagement ring back. "I just can't do this."

They were only a few weeks away from the wedding. Cade assumed the stress of planning everything was getting to her.

"What do you mean? You want to elope?" He smiled. Planning a wedding had begun taking its toll on him too. This was great news.

A long silence filled the space between them. The smile on Cade's face melted as he realized this wasn't about the wedding.

"No, Cade." Tears ran down Janna's cheeks as she shook her head. "I mean I can't do this—I can't marry you."

Cade took a breath and tried not to overreact. "I . . . I don't understand . . . I mean we're planning a wedding, Janna. I just put a down payment on a house. What do you mean you can't marry me?"

Janna put her face down into the palm of her hands and sobbed softly. Cade put his arm around her and pulled her close to him, stroking her soft, sun-kissed curls. She smelled like honeysuckle. To his surprise, she let him hold her and even leaned into him for comfort.

"Let's both take a deep breath and talk through this a minute." He kissed the top of her head. "Obviously, you're overstressed from all this wedding planning, but I can help you with whatever you need."

She lifted her tear-streaked face and stared at him for a moment. She seemed to be considering his proposition, which Cade hoped meant she wasn't serious about what she'd just said.

Janna sighed. "It's just I've been thinking over all this and . . . I can't live here anymore. I look around and I see all these people who have lived in Shady Grove their whole lives. They've known the same people and done the same things. They never go anywhere. They never venture out of their safe little bubble, and I don't want that to be my life, Cade. There's so much more I want to do."

He tried to wrap his mind around what she said. She loved this town. Where was this coming from?

"Cade, you're lining up a job here. Your family is here. I can't ask you to leave all this. It wouldn't be fair to you. But I can't stay. I just . . . feel trapped." She balled up her fists and held them to her chest. "I can't breathe here. I feel like if I stay, I'll smother."

"We can go anywhere you want, Janna." Cade swallowed the lump of desperation rising in his voice. "You just name the place, and we'll go there after the wedding. It's probably not too late to get out of the loan agreement."

Janna shook her head again. "No, Cade. You're not listening to me. This is something I need to do on my own. I've always had someone else making decisions for me. It's time for me to make my own way. Without anyone's help."

A stabbing pain shot through Cade's chest. "You mean without me." He removed his arm from her shoulders. "So, what are you saying? We're not getting married, and that's it? Janna, there's got to be something I can do . . . I mean this can't just be *over*. I love you."

More tears poured down Janna's face, and Cade could tell this hurt her as much as it hurt him. Maybe she hadn't completely made up her mind yet. He could still talk her out of it.

He ran his hand over her hair again and cupped her face in his hands. "We can figure this out, Janna. We can decide together where to live and what kind of life we're going to have. We *can*."

Janna pulled away from him and got up from the swing. "It won't be that simple, though. You know that. Your whole life is here, Cade. Your friends, your family."

"Yours are too. You would be able to just up and leave all of them behind?"

"It's different for me, Cade." Janna avoided his eyes, looking out into her parents' front yard. "I look around here and all I see are people who are perfectly content with meaningless, mediocre lives. I need more of a challenge in my life. I need to know I'm making a difference, and I can't do that here."

Mediocre. That's what she thought of the people in this town? That's what she thought of *him*?

He rested his elbows on his knees and rubbed his palms together, while he stared at the floor. "What about me, Janna? Is that what you see when you look at me? Mediocrity? Someone who's going nowhere?"

"No, Cade, that's not what I meant. It's just . . . I'm twenty-two, for heaven's sake. There are a lot of things I haven't done, things I haven't seen. If we get married now, I won't have a chance to experience anything else. I'll know exactly what my life will hold for the next sixty years."

"You feel like I'm holding you back. Is that what you mean?" His voice rose as his confusion turned to anger. "Then why did you say yes, Janna? If I'm just this big anchor dragging behind you, why didn't you turn me down when I asked you to marry me?"

Janna wiped the tears from her cheeks, but her voice still quivered. "Because I love you, Cade. I do want to marry you, just not right *now*. I think we both need a little more life experience before we can truly be ready to make a permanent commitment."

"So, what's the plan? We wait a few years, let you go experience life a little more, and then we see if we still feel the same way about each other?" Cade narrowed his eyes.

Janna's voice remained calm. "My aunt said I could come stay with her for a while in Wilmington until I decide what I want to do. She's been trying to get me a job down there. I've already talked to her supervisor, and she has offered me an entry level position."

Cade put his face in his palms and rubbed his forehead. What could he say to make her stay? She had already been making plans to do this for a while—she'd just waited until tonight to reveal it to him. His chest tightened, like he'd stopped breathing.

Janna avoided his gaze again. "I don't think we should contact each other for a while, either. I think it'd just be easier that way."

Cade laughed but was not amused. "Easier. There's nothing easy about this, Janna. Do you hear yourself? Basically, you're saying this is it. We're over. And maybe in a few years, when you've seen if there's anything better out there, you'll give me a call."

"Believe it or not, I'm doing this for you." Janna's tone became indifferent. "You shouldn't be with someone who doesn't want the same kind of life as you do. Otherwise, you'll always be disappointed in your differences and that person will never be enough for you. You deserve someone who's enough for you, Cade."

Cade stood from the swing and grabbed Janna by both hands. "Think about what you're doing. Think about what you're saying. Why don't we just postpone the wedding for another six months to give you time to think? Everything can just go back to the way it was before I proposed."

Janna pulled her hands loose from his. "I'm not going to feel any different in six months, Cade. I've already thought this through. I'm sorry. I can't marry you." She wiggled the engagement ring off her finger and pushed it into Cade's palm.

He was speechless. This wasn't happening. He must be stuck in a bad dream. If only he'd just wake up.

Things weren't supposed to go this way. He loved her, she said yes, how could this be the end? He stared at the ring in his hand.

Janna had stopped crying. In fact, she looked like everything was fine with her, despite the bombshell she'd just dropped. Her reaction angered Cade, who suddenly felt a strange compulsion to take what he thought Janna owed him. He grabbed her by the shoulders and kissed her forcefully. Pulling away, he let rage fuel his last words to her, "Enjoy your new life experience."

***

Brian exhaled his surprise. "Those were your last words to her? Wow. Harsh. No wonder she didn't speak to you for seven years, dude."

"They weren't supposed to be the last words." Cade still felt guilty for how he'd treated Janna that day. He knew it was wrong when he did it, but he was so hurt and angry the only thing he could think to do was to hurt her back. It seemed so childish now. Time had given him a lot more perspective than he'd possessed back then. He realized now Janna was just trying to do what was best for both of them.

Cade flashed his turn signal and made a left onto Brian's street. "I spent the whole night awake thinking about everything. I went over to her house the next day to apologize and try to convince her to stay, but her mom said she had packed up the night before and left for Wilmington early that morning."

"So, you didn't try to go after her or anything? Did you try to call her in Wilmington?" Brian asked, proving his wife wasn't the only nosy one in the family.

"She said it'd be easier not to talk, remember? I got to thinking about it and thought maybe I held on too tightly to her or something, like maybe this town didn't smother her, I did. I decided to give her some space for a few months. Then Mom died and everything with Janna just went to the wayside." Cade sighed.

"Why do you think she stayed away so long? Stacy kept in touch with her through a few emails. I know she said Janna's parents visit her a few times a year, but this is really the first time Janna's been back here." Brian pursed his lips and rubbed his chin. "Sounds like something bigger was going on with her besides the fact she wanted a few more adventures before she got hitched. I mean, why wouldn't she come back for your mom's funeral?"

Cade shrugged as Brian's house came into view a few yards in front of them. "That's one thing I'll never understand. Janna and Mom were so close. I don't know if it was too hard for her to get away from work or if her mother didn't tell her in time. I don't know, maybe she just couldn't be around me after the way I left things."

"Well, at least something good came out of the end of your relationship with Janna." Brian sounded optimistic as they pulled into his driveway.

"Oh, yeah, what's that?" Cade shot him a sideways glance.

"I got a great deal on our first house." Brian grinned and climbed out of the passenger seat.

"Yeah, because that's what's important in this story." Cade rolled his eyes. "Tell Stacy I said 'Hello.'"

Brian turned around and propped his elbow on the rim of the passenger door. "Why don't you tell her yourself tonight at dinner? I just remembered my mission was twofold: find out what happened between you and Janna *and* invite the two of you, and the little girl, too, I guess, to supper."

Cade tilted his face and shook his head. "Um, I don't know."

"Oh, c'mon." Brian leaned in and unfolded a thick layer of guilt. "You bailed on us last night, and I just spent my hard-earned day off helping you find vital evidence for a missing persons case. I think it's the least you could do. Besides we have a ton of leftovers from last night. It'd be a shame to let good hamburgers go to waste."

Cade laughed. "I'd like to, man. I just think it might be a little too weird—"

Before he could finish protesting, Stacy stepped out onto the wide wraparound front porch of the house Cade originally chose for himself and Janna to share. She waved and walked down the steps to greet him. "Cade, did Brian remember to invite you to dinner tonight?"

"Don't worry, Stace, he followed your specific orders, down to the last detail." Cade lifted his hand to his forehead and gave her a mock salute.

Stacy had invited him to dinner numerous times over the last few years, but he somehow managed to avoid eating there, with the exception of their annual Fourth of July barbeques. Even then, he stayed outside the whole time and left early so he wouldn't be invited into the house. He thought it might be easier to just accept an invitation from Stacy this time than to try to come up with another lame excuse.

Despite the reputation redheads usually have for being temperamental, Stacy was always so sincere and sweet when she'd invited Cade over before and even more gracious when he declined. He wasn't sure Brian ever told her how he purchased their home so inexpensively, and she seemed oblivious to why it might be hard on Cade to be there, so he didn't think he could avoid eating with them this time around.

Cade smiled. "Do you need me to bring anything?"

Stacy's face perked. "Just Janna and yourself. Oh, and Brian said you were babysitting a little girl this weekend. You should bring her, too. We just love kids, don't we, honey?"

Brian draped his arm across Stacy's neck. "Yep, and one day soon, we'll have a whole yard full of 'em, so I guess we better start practicing now."

"The three of us will see you tonight for dinner, then." Cade nodded. "What time?"

"How about seven?" Her voice held the same exuberance as it did every time she tried to set Cade up with one of her friends.

"Seven sounds great. See y'all later."

"See ya," Brian said.

Pausing at the end of the driveway, Cade watched Brian and Stacy walk to the front porch together with their arms around each other. He envied the closeness they shared. Although he had been pursued by several of the women in town after he joined the police force, he'd never met anyone who could make him forget how he felt about Janna. He might have picked up on the wrong signals yesterday, but he sensed she'd come back for more than just regaining her bearings after a rough case.

He'd need some assistance to discover the real reason for Janna's sudden return. "Whatever the reason, Lord, I need your help. I know you got her here, but what do I do now? She seems to have lost who she used to be. She's guarded and closed off now. Not at all like the girl I used to know."

A crazy idea sprung into Cade's mind. Perhaps now was a good time to remind her of who Janna Petersen was and what they used to have.

***

The sun shone brightly through the curtains in Janna's bedroom, beckoning her to wake up and enjoy its warmth. She rolled over, expecting to find Grace tucked under the covers beside her like she had been last night. Instead, the little girl's side of the bed was empty. In fact, it looked as though she'd made it up perfectly before she left the room. Janna sat up and rubbed her eyes. The smell of bacon drifted up the stairs and into her bedroom. Grace must have been hungry and headed down for breakfast.

Breakfast sounded pretty good to Janna too, so she made her way down to the kitchen. Her mother was busy at the stove. Grace, dressed in her now-clean purple sundress, sat on a stool at the island, swinging her legs and enthusiastically filling her mouth with bites of pancake.

Janna smiled, noticing Grace wore the purple flip-flops Cade had picked up for her. Her mother had also braided her hair and tied the end with one of Janna's old hair ribbons. Mom really did keep everything.

Grace looked up at Janna and smiled, her cheeks full of the pancake man Janna's mom had created for her. Janna put her arm around Grace and gave her a little "Good Morning" squeeze.

"You hungry, Jan?" her mom asked, placing two pancakes and three slices of bacon onto a plate for her daughter.

"Mom, this looks great." Janna accepted the plate from her mother. She took a seat at the island and glanced around the kitchen. "Where's Dad?"

"Oh, he's playing in the Fourth of July golf tournament this morning. He said he had a few stops to make on his way home from the course afterward, but he'll probably be back before lunch."

Janna stared at the food on her plate. In efforts to keep her figure slim, she had avoided real bacon over the past several years and tried to keep track of her calories and fat intake every time she ate. But trying to control everything all the time was becoming tiresome.

It may be only a small step, but she was taking a bite of this bacon and would not think about anything but how delicious it tasted. Taking in the smell of pancake batter and butter as it danced around the kitchen, Janna closed her eyes. She sunk her teeth into the slice of bacon and savored the crisp edges as they melted away into a salty, smoky flavor. She sighed and picked up another piece. This one tasted like maple syrup and brown sugar, her mom's "special" bacon.

Before Janna could stop herself, she let out a satisfied, "Mmm."

She opened her eyes to find both her mother and Grace staring at her with amused expressions on their faces. Her mother's head tilted to the side, no doubt trying to decipher her daughter's peculiar reaction to a few slices of bacon. Grace put her hand over her mouth and giggled. It was the first time Janna heard Grace make any noise. She patted Grace on the head and looked at her mother. "Sorry, it's just that I haven't had bacon in a while. I'd forgotten how good it was."

Grace smiled at her again, taking a piece of the bacon from her plate and putting it onto Janna's.

Janna laughed. "Thanks, Grace."

The doorbell chimed through the house. "It must be Cade," her mother said.

Grace hopped down from her stool and raced to the front door. Janna shoved the last piece of bacon from her plate into her mouth and followed Grace.

Grace pulled the door open and Cade looked down at her, surprised. He must have been expecting someone much taller. The little girl held her arms up for Cade to lift her. He picked her up, and she hugged his neck. Janna watched their interaction from the entryway. Grace held out one of her feet to show Cade how nice his gift looked on her.

"You like them?" He smiled at her and looked at Janna. "Mornin', Janna. Sleep well?"

"Yeah, thanks." She gestured with her hand. "Come on in."

He scraped his feet on the welcome mat before stepping into the house. Janna closed the door behind him. "Did you and Brian find anything?"

"Strangely enough, we did." He placed Grace back down. "I just don't know what it means." Cade sniffed the air. "Is that bacon?"

"Oh, yeah. Mom made breakfast." Janna adjusted the edges of her pajama top. "Would you like some? You must be starving after searching the cornfield all morning."

"Sure." He nodded and raised his eyebrows at Grace. She took his hand and pulled him toward the kitchen.

Crossing paths with Janna on the way, Cade smiled, staring at her hair and patting her on the shoulder. "That's a nice look, Alfalfa."

Janna walked to the mirror on the wall to get a glimpse of what he was talking about. She must have wriggled around in her sleep last night, causing the curls on the back of her head to get smooshed together and stick up like stalks of curly wheat. She didn't feel embarrassed by her hair faux pas, maybe because she knew Cade was having fun with her, but she did smooth it down before following Cade and Grace into the kitchen.

Her mother looked up from the stove as the three of them entered the kitchen. "Good mornin', Cade. Would you like some coffee?"

"Yes ma'am, I'd love some. Black is fine."

Janna's mother loaded up a plate with a stack of four pancakes and several slices of bacon and placed it in front of the spot Grace had vacated at the sound of the doorbell. After reaching for a yellow ceramic coffee mug from the cabinet beside the stove, she walked to the coffeemaker, picked up the pot of fragrant brew, and filled Cade's mug to the brim.

"Wow! Mrs. Petersen, you have outdone yourself. This is a breakfast feast." Cade pulled his wallet and keys from his back pocket and placed them on top of the island as he sat down. He took a sip of coffee, while Grace climbed onto the stool beside his.

Janna tried to camouflage a pleased grin with her hand. It was sweet of him to make a big deal to flatter her mother.

Her mom ate up the attention. "Oh, Cade, you're too much." She swatted her hand at him. "But you're welcome." She looked at Janna and seemed to be trying to gauge her reaction to Cade being there.

Janna felt her mother's stare burning a hole into her forehead. She diverted the attention back to Grace's situation. "So, you were saying you and Brian found something out there in the cornfield?"

"Oh, yeah." Cade swallowed a bite of pancake and pulled his cell phone from his pocket. He pressed a few buttons before holding it up for Janna and her mother to see.

Janna leaned in for a closer look at the picture. "What do you think it means? Do you think someone is coming back for Grace, and they were trying to let whoever found her know?"

"You know what . . ." Janna's mother interrupted, scooping Grace up from the stool. "Little pitchers have big ears, so why don't I take Grace up to brush her teeth while you two talk?"

Cade watched them go up the stairs. "I thought so at first, but after looking through the rest of that dilapidated old house, I'm not so sure. If someone told her to stay there, wouldn't they have left some food or a blanket or something?" He shrugged. "I'm thinking it might be some

161

kind of warning . . . like if she didn't stay put and wait for whoever left her there, they were telling her they would find her anyway. What do you think?"

Janna grimaced and shook her head. "It's hard to say, Cade. If the message was intended for Grace, she's probably the only one who knows what it means."

"That's what I was afraid of. I really need her to communicate with us. Do you think you could see if she'd open up to you? We could show her the picture of the message on the door and see if it sparks something in her. Unless you think it'd be too traumatic for her." He let out a sharp breath. "I'm at such a loss here, Jan. This is really more your area of expertise."

Janna wondered if he meant to shorten her name like he used to when they were teenagers. "I don't know if I'd call me an expert, but I'll try talking to her if you think it will help."

Cade stared at Janna for a moment. He seemed to be debating whether he should say what else was on his mind, but he would have to wait to share his thoughts. Janna's mother and Grace returned to the kitchen.

"Show 'em your nice clean teeth," her mother instructed.

Grace obeyed, lifting her lips and pressing her top and bottom teeth together to show off her freshly polished pearly whites.

Cade made a production out of his inspection by gently grabbing Grace's chin and moving her face to check one side and then the other. "Very nice." He pulled her up into his lap.

"Listen, Grace, we need to talk to you for a little bit about what happened to you, okay? Now, you won't get in trouble for anything you tell us. We just want to help you." Cade glanced up at Janna and widened his eyes, signaling for her to jump in.

"That's right, Grace." Janna leaned over and smoothed a stray hair away from Grace's face. "Can you tell us anything about your family? Did your mommy or daddy bring you out to a house in the field?

Grace looked at them both and sighed.

"Mom, could you find some blank paper and something to write with, please?"

"Sure." Her mother headed toward the living room.

Janna returned her gaze to Cade's face. "It might help her to draw what happened if she doesn't want to talk about it."

163

He nodded, as her mom returned with some white paper and Janna's old lunchbox full of crayons. She placed the paper onto the island in front of Grace.

Janna ran her hand gently over Grace's braid. "Honey, we need to know what happened to your family." She pulled out a handful of different colors and spread them across the top of the paper. "Could you draw us a picture of how you got to the cornfield?"

Grace sighed again and looked solemnly into each of their faces. She nodded and began to color the top of the paper a sky blue. They watched as she drew clouds, some cornstalks, and a house. The details were a little rough, but there was no doubt that she'd at least seen the old farmhouse before. Janna exchanged bewildered looks with her mother and Cade while Grace finished the last touches of her diagram.

She pointed to the sky in the picture, then to the house, and then to the cornfield.

"In the morning, someone dropped you off at the house, and then you went to the cornfield?" Janna's forehead wrinkled.

Grace nodded but continued to point to the old farmhouse. She moved her drawing and took another piece of fresh paper from the pile. She drew a door, just like the one Cade had snapped a picture of on his phone, and pointed to the bottom of it.

"Grace we'll find you." Cade repeated aloud. "You saw the message there, right? Who will find you, Grace? Is someone coming back to take you home?"

Grace raised her head up and down slowly, indicating Cade was right.

"Who, Grace? Can you draw them?"

She shook her head "No" this time, gesturing with her hands. They watched carefully as she made a square using her index fingers and thumbs. She lifted the index finger on her right hand, pressed it back down, and made a clicking noise with her tongue.

"Yes, Grace. We need you to draw a picture." Janna looked at Cade for help.

He pulled something from his pocket and laid it out in front of Grace.

"Grace, do you have a picture of who brought you to the house? A picture? Like this." He pointed to the old, yellowed photograph he'd placed on the island.

Janna read the names to herself and looked at him. There was something else scribbled on the bottom of the photograph, but she had a hard time making it out without her contacts. She hoped Cade had an explanation to share with her later about where he'd found the photograph and why he'd brought it back with him.

Grace's shoulders slumped and she shook her head in frustration. She pushed the drawings away from herself with some force, accidentally knocking Cade's keys and wallet off the island and onto the floor.

"Whoops. I'll get those for you," Janna offered. She walked around him to retrieve his things from where they'd landed on the other side of the island. She squatted down to pick up his keys first, which had gone farther due to their lighter weight. As she reached over to grab his wallet, her breath caught in her chest. In the fall, his leather wallet had unfolded, and there in the center was another picture. A picture of Janna.

~11~

A photograph of her younger self stared back at Janna, her eyes holding the exuberant glimmer of a girl in love. It was taken at the county fair, the day after Cade proposed. Her long curls were full, and she was wearing the same pink shirt she'd worn last night. Grinning from ear to ear, she was holding up her left hand. A sparkly oval-shaped diamond gleamed on her finger in the sunlight. She'd been so happy in that picture. They'd taken other pictures that day too—Janna and Cade smiling at each other, holding hands, kissing on the Ferris wheel. As much as she hated to admit it, the memories attached to those pictures had been ever present in Janna's thoughts the past few months. Now it seemed they'd also been on Cade's mind. Why in the world did he still have this in his wallet?

Cade's voice jolted her back into the present. "Uh, Janna, you okay down there?"

"Oh, um, yeah." She closed the wallet and scrambled to stand back up. "Here you go." She placed the wallet and keys on the island in front of Cade and looked up at him casually, trying not to let him see she'd discovered his secret.

Cade lifted Grace from his lap and seated her on the stool beside him. He rose from his seat and took a step toward Janna, gently grabbing her by the arm and pulling her to the other side of the kitchen.

"You know," he whispered, "It seems like this may be too much for Grace right now. She's made it clear someone would be back for her. Maybe she'll tell us more if we stop pushing her so hard. What do you think?"

Janna kept her voice low, too. "You're probably right. Besides, judging from her last reaction, she's getting frustrated with the fact we don't understand what she's trying to tell us. We could give her a break and go visit your father for a while. Who knows, she may just need more time to process what happened to her."

Cade turned back around to Grace. He inhaled, clapped his hands together, and released a short breath. "Well, how 'bout we take a break from all this and go for a little trip to see Dad. Would you like that, Grace?"

Grace seemed to perk up at the idea of leaving arts and crafts time to do something more social. She hopped down from the stool and walked to Cade's side, indicating she was ready to leave. Cade leaned over, retrieved the picture of the Dellingers from the top of the island, and put it back in his pocket.

"You ready?" He grinned at Janna.

"Yeah, just let me run upstairs and get my purse." Janna walked to the base of the steps leading upstairs from the kitchen. She stopped and looked down at her oversized blue T-shirt and matching flowered pajama pants. "I should probably change too, huh?"

Janna turned around and exchanged a smile with Cade before she took the stairs two-by-two.

***

"Would you mind if I rolled down the windows?" Cade asked as they drove from Janna's house to the Shady Grove Senior Center. "It's been so unusually pleasant out the past few days after the morning humidity clears. It'd be nice to enjoy it on our ride over."

"Yeah, that's fine." Janna gazed out the window.

Cade figured the wind blowing through the car would take the pressure off them to fill the silence.

He wondered if Janna felt nervous about seeing his father. He knew his dad wouldn't remember her anyway, but maybe he should make her aware of how bad the situation could be.

"I want to warn you about a few things before we go see Dad." Cade squeezed the steering wheel. "He's been having some . . . uh . . . difficulties the past few weeks. He doesn't remember Mom's not around anymore, and sometimes he asks about her. It's usually easier to just play along with whatever memory he's having than try to explain things to him—"

"Listen, Cade, I'm so sorry about last night, at dinner, I—" Janna lifted her hands and let them drop into her lap as she sighed. "Mom didn't tell me . . . I mean I didn't know anything about your dad, and yeah, Mom should have told me, but . . ."

Cade glanced in the rearview mirror and watched Grace drop her forehead into her palm and shake her head. She must have felt as bad for Janna as he did sometimes.

"Janna, you don't have to explain anything." He swatted his hand through the air. "It's already forgotten, okay? I just wanted you to be prepared before we go see Dad, that's all."

"Okay." She nodded and seemed to turn her attention back to the passenger side window.

***

Janna had been unable to focus after seeing her picture in Cade's wallet. Perhaps her mother had been right. Seven years is a long time to wait for someone. If Cade had been carrying that picture around since then, it had to mean he still thought about her. Maybe he didn't hate her as much as she'd been imagining all these years.

She turned to look at Grace in the backseat, who had fallen asleep as they rode. "So." She rubbed an imaginary spot of dirt off the dashboard. "I'm curious about something."

"Yeah, what's that?"

"It's just . . ." Janna rubbed her hands together. "I haven't heard you mention you were seeing anyone. I know it's really none of my business . . . but are you?" *That was about as eloquent as her apology earlier.* "What I mean is, it wouldn't bother me if you were. You can date anyone you want; it doesn't matter to me." She fanned the air from the passenger side window toward her face.

171

The sides of Cade's mouth turned upward as Janna tried to backpedal, but he kept his eyes focused on the road. "Clearly." He chuckled. "Actually, I wasn't sure when to bring this up, but yeah, there is someone special in my life."

"Oh." Janna heard the pathetic disappointment in her own voice, but hoped Cade wouldn't notice. She tried to look happy as she turned to him. "That's really great. Who is she?"

"You remember Candace Mabry?"

"The pastor's daughter?"

Janna thought about what Candace Mabry had been like in high school. She couldn't imagine how the girl she remembered could've become Cade's type. Although, in seven years time, his type may have drastically changed.

"Yeah, the one who used to be in science class with us," Cade said.

Janna shot Cade a skeptical look. "The one with all the tattoos and piercings?"

"Mm, hm. That's the one."

Janna winced, wrinkling her eyebrows in disgust before she could stop herself.

Cade's face broke into a huge grin, indicating his tattooed sweetheart was just a joke. He filled the car with his hearty, resonating laughter.

Janna swatted his shoulder with the back of her hand. "Oh, shut up." She was comforted by the fact her unfiltered responses didn't seem to offend him.

Cade smiled. "What? You know I've always had a thing for girls who can pull off a skull and crossbones tattoo *and* a nose ring."

Janna laughed and relaxed her shoulders.

Cade shrugged. "There have been a few girls who showed some interest in me after I officially joined the police department, but it was all just an attraction to the badge I'm afraid."

"I wouldn't be too sure about that." Janna blushed as the words escaped her mouth. Why was she having such a hard time keeping her thoughts to herself?

Cade only smiled again, pulling into a parking spot near the entrance of the center.

"Well, whatever the case is, I guess I've just never found a woman in this town with much substance."

Janna wondered if he included her in that count. She made it seem like she'd left town to find more substance, so maybe he was subtly referencing the reason she'd given him for leaving.

They climbed out of the car, and Cade woke Grace from her nap.

"Grace, you want to go inside and meet my dad?"

She rubbed her eyes and nodded.

They checked in at the front desk and were informed it was recreation time. Most of the patients were in the common area. Janna followed behind Cade, who held Grace's hand as they walked past several people sitting in wheelchairs in the hallway. The walls in the whole place were a dull, eggshell white, and the air smelled like rubbing alcohol and lemon-scented cleaning solution.

Several nurses sat talking to patients who were playing checkers or watching television as Cade, Janna, and Grace passed through the door into the common area. A man in a wheelchair rolled himself across the room with his feet, almost bumping into the back of Janna's ankles.

"Watch out, Jerry," Cade said, redirecting the man's wheelchair. He whispered to Janna, "You have to watch out for him. He'll run right over your toes."

Smiling uncomfortably, Janna nodded and glanced around the room. After a few seconds, Cade seemed to spot his father. Still holding Grace's hand, Cade walked toward a man who sat in a rocking chair facing the courtyard outside. Janna followed closely behind him. The man turned at the sound of Cade and Janna's footsteps.

Janna hadn't see Bill Thompson since she was twenty-two, but she wasn't prepared for how much his appearance had changed in just a few short years. He was only a year older than her own father, but he was so thin now. His skin adhered tautly to his face, and she could see the dark circles beneath his eyes. His brown hair was now sprinkled with gray around his temples, and he stared distantly out the window.

"Hey, Dad." Cade gently placed his hand on his father's shoulder. Mr. Thompson didn't respond.

Janna turned around in time to see a woman dressed in pink scrubs come up from behind them. Her hips swayed when she walked and her eyes were wide as if she were stuck in a state of perpetual surprise.

"He's had a pretty good day so far, Cade," the woman said a little too enthusiastically.

"Oh, hey, Kristin." Cade turned around. "How did he do at breakfast this morning?"

"He's getting some of his appetite back, I think. Isn't that right, Bill?" She leaned in closer toward Cade as she addressed his father.

Janna rolled her eyes. *Oh, brother.* Janna wondered if Cade considered this woman one of substance. He didn't seem to mind her drooling all over him now.

Cade remembered his manners. "Janna, this is Dad's nurse, Kristin. Kristin, this is Janna."

"Oh," Kristin said, her face dropping. "Is this your girlfriend?"

Now it was Cade's turn to blush.

"We're just friends," Janna answered plainly for him.

"Oh. Well, it's nice to meet you." Kristin's tone rose when she realized Cade's relationship status hadn't changed. "I'll leave you alone to visit with your father, but y'all just let me know if you need anything, okay?" Her voice was thick and sweet, dripping like molasses as the last word rolled from her tongue.

"Okay, we will." Janna pasted on the best fake smile she could muster.

Cade pulled up two chairs for Janna and him to join his father. He lifted Grace onto his lap, while Mr. Thompson continued to stare out the window.

"Dad, this is Janna. You remember her, don't you? She's Calvin Petersen's daughter." Cade looked at Janna as they waited for a response. "She's back in town for a visit, and she wanted to come see you. And this is Grace. We're taking care of her for a little while, and we thought you might like to meet her."

176

Mr. Thompson turned to look at Janna and Grace. He seemed to understand what Cade said.

"Very good." Mr. Thompson's voice was slow but clear. His eyes looked hazy, like his mind was somewhere else as he stared at Grace for a moment.

Cade leaned over and whispered to Janna, "Sometimes his meds make him sleepy, so I'm not sure if he really knows what's going on right now."

Janna nodded her understanding. "Mr. Thompson, my mother asked me to tell you 'Hello.' Do you remember Julia Petersen? She says she hopes you're doing well." She smiled but didn't know what else to say.

They were all silent for a moment. Grace wriggled down from Cade's lap, walked over to Mr. Thompson, and held out her hands. She must have wanted to sit with him now.

"Grace," Cade gently reprimanded. He leaned forward to pull her back, but Janna placed her hand on his forearm, catching his attention.

"Look," she whispered, pointing to Mr. Thompson. He looked down into the little girl's eyes, the edges of a smile forming on his previously solemn face.

The sun began to stream in more heavily through the window where they sat, illuminating Mr. Thompson's face.

He scooped Grace up and sat her securely in his lap. She leaned back comfortably onto his chest.

"Where'd she come from?" Mr. Thompson asked.

***

Cade stared at his father for a minute, trying to determine if his dad was truly cognizant of what he shared with him or if he was having some sort of flashback about his mother. He'd been doing that a lot lately.

"Uh." Cade exchanged a look with Janna, who seemed to be thinking the same thing as he was. "You mean Grace? She was out wandering Harold Dellinger's field yesterday morning. We're trying to find her family right now. We think she got lost from them somehow."

Cade watched as the haze cleared from his father's eyes.

"She's not lost." His dad tilted his head. "She's exactly where she's supposed to be."

Cade let go of a breath. "What do you mean, Dad?"

"She's supposed to be with you, Son." His father shifted Grace in his lap and stared into Cade's eyes. "She's been looking for you, and she finally found you."

Cade glanced at Janna, hoping she might have some idea of what his father was trying to say, but the look on her face didn't offer him much clarity.

Leaning forward, Cade studied his dad's face. "Who found me, Dad? Who are you talking about? Grace? Mom?"

His father shook his head. "No." He pointed at Janna. "Her."

Janna's mouth fell open as Cade tried to clarify some details for his father. "Dad, you're not making any sense. Janna wasn't lost this morning. Grace was."

Cade touched his hand lightly to the back of Janna's shoulder. "I'm sorry. He's confused or something. I don't think he knows what we're talking about."

"That's okay." Her voice sounded robotic. Maybe she was just shaken up by his father's claims.

"I know exactly what we're talking about," Dad raised his voice indignantly. "Miranda would understand what I'm trying to say. Where's Miranda?"

He sprang from his chair, almost dumping Grace into the floor. The little girl calmly stood beside the rocking chair watching while Cade's father began to wander the common area, calling loudly for his wife.

"Miranda, he won't listen to me. You need to come talk some sense into him. Miranda!"

179

Cade jumped up from his seat a little quicker than Janna and walked slowly toward his father, hoping to calm him down.

"It's okay, Dad. You need to be quiet now, though." Cade pressed his hands down, a gesture he hoped would lower his dad's voice. "You're going to upset the other people in here." He looked around. Some of the more coherent patients in the recreation area had stopped watching television and turned around to stare at his father. Why did every visit have to turn into a spectacle? This was too much to handle.

"Miranda!" his father bellowed again.

Kristin rushed over, calling out to two orderlies who were standing in the corner of the room. Cade didn't remember seeing them when they walked in. Neither of them looked very big. He wondered if they would be able to control his dad if he became violent. They each grabbed one of his arms and spoke soothingly to him.

Kristin kept her voice low and soft and shot Cade a sympathetic look. "It's okay, Bill. Miranda's not here. Why don't we take you back to your room for a little while? I think maybe you've had too long of a visit today."

"I'm fine." His father pulled his arms away from the orderlies' grasp. "I'm just tired, and I want to see Miranda. If she were here, she could help him understand. She could help him see."

The shorter, light-haired orderly patted Cade's father on the back. "We know, Bill, but right now I think it'd be best for you to rest in your room. You can explain everything after you've had some rest."

His dad sighed. "I guess I can just tell you later." He looked sleepy again, and the haze returned to his eyes.

"Michael and Gabe will walk you back to your room now, okay?" Kristin said, as if speaking to a child. "I'll call one of the doctors to come check on him." She walked to a white phone on the wall.

Just before Cade's father passed through the door, he removed himself from the orderlies' grip one more time and spun around, pointing his finger sharply at Cade like a warning. "He brought her here for you, Son. The sooner you realize that, the better off you'll be."

~12~

Janna glanced sideways at Cade, who stood frozen as the doors closed behind his father. She wished she could think of something to say, but Mr. Thompson's parting words had left her speechless too.

Kristin walked back over to them, shattering the eerie silence that hung in the air. "I'm sorry, Cade. He seemed to be doing well this morning." She put her hand on Cade's shoulder. "I'll talk to the doctor about adjusting his medications again. Maybe that will prevent other outbursts like that from happening in the future."

Janna tried not to fixate on the fact that Kristin's hand remained on Cade's shoulder, stroking it sympathetically. She felt Grace brush past her, bumping into her purse. Kristin retracted her fingers as Grace took Cade's hand. He looked down into Grace's face.

"I'll come back tomorrow and see if he's doing any better," Cade said without looking up. Janna could tell he was somewhere else.

"We can go now." Cade lifted Grace into his arms and began walking through the common area and past the reception desk. He moved so fast that Janna had to jog slightly once they reached the parking lot, just to catch up with him. Grace stared at her over Cade's shoulder.

When they reached the Wrangler, Cade unlocked Janna's door and opened it for her before loading Grace into the seat behind her. Janna watched him via the side and rearview mirrors as he walked around to his side. She could hear his shallow breaths as he climbed into the driver's seat, buckled his seatbelt, and tried to insert the key to get the engine started.

He was so agitated the key missed the opening as he tried unsuccessfully to jam it into the ignition several times. Janna could see he was in no shape to drive after his dad's erratic behavior. She reached over and pulled the key from his hand.

Cade released his grip around the key and let her take it. He unbuckled his seatbelt and slung it full force into the door, sending a loud metal racket through the vehicle. He gripped the top of the steering wheel with both hands and slumped over, resting his head on his wrists. "You know, this is just so . . . unfair," he said, still leaning over the steering wheel and staring at the floor mat. "That's what it is. It's just flat out unfair."

Janna wished she could think of something comforting to say. Her last few attempts to say the right thing hadn't gone so well. This time she'd take the silent route.

Cade jerked up from his position and dropped his hands in his lap, surprising Janna. "First, I lose my mom with no warning at all. Now I'm losing my dad slowly but surely, too. He loses his wife, but he can't even remember it. Maybe it's lucky he can't remember because then he doesn't have to grieve. He doesn't even have to miss her. For heaven's sake, he still thinks she's here!" He banged his fist on the middle of the steering wheel, accidentally hitting the horn. The sharp sound announced his anger to the parking lot.

Janna could tell Cade had been holding these feelings in for quite a while. Maybe that's what he meant yesterday at Mrs. Keever's when he'd said people wanted to talk about things and just wanted someone to listen. She was glad he'd chosen to share all this with her. Or maybe he'd just held it in so long he couldn't contain it any longer.

She reached out to place her hand on his shoulder but pulled back right before she made contact. The solace of someone's touch, no matter how well-intended, was only temporary. It might be better for Cade to release all the exasperation he felt and get it out of his system for good.

"I'm so tired, Janna. You know what I mean?" He turned toward her. "Not physically, but mentally and emotionally tired. I'm tired of not understanding anything. I'm tired of constantly having to battle with bitterness all the time. I'm tired of feeling mad every time I pray. I mean, I know God is supposed to work out everything for good for those who love Him, but what good has come of all this?" His steely blue eyes begged for an answer.

Janna turned away from his pleading face and played with the keys. "You know, I've been thinking a lot of the same things lately. Like why good people have to suffer sometimes. I still don't know the answer. I'm sure if you asked my mom, she could come up with a Bible verse to explain it."

"First Peter chapter five, verse ten," Cade said with an odd certainty.

Janna laughed, surprised. "Wow, Billy Graham. What'd you do, memorize a concordance?"

Cade shook his head but didn't laugh. "I recently read a verse like that." He pulled the picture of the Dellingers from of his pocket and laid it in Janna's lap.

With her contacts in now, Janna could read the verse. "It seems kind of ominous for a wedding photo, don't you think?"

"Who knows? Maybe something happened to one of them before they got married. Maybe one or both of them suffered a while because of something they did, and they felt their marriage was God's way of making them perfect again. I sure wish some of my dad's suffering would stop. You're lucky in that respect, Janna." Cade smiled. He seemed to be calming down.

"I know." She hung her head. "I think I've taken that for granted lately."

Cade didn't reply, but Janna knew he was thinking she could easily remedy that problem. After all, her parents were both alive *and* well. Having seen Mr. Thompson in the condition he was in now, she felt guilty for staying away from Shady Grove for so long. She made a promise to herself to sit down with her parents and thank them for their support. She also needed to ask their forgiveness for keeping them at arm's length all these years. They had done nothing to deserve it.

"Well, I guess we'd better be getting back to your parents' place. I don't want to monopolize all your time while you're here." Cade held out his hand for the key.

"Are you sure you're okay to drive?" Janna pulled the key to her chest protectively.

Cade rubbed his hand over his hair. "Yeah, I'm fine now." He thrust his hand out for the key again.

Janna caught a glimpse of Grace in the rearview mirror and noticed she studied them closely from the backseat. Another smile spread across her face, but it seemed neither amused nor mischievous. Janna thought she looked pleased, although she wasn't sure with what.

Cade's fingers brushed slightly against Janna's as she placed the key into his palm. He started the engine and pulled out of the parking lot. Neither one of them spoke for a few minutes, the gentle hum of the engine making their lack of words more comfortable.

Janna glanced back at Grace in the rearview mirror again. Now the girl stared out the window contentedly, enjoying the trees' reflections as they flashed across the glass.

"Oh, I forgot to tell you earlier. Brian and Stacy asked if we'd like to have dinner with them tonight. They said we could bring Grace along, too. Would you be interested?" Cade's tone gave nothing away about his own preference for the evening.

"Um, sure," Janna answered a little too quickly.

"Okay, great. I can drop you and Grace off at your parents' for a little while. Give you both a chance to eat lunch and maybe squeeze in a nap. Actually, there's probably something I should tell you before we commit to dinner at Brian and Stacy's tonight." Cade sat up straighter in the driver's seat.

"Oh really, what's that?" Janna asked absentmindedly, as something outside the car sparked her interest more than their conversation.

"Well, the house that they're in—" he began.

As they neared Shady Grove Community Church, Janna interrupted him. "Wait a minute." She placed her hand lightly on Cade's forearm. "Let's stop and see your mom."

Cade didn't respond, but he followed Janna's directions and turned into the parking lot of the church. Pastor Mabry's car was the only other vehicle there.

Janna was the first one to exit the car, plowing her way purposefully toward the cemetery.

***

Cade took his time getting Grace from the car. He wasn't sure he was prepared to witness Janna visiting his mother's grave, but he received comfort from the presence of

Grace's little hand in his as they walked toward the side of the church.

Janna had already entered the cemetery by the time Cade and Grace made it up to the sidewalk in front of the church. They had almost caught up to her when Pastor Mabry exited the main sanctuary doors. He smiled when he saw Cade and his small companion.

"Mornin', Cade." Pastor Mabry held a Bible underneath his arm. Cade wondered if it was a requirement for all pastors to carry one with them. The two men shook hands, and Cade introduced Grace.

"I found her walking in Harold Dellinger's field yesterday morning."

"Hi there, Grace." Pastor Mabry patted her on the head. She smiled at him. "How long is she staying with you?"

Cade shrugged. "Right now, she's actually staying with Julia and Calvin Petersen. Their daughter is back in town for a visit. She's a social worker. Or at least she used to be. She's helping me care for Grace until the county social worker gets back from vacation."

"Oh, you mean Janna? I haven't seen her since you two . . . uh . . . well, since you two came to me for premarital counseling. I didn't realize you two still talked."

"Actually, we haven't. Well, not in the past few years anyway. She happened to be in town visiting her parents and I needed someone with expertise in dealing with children, so I asked for her help."

"I see." Pastor Mabry looked at Grace and followed the path of Cade's stare to Janna. "Can I give you some unsolicited advice?"

Cade smiled. "Sure."

Pastor Mabry put out his hands to illustrate his point like he did on Sunday mornings. "In my experience, I've found things like this don't just happen by accident. There's usually a reason for everything—whether we see it or not, Son."

Hearing the word *son* brought his father's final words echoing back to Cade's mind. *He brought her here for you, Son.*

After what he'd just experienced at the Senior Center, he wasn't sure he was in the mood for one of Pastor Mabry's sermons after all. "I'll keep that in mind, sir."

The pastor seemed to sense the tension rise in Cade's voice. "You're welcome to pray in the sanctuary, if you'd like. It'll be open the rest of the evening for anyone who wants to pray. Lots of folks around here have family in the military. The Fourth of July is often a reminder of the price their loved ones are paying for this country."

"Okay, thanks Pastor Mabry." Cade offered his hand this time as a parting gesture.

"You take care, Cade. You too, little one." The pastor smiled one last time at Grace before unlocking his car and climbing into the front seat.

Cade watched him disappear from the parking lot and thought about what Pastor Mabry said about things not just happening. He began to think the pastor may be right. He just hoped the reason for all the things that had been going on was a good one.

Cade and Grace continued toward the cemetery. Janna was kneeling by his mother's headstone. He thought he heard her say, "I knew you would understand."

Cade's steps startled her and interrupted the rest of her conversation with his mom. "You okay?" he asked.

Janna's eyes were red from crying. "Yeah." She sniffed and wiped her cheeks. "I just realized how much I've missed your mom. You never felt like you had to explain yourself to her, ya know?. She just got you."

She stood up and Grace stepped forward, taking her hand and creating a bridge between Janna and Cade as they all stood facing his mother's memorial.

"I know what you mean." He smiled, running his hand across the smooth, cold top of the grave marker. He looked down at the ledge surrounding the headstone. The jar of peonies was gone.

"I've been meaning to ask you something. Did you come by here earlier to see Mom?"

Janna gave him a puzzled look. "No, why?"

"It's just I stopped by here yesterday, and I noticed a jar of peonies on her grave. Today they're gone. And, I don't know . . ." He shrugged. "I thought maybe you put them there."

"What makes you think it was me?"

Cade couldn't decipher her tone.

"Because I know peonies are your favorite too."

Janna smiled, dabbing the mascara that had smudged under her lower lid. "How in the world did you remember that?"

"I've got a really good memory." Cade raised his eyebrow, recalling his plan for reminding Janna of who she used to be. "In fact, I think you'd actually be surprised at all the things I remember about you."

"Oh yeah?" Janna put her hand on her hip. "Like what?"

"Well . . . like, your favorite color is purple."

"Gee, how'd you figure that one out?" Janna lifted the sleeve of the lavender shirt she wore.

"Oh, that's not all." Cade cocked his head to one side and grinned. He could tell he had piqued her interest.

Janna rolled her eyes and laughed. "Well then, please, tell me what else your phenomenal memory has kept locked away in that head of yours all these years."

"Let's see." Cade rubbed his chin and stuck out his lips. "Your favorite food is macaroni and cheese. You had a pet hamster named, uh . . . uh." He snapped and pointed his finger to the sky. "Lester! You got him in the fifth grade and had him for two years before you and Stacy set him free. Poor Lester never had a chance with all the neighborhood cats." Cade shook his head in mock grief.

"Is that all you remember?" Janna dismissed his prowess with a swat of her hand.

"Hold on a minute. You didn't let me finish." He tried to hide the smile tugging at the sides of his mouth. "Oh, yeah and you're deathly afraid of heights. No matter how much we begged, you'd never ever try the rope swing hanging out over Hollow Creek."

Janna scoffed. "I just didn't think that thing was tied to the tree securely enough. And besides, what's so great about dropping into that muddy, old creek anyway?"

"I hoped you'd say something like that." Cade grinned.

"Why?" She seemed scared to know the answer.

"Oh, you'll see. Let's head back to the car."

***

"I cannot believe I let you drag me all the way up here." Janna huffed as she climbed up the side of the hill facing Hollow Creek.

Truth be told, the "creek" wasn't a creek at all. It was actually part of the river that had been dammed up to help run one of the old sawmills when it was still in existence.

They reached the top of the hill, and Cade placed Grace on the ground so they could all survey the area. Janna caught her breath as she stared out over the creek. The old rope swing still hung over the water from a huge oak limb. She noticed that even the piece of wood someone had tied to the bottom of the rope to stand on remained intact, even after all the years that had passed.

"Wanna give it a try?" Cade's crooked smile was disarming.

In the past, Janna would've let her fear control her and turned him down, but strangely she felt like she had to do this.

"Here, hold these." She took off her shoes and shoved them into Cade's arms.

Janna intrepidly released the part of the rope looped around a nail at the base of the tree and pulled the swing to her. She climbed up on an old stump that people were supposed to jump from and placed one foot on the piece of wood at the bottom of the rope swing, steadying herself for takeoff.

She lifted the other foot onto the piece of wood and swung out wide over the creek. Her stomach hit her throat as she felt both feet leave the safety of the stump. She wanted to scream, but nothing came out.

Cade let out a whoop, cheering her on as she swung back and forth like a pendulum. Janna could see Cade and Grace watching her from the hill, as she swang toward them and then away, gliding over the middle of the creek. After her stomach settled, it actually felt nice up there above everything, with the wind in her hair.

She heard Cade say, "Let go, Janna," and despite all the instincts in her body telling her to do otherwise, she listened to him, releasing her grip on the rope swing and dropping feet first into the cool, muddy water.

"Janna!" Cade shouted, his voice echoing off the trees surrounding the creek.

She was underwater for a few seconds but swam to the surface quickly after her initial drop. The water felt like a second baptism as Janna leaned back and immersed the back of her head in its slow current. She felt like the water washed off all the dark things she had been dealing with the past couple of months, which seemed ridiculous considering the muddiness of the water. She felt like she could breathe better and see more clearly.

"Well, what are you waiting for?" Janna called back to Cade and Grace. "If I can do it, you certainly can too. C'mon, the water actually feels great."

Janna watched as Cade removed his shoes and Grace's, flinging them aside. He pulled the swing back to them and stepped onto the stump with one foot.

"You ready?" he asked Grace.

She nodded and grinned. Cade jumped onto the swing, and they glided across the air over the water.

"Hold your nose," Janna heard Cade warn Grace, right before he let go and dropped them into the water below.

They came up faster than Janna had, and Grace pushed herself away from Cade, proving she could swim on her own.

Cade swam toward Janna, smiling. "I guess I stand corrected, Petersen. I didn't think you had it in you. What made you decide to jump in after all?"

"What do you mean? Oh, you're trying to be funny, is that it? You told me to jump in, knucklehead, so I did." She splashed some water his way.

"Knucklehead?" Cade pretended to be offended. "Wait a minute, what? I didn't tell you to jump in."

"Okay, well you said 'Let go.' Same difference." Janna kicked her feet to keep her head up higher above the water. "I just thought you were right. I need to let go every once in a while. I guess I figured doing it while I'm swinging above a deep pocket of water is probably one of the best ways to accomplish that."

"Well, I'm glad you felt like loosening up a bit, but Janna, I really didn't say anything." Cade shook his head.

"Oh right . . ." Janna rolled her eyes. "It must have been Grace, then."

"I'm being serious Janna. I don't know who it was you heard, but it wasn't me. I know that for sure."

Janna was ready to argue with him but noticed Grace no longer swam around them. "Where is Grace?"

They both turned around looking for her, but she was nowhere to be seen.

"Grace!" They called out simultaneously before Cade dove underwater. Janna stayed above the surface, scanning the sandy rim that lined the creek.

After a few moments, Cade came up for air and exchanged a frantic look with Janna.

"Did you see her?" Janna asked, panic filling her chest.

"No, but she was swimming fine here just a minute ago. Keep looking."

They both dove in this time, but Janna swam in the opposite direction of Cade. The murky water made it impossible to see anything. Janna resurfaced again, followed promptly by Cade.

They both cupped their hands around their mouths and yelled loudly, "Grace! Grace!" All around them the water was silent and only the whisper of the wind in the trees answered their calls.

~13~

"What do we do?" Janna screamed.

Cade didn't answer but made a full turn around in the water, frantically scanning the surface. "She was just here a minute ago. Wouldn't we have heard her splash around if she started to struggle? Grace! Grace!"

Cade took another deep breath and dove under again. Janna stayed above the muddy brown water this time, in case Grace surfaced momentarily.

"Grace! Where are you? Grace!" Janna's own voice repeated a second call for the little girl as it bounced off the trees around them. Cade had been underwater for at least two minutes by her estimation. She didn't think it was normal to hold your breath for that long and began to worry he had disappeared under the water like Grace. What would she do if he never came back up either?

Cade finally returned to the surface for air a third time. Panic spread across his face.

"I can't—I don't . . . see her." He put his hand on his chest and gasped in air. "I don't know what happened to her. It's like she just . . . vanished."

"Maybe we're panicking over nothing." Janna tried to calm herself so she could think more clearly. "I mean maybe she just swam to the side of the creek and got out to dry off."

"Then where is she, Janna?" Cade raised his voice, its tone shifting from fearful to angry. "I never should have brought you out here. What was I thinking?"

"Well, I should never have told you to jump in the water with her." Janna pushed her wet hair out of her face. "If something happened to Grace because of this, it'll be all my fault."

"Lord, please don't let anything happen to Grace." Cade lifted his face toward the sky. "Please. Show us where Grace is."

Janna and Cade both heard some rustling in the trees above them and looked up to the ledge where they had jumped from the rope swing. A large flock of doves, startled by something, flew out from the trees like white missiles, filling the air with the sound of their flapping wings and staccato calls. Grace stood on the ledge above the creek, staring down at them. Her lavender dress was almost completely dry now, the wind ruffling it slightly at the hem.

Cade put both hands up and motioned to her. "Stay put, Grace. We're coming up there to get you." He pressed his hands together and looked to the sky again. "Thank you, Lord."

"How did she get up there so fast?" Janna's confused face mirrored Cade's.

"I don't know. We didn't take our eyes off her for more than a second or two."

They swam to the bank of the creek and climbed out. Water droplets raced down Janna's legs. She smoothed her hand over her jeans, pressing out what little water she could, before they began the brief but strenuous trek back up to the ledge.

"Don't go anywhere, Grace." Cade called up the hill again. "Stay right where you are and we'll come get you, okay?"

They reached the top of the hill, where Grace remained standing perfectly still. She must have taken Cade's instructions literally. She turned slightly at the sound of Janna's foot snapping a twig on the ground.

Cade reached Grace first and bent down to her eye level, his voice serious yet gentle. "You can't go running off like that, Grace. You scared us to death, kiddo. We thought you were gone or something bad happened to you. You understand?"

Grace nodded and smiled, taking Cade's outstretched hand. He grabbed his shoes and her flip-flops with his free hand, while Janna took a minute to sit down on a nearby rock and put on her sandals before they headed back down the hill.

She purposely lagged behind as the trio walked back to the car. Her wet clothes stuck to her slim frame. She discreetly wrung the remaining water out of them and straightened her shirt before Cade caught a glimpse.

Once they made it back to his Wrangler, Cade retrieved two ratty-looking old towels from the backseat. "Here," he said, handing one to Janna. "They're old, but they're clean."

Janna wrapped the towel around the ends of her hair and squeezed the water out, while Cade ran the other towel over his head and rubbed vigorously.

After opening the passenger door, Janna folded her towel and placed it on the upholstered seat before she sat down. Cade put Grace into the backseat and climbed in the driver's side.

"I'm sorry I yelled at you back there." Cade's eyes filled with remorse. "I just freaked out when we couldn't find Grace. I was afraid my intentions for bringing you here had clouded my good judgment."

"It's okay. I was pretty frantic myself. I'm just glad we found you, Grace." Janna reached into the backseat and tickled the girl's toes.

"Could you roll down your window?" Cade pointed to Janna's door before he rotated the handle on the driver's door. "Maybe our clothes will dry while we ride."

The wind picked up its pace inside the car as they headed back to town. It caught the edge of the Dellingers' wedding photo and lifted it from the dashboard where Janna had placed it earlier. With both windows down, the air whipped the old photograph around the front seat.

Janna wrenched forward and grabbed for it, but it slipped through her fingers and was sucked out the driver's side window. "Oh no!" Janna turned around to see where the photo went but couldn't tell if it had landed on the road or still sailed on the wind. "Should we go back and get it?"

"Nah. It's probably long gone now." Cade leaned to his left, checking the side mirrors. "Hope Harold Dellinger won't mind we lost his grandfather's wedding photo. It's been in the old house so long, he's probably forgotten about it anyway." He seemed to sense her distress. "Don't worry about it, Janna. It doesn't mean anything to anyone or they would've taken better care of it. Or they would have at least held on to it. Really. It's just a picture."

Janna wondered if he felt the same way about the picture of her in his wallet. Was it just a picture, or was the fact he'd held on to it a sign his feelings for her hadn't changed?

***

The aroma of warm cookies greeted Janna and Grace as they came in through the back door and entered the kitchen of Janna's parents' home. Her mother bent over a cookie rack by the stove, squeezing red, white, and blue icing over one cookie at a time as they cooled. There were at least six dozen already-decorated cookies resting on sheets of wax paper on the island.

Janna took in a big whiff of the sweet, sugary air. Grace, who seemed to be observing her, followed suit with a tiny sniff, causing Janna to laugh and declaring their presence to Janna's preoccupied mother.

"Oh, honey. Do you think you could run to the store and pick up some streamers for our booth? I thought I'd have time to go later, but I—" Her mother stopped mid-sentence, looking up and examining the state of her daughter's clothes.

Janna pressed her lips together like a little kid who'd ruined their "good" clothes playing outside. "Um, we went for a little afternoon swim."

She knew her mother disliked dirt or germs being brought into her clean house and held her breath as she waited for her mom's reaction.

"I see that." A smile played at the corners of her mother's mouth. She seemed to want to comment further, but instead she refocused her attention on icing the cookies. "Is Cade with you?"

"No, he just dropped us off before he went home to clean up and change. He'll be back around dinner. We're actually going to Brian and Stacy's for supper."

"Oh, how nice." Her mother jerked up the icing bag in her hand so quickly a blob of icing plopped onto the counter.

"I can still go pick up the streamers if you want me to."

"No, honey. It's alright." Her mother set down the tube of icing and wet a dishrag from the sink. "You need to get cleaned up and changed for lunch. I'll have your father pick some up on his way over to the parade." Mom wiped the icing from the countertop. "You, Cade, and Grace are coming by the hospital's booth after dinner, right?"

The town's annual Fourth of July festivities always included a parade featuring local politicians and business owners as well as the local Shriners in their fancy go-karts. After the parade, which usually lasted only about fifteen minutes, locals and visitors alike were invited to check out the booths sponsored by local charities and a few for-profit business ventures that lined half of Main Street.

Janna's mother took charge of Shady Grove Memorial Hospital's booth each year. Considering all they did was hand each person who stopped by an embellished sugar cookie and a brochure about the latest addition or update to the hospital facilities, all her efforts seemed like a waste of time to Janna.

"Yeah, Mom, we'll try to stop by." Janna tried to be vague yet still sound optimistic about their plans including a stop at the festival. "I'm sure Brian will be riding the truck with the other firefighters, so I bet we'll go with Stacy to the parade after dinner anyway."

"Good." Her mother rinsed the dishrag in the sink and hung it over the faucet head. "Before I forget, I found the cutest dress for Grace to wear tonight. It's laying on your bed upstairs."

"Thanks, Mom." Janna smiled, picturing the kind of dress her mother would have chosen for the Fourth of July. She hoisted Grace onto her hip and carried her up the stairs to her bedroom.

Janna knew they probably needed to shower and change before they got in a quick nap, but exhaustion hit too quickly to think about the ramifications of lying down on the bed in dirty clothes for a few minutes.

She lifted Grace onto the bed and laid her down gently before curling up beside her. Grace lay staring at Janna for a few moments before nudging closer to her and softly stroking her hair like she'd done with Mrs. Keever. Janna smiled at the girl's sweet gesture. Janna's eyelids grew heavy, and before she knew it, she'd drifted out of the real world into the land of dreams.

***

This dream held a sharp contrast to the nightmare Janna had experienced the morning before. She was swinging over Hollow Creek and dropped down into the cool water, just like she had earlier that day, except this time she

207

struggled to swim out of the cloudy water. She felt the burning pressure in her lungs again and knew she would run out of air soon. Hands pressed on her shoulders, too, but this time when she grabbed for them, she felt them pulling her toward the surface of the water, rescuing her. The murky water around her became crystal clear. Someone above her was trying to lift her from the water to safety. It was Cade.

"Don't worry, Janna." His blue eyes matched the water around her. "You're right where you're supposed to be. He brought you here for me."

Janna looked away from him for a moment at the sound of a flock of doves in flight. When she looked back, Cade disappeared, and the surface of the water became blanketed in bright pink peonies. She reclined back in the water, fragrant peonies swirling around her head. Her feet floated to the surface, and she watched as a beautiful monarch butterfly landed gracefully and sat perched on her toe, fluttering its wings.

***

The wall clock chimed loudly, breaking into Janna's peaceful dream and startling her awake. Grace was still staring at her the way she'd been when she fell asleep. *Had she slept at all?*

The clock read 3:54 p.m. Janna had slept through lunch, which explained why her stomach churned now.

"Grace, why don't you stay up here for a minute. I'll go down and get us a snack before we get cleaned up."

Grace nodded.

Janna's mother had finished icing the cookies and sat at the kitchen table working on paper flowers for the hospital's booth.

"Mom, I'm gonna make up some sandwiches for Grace and me before we get ready."

"Okay, hon. There's peanut butter in the cabinet over there and preserves are in the fridge. I came up to check on you earlier, but you looked so peaceful sleeping, I couldn't bear to wake you up. Did you get some rest?"

"Yeah, actually, I do feel pretty rested." Janna smeared peanut butter onto two slices of bread. "I had a weird dream, though."

She walked to the refrigerator and retrieved a jar of her mother's homemade peach preserves.

Her mother kept her eyes on the paper she was folding. "Oh, really. Was it a bad dream?"

"Um, no, not really. Just weird. By the way, do you remember the report I did on butterflies in the sixth grade?"

Her mother smiled at the memory. "How could I forget? You brought home a ribbon from the science fair with that project."

"You don't still have it somewhere, do you?" Janna licked the remainder of the peanut butter and preserves mixture from the butterknife in her hand.

"You know I never throw anything of yours away. I think it's upstairs in a box in your closet. Why?" Her mom looked up in time to catch her daughter's method for cleaning utensils. "Oh honey, don't lick the knife like that. I did not raise you to do that sort of thing."

Laughter burst from Janna's mouth at her mother's assessment of her manners. She finished the sandwiches, placed them on a dinner plate, and poured two glasses of milk for Grace and herself. Leaving the sandwiches and milk on the side of the island, she walked to her mother at the table, put her arm around her shoulders and gave her a squeeze.

"Thanks for teaching me the right way to do things, Mom. Even if I don't always follow your rules, I do remember them often. And thanks for always keeping the important things."

"Like butterfly reports." Mom patted Janna's arm, more than likely to get her daughter to remove her creek-stained clothes from her personal space. "You're welcome, sweetheart. Speaking of which, I put some coloring books and your old crayon box inside the window seat if Grace wants to color later."

Janna picked up their snack and turned to head upstairs. "Okay."

"Oh honey," her mother said before Janna made it out of the kitchen. "Could you put your bedspread in the laundry room after you're done getting ready? I need to wash it before those mud stains from your clothes set in."

Janna suppressed a smile. *That didn't take long.* "Sure, Mom. I'll even stick it in the washer for you."

Once upstairs, Janna set the milk on the nightstand and placed the sandwich plate in front of Grace on the bed. Grace stared at it.

"Aren't you hungry?" Janna picked up her own sandwich and took a bite.

Grace sighed and looked out the window.

"Okay," Janna shrugged, relocating the plate to the bedside table with the milk glasses.

She finished her sandwich and gave Grace another bath. Once she had dressed Grace in the American-flag-inspired dress her mom had chosen, Janna went to the window seat and opened the lid, grabbing one of the coloring books and the box of crayons. Janna closed the lid and sat Grace on the seat's cushion, facing the front yard.

"Grace, can you color a picture for me while I get ready? When I'm finished, you can show me what you've created, alright?"

Grace nodded before Janna walked to her closet to pick out something to wear. Cade had seen her in a pantsuit, an old outfit from college, her pajamas, and a muddied T-shirt and jeans. Now she really wanted to wear something nice. Not too fancy for dinner, but something that would make him take notice of her.

"Wait a minute, what am I doing?" she said aloud. "Why do I care if Cade takes notice of me or not? I'm being ridiculous." Janna shook her head. "We're not kids anymore, and I'm certainly not the same girl Cade knew back then. I've just gotten caught up in old feelings, that's all."

Still, he did have her picture in his wallet. If she was being honest with herself, it wasn't *all* nostalgia she was feeling either.

Grace let out a frustrated sigh from behind her, interrupting her reflection, and Janna turned around in time to see her shaking her head in disdain. Something must have been harder to color than she'd expected.

Janna reached for a cotton blouse hanging in the closet. The hanger slipped off the closet rod and the blouse crumpled to the floor. She bent down to pick it up and saw the box her mother had been talking about. *Janna's School Stuff* was scribbled across the front in blue marker. Janna pulled the box out and opened the top. Inside were old report cards, valentines from classmates, her tassel from graduation. She dug a little deeper until something poked into her finger.

It was her report on butterflies. She'd forgotten she'd made a little butterfly for the poster board display. Her mother helped her fashion it out of orange tissue paper and toothpicks, which must have been what poked her finger. Pulling the butterfly out, she swirled it around by one of the toothpicks.

Janna reached back into the box and pulled out the report that had earned her a second place ribbon. She had been obsessed with butterflies as a child and completed more research for that project than she had for most of her papers in college. Her mother even planted flowers in the window boxes outside her room that were supposed to attract butterflies so Janna could study them up close. She scanned the report, reading aloud as she noticed amusing details she'd included.

"Monarch butterflies are one of the few species of butterflies that migrate to warmer climates for winter." The words were written in a child's scribbly handwriting beside a map of the butterflies' migratory pattern. It didn't appear she had quite mastered cursive at that point in her academic career. The "i" in butterflies looped around and was missing the dot at the top, making the word look more like *butterflees*.

Janna chuckled and read the other little facts sprinkled across the poster board. "The monarch goes through four stages in its life cycle. Monarchs like to suck the nectar from plants using their straw-like noses. These butterflies also symbolize transformation or change."

The clock on the wall chimed again. Four thirty. "Ooh, I'd better hurry up." Janna shoved the report and the rest of her childhood memories back into the box. She'd have to reminisce later. Choosing a different shirt that brought out her eyes, along with a pair of semi-casual black capris, she rushed to the bathroom to get ready.

Janna emerged from the steamy room twenty minutes later, dressed in her dinner attire. She'd decided to let her hair air dry. She was getting used to the way it looked with curls again and Cade seemed to admire it that way, so she figured it couldn't hurt. She dug a pair of silver hoop earrings out of her makeup bag on the nightstand and walked over to the full-length mirror to examine her completed look.

"Well, I certainly don't look like the girl in Cade's wallet anymore, but I think I've made some stylish changes over the years." She scrunched up a few waves around her face. "A nice transformation, just like the monarchs."

The leftover steam from the shower filled Janna's bedroom, making it feel hot and stuffy. Janna walked across the room and unlocked the three windows in front of the window seat. She pushed each window open and felt the relief of a light breeze as it danced through the room.

"What a great afternoon." Janna breathed in and out methodically. "Hard to believe it's July with the temperature this pleasant."

She looked down at Grace's coloring book, which lay closed on the window seat cushion. Bending down, Janna picked it up.

"What did you color for me, Grace?" Janna thumbed through the first few pages.

It looked like Grace had time to color more than one. Janna continued flipping pages and discovered every single picture in the entire coloring book was filled in. Not one color out of the lines.

"Wow! I must have been in the shower longer than I thought." Janna looked at Grace, who gazed out the window at a couple of butterflies fluttering around the vibrant zinnias in the window boxes.

"Aren't they beautiful, Grace? My mom plants those flowers every year to attract them to the window."

As Janna and Grace admired them, one of the butterflies ducked below the open window and entered the bedroom. It flew around for a minute, like a lost leaf blowing in the wind, finally settling on Grace's tiny index finger. She held the yellow butterfly on her finger and studied it carefully.

Janna smiled. "Don't move, Grace. Let me get a picture of you."

She took a few steps backward to her purse hanging over one of the bed posts and rummaged quietly for her cell phone. She didn't want to scare the butterfly away before she could get the shot. When she turned around to take the picture, she saw that would not be a problem.

Grace, who sat completely still on the window seat, was covered head to toe in butterflies. Yellow tiger swallowtails clung to the stars and stripes on her dress like fluttery ruffles. Black swallowtails with blue and orange dots covering their wings were lined up on her petite arms like sleeves, and orange monarch butterflies were swaying in her long, sandy hair as it flowed down her back. They all seemed to be hearing the same song as they pulsed their wings back and forth in synchronized cadence.

Janna stood dumbfounded for a moment, almost forgetting the phone in her hand. She thought it might be a good idea to get a picture for proof her eyes weren't deceiving her.

Grace seemed to be enjoying her experience with nature, grinning as Janna continued taking pictures.

The doorbell chimed through the house, sending the butterflies into a frenzy of color. They flew up from Grace's body and out of the three open windows in an orderly procession.

"Janna, could you get the door?" her mother called from downstairs.

"Okay, Mom," Janna said in a daze, her eyes wide.

She laid down her phone and walked over to Grace. The girl stared deeply into Janna's eyes the way she had when they'd first met. Janna couldn't tell if she was upset, exhilarated, or in shock. "Are you okay, Grace?"

Grace nodded, another wide grin spreading across her face. Janna quickly closed the windows and locked them before grabbing her phone from the bed.

"C'mon," she said, holding out her hand to Grace. "Let's go see who's downstairs and then we'll show these pictures to Mom."

Janna's mind raced in a million different directions as she and Grace headed down the front staircase. *What just happened?*

Before she could come up with a reasonable explanation for the surreal moment upstairs, they had reached the front door. Janna opened the door to greet their visitor, only to discover they must have gotten impatient waiting for her and Grace to answer the door and left.

Janna stepped out onto the porch and walked down into the front yard. She moved to the sidewalk in front of the house, scanning the street for a familiar car or someone strolling down either end of the sidewalk. Nothing.

She turned around and trekked back to the porch, smiling at Grace who stared at her through the screen door. When she noticed the gift someone had left behind, Janna forgot about the cell phone in her palm. She released her hold of the phone, dropping it to the porch floor, and gasped as she heard the display screen crack.

A mason jar full of bright pink peonies sat beside the welcome mat. She moved closer, trying to make out the note attached to the rim of the jar. The small piece of paper contained two words, *Let Go*, and beneath them was written a very familiar Bible verse reference, *I Peter 5:10*.

~14~

"Can I help you?" the receptionist at the Shady Grove Senior Center asked Cade from behind the plexiglass window. She must have been a temp because he didn't recognize her.

"Yes, ma'am. I'm here to see my father, Bill Thompson."

The receptionist thumbed through a binder on her desk and looked up at him. "Actually, he has a visitor right now, but as soon as he leaves, you're free to go in and visit with your father."

"Okay, thanks." Cade sat down in a chair by the window in the waiting area. Three other people came and went through the waiting room door before Cade was able to go back to his father's room.

"You can go back now, Mr. Thompson." The receptionist buzzed the door open to let him enter as Calvin

Petersen emerged from the door to the common area on the other side of the room.

Cade stood. "Mr. Petersen?"

Calvin gave him a nod. "Cade."

Both of them exchanged pleasantries before Cade worked up the courage to ask Mr. Petersen how his dad was doing.

"Fine," Mr. Petersen said in that no nonsense way of his. "He seems more like himself this afternoon."

"Good." Cade relaxed his shoulders and crossed his arms over his chest. "It's just when we stopped by here earlier this morning, he had some sort of episode and had to be escorted back to his room."

"Do they know what caused it?"

"They think it might be the medications he's on now." Cade rubbed his cheek, deciding if he should tell Mr. Petersen how bad things had become recently. "It worries me a little that he seems to get more agitated and confused every time I see him. This morning makes the third time this week he's called for my mother like she's still here."

"Have you talked to Bill's doctors?"

"I have another appointment with them next week, but so far they don't seem to know what's triggering the rapid progression of the disease."

221

"You'll keep me posted on what they tell you?" Calvin looked at his watch.

"Yes, sir."

"I should really get going now, I suppose. If I don't get home soon with some patriotic streamers in hand, I might get a scolding from Janna's mother." Calvin smiled. "I trust we'll see you tonight at the Fourth of July festivities."

"Probably."

The two men nodded goodbye, and Cade walked down the hall to room 310. He could hear voices coming from the other side of the cracked door and leaned in to see if his dad was actually talking to someone or having another imaginary conversation with his mom.

"Your days will become easier, Mr. Thompson. I promise. Remember the battle doesn't always go to the strong, but sometimes we do get lucky, if that's what you want to call it," a familiar voice said.

Cade knocked lightly on the door before opening it. He recognized the face that went along with the voice as one of the orderlies who tried to calm his dad down earlier that morning—the taller, dark-haired one.

The orderly looked up and smiled at Cade. "Good morning."

"Good morning. I'm Cade," he said, holding out his hand.

The orderly reached forward, shaking Cade's hand firmly. "Yes, I know. Mr. Thompson talks about you all the time."

"He does?" Cade cleared a tremor from his throat. "What does he say?"

"Let's see," the orderly propped another pillow behind his father's head. "He's told me you work for the Sheriff's Department. You're taking care of the house for him while he's here, and that he and Miranda are so proud of you."

"Oh." Cade's optimism quickly melted away. He had hoped for something a little more substantial than that.

"I'm sorry, I don't remember seeing you around here before this morning in the common room. What's your name again?"

"Michael." He smiled. "I'm new."

"Oh, then you may not know the answer to this question, but I'll ask you anyway." Cade glanced at his father, who stared out the window at something no one else could see. "Have you seen a lot of patients like this before? You know, people who are still kind of young suffering from a disease typically found in older patients?"

223

"Well, early onset Alzheimer's is not that common, but it is linked to a specific set of genes. Someone with those genes always has a chance of developing the disease." Michael grabbed a blanket from the end of the bed and draped it over Cade's father's legs. "At this time, there seems to be no conclusive evidence to help doctors know who will end up with Alzheimer's."

Encouraged by the orderly's medical knowledge, Cade asked, "Does it usually progress so quickly? I mean I know he's getting up there in years, but they diagnosed him at sixty. It's only been six and a half years and now he's . . ." He flipped his hand toward his dad.

Michael looked to Cade's father and then back at him. "I know it's very difficult for you to see your father like this, but you've got to remember he still has things to tell you. Things he wants you to hear. You've just got to listen more closely now."

Cade pursed his lips together and nodded in agreement.

"I'll leave you two alone." Michael smoothed out a wrinkle from the bottom of the bedspread. "If you need anything, just ask."

"Thanks," Cade said. "It was nice to meet you."

"You too, sir." Michael pulled the door shut as he left the room.

Cade walked around his dad's bed and sat down on the edge by his feet. "Hey, Dad. How are you?" He patted the blanket Michael had laid across his dad's legs. "I saw Calvin came by to see you earlier. Did you have a nice visit with him?"

His dad gaped at him blankly

Cade checked to make sure the door remained closed. "What was your friend Michael telling you before I came in? Something about things getting easier?"

The fog from his father's eyes cleared a little like it had earlier that morning before his outburst. He sat up straighter in his bed and leaned forward, placing his hand on Cade's shoulder.

"I'm proud of you, Son. I don't tell you enough, but your mother and I are very proud of the person you've become."

Cade perked up for a moment until he realized he'd heard those words before. His father had told him the same thing the day he graduated from the police academy. Seeing Cade must've triggered an old memory.

"Um, thanks, Dad." Cade put his fingers on either side of his temples and rubbed his forehead. "I've always tried to be someone you could be proud of."

"Your mother would be glad to know you found her again."

"Who, Dad?"

"The Petersen girl." His dad removed his hand from Cade's shoulder and reclined against his pillows. "Miranda always liked her. Said she hoped the two of you would work it out someday." He smiled. "I guess you did."

"Dad, when did you talk to Mom about this?" Cade wasn't sure if his father was in the past or present time zone.

"We talked about it after the two of you broke your engagement. Seemed like such a pity to us both." His father spoke so clearly. Cade thought he may have heard him wrong. Maybe he was just listening more closely now, like the orderly had suggested.

"Dad, do you remember what happened to Mom?" Cade knew it was risky to test the waters of his father's clarity any further, but his window of opportunity could close at any moment.

His father turned and stared out the window again. Cade feared he had lost him. The room grew quiet for a few seconds.

226

"Miranda came to help me stock the shelves after church. There was going to be a big sale that Monday. She complained of a headache, so I gave her some aspirin. She didn't say much while she worked, so I assumed her headache went away." His father swallowed hard but continued, his voice quivering slightly. "We were pricing chicken feed. She put a price sticker on one of the bags. She took a few steps back, put her hand to her head, and sat down on the floor. I called her name, but she didn't answer. I heard her sigh, and then she sort of slumped over on her side."

A tear dripped down Cade's face, darkening his light blue shirt. His father had correctly recounted what happened to his mother. He knew the rest. Dad called an ambulance, then he'd called the diner where Cade was eating lunch with Brian and Stacy. The EMTs rushed his mom to the emergency room where doctors informed them both there was nothing they could do for her. Miranda Thompson had died of a brain aneurysm at the age of fifty-seven.

Cade's father wiped the tears from his face with the back of his hand. "Let's talk about something else now," he said, looking out the window again.

"Okay, Dad. What would you like to talk about?" Cade silently thanked God for a sign his father hadn't left him completely.

"How's Brian doing?" His dad's streak of lucidity hadn't run out yet.

"Uh . . . he's doing fine. Actually, Janna and I are having dinner with him and Stacy tonight."

Cade still didn't know if this conversation was really happening or if it was some fantasy in his mind. Like maybe he was having the conversation in his head and his dad really just sat there listening. At this point, he wasn't sure, but he also didn't care. He hadn't had a real conversation with his father in several years and, fantasy or not, he wouldn't let this moment pass him by.

They talked for the next half hour, until Cade caught a glimpse of the clock on his dad's bedside table.

"Dad, it's been great talking to you, but I'm supposed to pick Janna up soon, so I probably need to go." He leaned over and hugged his dad tightly.

"It was good talking with you too, Cade."

Cade turned to leave but froze when he saw the gift someone left his father on the dresser by the door. "Dad, where did you—" Cade raised a finger toward the dresser.

"Those are supposed to be good luck. At least that's what Michael told me," his father replied.

"Is that right?" Cade stood immobilized for a moment, trying to make sense of what he saw. A jar of peonies stared back at him from the dresser.

***

"Janna, those are beautiful." Her mother looked up from her paper flowers as Janna carried Grace and the jar of peonies into the kitchen. "Did the floral delivery service leave those at the door?"

"I don't really know." Janna wrinkled her eyebrows. "I didn't get to the door in time, and whoever put these on the porch left before I could ask who they were from."

"Oh, honey. They're probably from Cade." Her mom's eyes lit up. "He's trying to woo you back."

Janna tilted her head and shook it slowly. "No, I don't think so."

"How do you know, sweetheart?" Her mother was practically giddy. "I'm sure he remembers that's your favorite flower."

Janna knew her mother possessed a very active imagination. She didn't feel like explaining that the same bouquet of flowers had shown up on Miranda Thompson's headstone, and Cade had accused her of placing them there.

"Was there a message or anything?"

Janna debated for a minute about whether or not to explain everything to her mother, but it all seemed too complicated. She would wait to speak to Cade before she or her mom jumped to conclusions.

"No, there wasn't a message exactly." Janna said, figuring the note was more like a recommendation than a message.

Janna held up the face of her now cracked cell phone, trying to divert her mother's attention elsewhere. "But whoever left those owes me a new phone."

"Oh dear. How did that happen?" Her mother ran her finger across the shattered glass face.

"I guess it surprised me to see flowers on the porch. I was still a little on edge from what happened upstairs, so I just forgot it was in my hand and dropped it."

Her mother's eyes grew wide as she leaned in closer to Janna. "What happened upstairs?"

"You remember all those flowers you keep planted for the butterflies?"

"Yes." Her mother lowered her eyebrows suspiciously. "You always loved to see the butterflies drinking nectar from them outside your window."

"Well, you got your money's worth because a whole swarm just came in through the windows when I opened them, and they all landed on Grace."

"What do you mean a swarm, like two or three?"

"No, Mom, I mean like dozens. Black and yellow swallowtails. Even some monarchs."

"Maybe it's a sign, honey." Her mom's voice perked up.

Janna rolled her eyes. "Oh . . . my goodness."

"No, I'm serious," Mom said, clearly undeterred by Janna's lack of respect for her theory. "Sometimes God gets our attention in unusual ways. What was the verse in Psalms about the stars tell his story or something? Let me go get my Bible." She got up from her chair and walked toward the living room.

It had been a weird enough day. Janna wasn't sure she wanted to hear more of her mom's theory on the butterflies, the peonies, or her relationship with Cade. Besides, Janna wasn't' sure she believed God spoke to people like that anymore.

Her mother flew back into the kitchen, Bible in hand, and began flipping through several pages in the middle of the leather-bound book. "Here it is. Psalm nineteen, verses one and two." Janna lifted Grace onto her hip and leaned over so they could follow along. She wasn't sure Grace could read, but she didn't want to leave her out. Grace smiled.

Her mother read the verse to them aloud. "See," she said. "It says everything displays the craftsmanship of God. Even the sky was created to make him known. Maybe God is trying to make himself known to you, Janna. You and Cade both. He's trying to tell you something."

Janna forced a breath through her tight lips. "Like what, Mom? Like Cade and I are supposed to be together? Is that what you're gonna tell me this all means?"

Her mom put her hands on her hips. "First of all, young lady, I don't appreciate the tone you're using with me. Secondly, I know you think I'm always pushing too hard, but you have to admit you and Cade have fallen comfortably back into step with each other the past couple of days." She scanned Janna's outfit. "And I see you've dressed up for dinner, so I can't be the only one who thinks there may be something left of what the two of you had."

Before Janna could respond, her father entered through the back door. His hands were full, carrying several bags filled with streamers. Cade came in behind him, his arms loaded with bags also.

"Look who I found in the driveway." Janna's dad held the bags up, waiting for his wife's approval. "Think these will be enough?"

"Just think about what God might have in store for the two of you, honey," Janna's mother whispered, before turning to look at the merchandise her husband had brought home. "That's all I ask. All we've ever wanted is for you to experience God's best for your life."

Janna closed her eyes and sighed. "I know, Mom." She opened her eyes and met her mother's pleading stare. "I promise I'll think about it."

Cade and Janna's father set the bags of streamers on top of the island.

Her mother remained the consummate hostess. "Would either of you like something to drink?"

"No thank you, dear." Janna's father leaned over and kissed her mother on the cheek. "Cade?"

"I'm fine, Mrs. Thompson, thank you." Janna watched Cade catch sight of the jar of peonies. "Janna, could I talk to you for a minute?"

"Yes," Janna's mom answered for her. "You kids talk. Calvin and I will head downtown and start setting up the hospital's booth. Maybe we should take Grace with us so you two can enjoy your visit with Brian and Stacy. She might like to see the festivities begin."

"What about dinner, Mom?" Janna tightened her arms around Grace. She enjoyed having the girl around as a buffer between her and Cade. She didn't want to go to supper at Brian and Stacy's without her.

"Oh, well, your dad was going to pick up some dinner at Mac's Diner for us anyway. He could just pick up something extra for Grace." Mom ran her hand over Grace's hair. "Would you like to come and help us set up the booth, Grace, or do you want to go to dinner with Janna and Cade?"

Grace didn't waste any time deciding and wriggled loose from Janna's hold and down to the ground. She walked over to Janna's mom and slipped her small hand into hers.

"Well, I guess that's that." Her mother's voice was triumphant. She scooped up a couple bags of streamers and turned to Janna's father. "You ready to go, dear? See you two after dinner." Mom winked at Janna.

Janna scoffed as Grace and her father followed her mom obediently out of the kitchen. She heard the front door close before either she or Cade spoke.

Cade laughed. "Well, it looks like we got the shaft on this one."

"Yeah, well, maybe she needed a break from us, but I have to admit I've enjoyed having her around."

"Me too." Cade smiled as a familiar awkward silence filled the kitchen.

"So what did you want to talk to me about?"

"Actually, it's about those." Cade pointed to the jar of peonies. "I stopped by to check on Dad on my way over here and a jar just like that, filled with flowers, sat on his dresser. I thought maybe you stopped by and gave them to him earlier, like you did with Mom."

Janna stared at the frilly pink flowers for a moment. "Cade, I hate to tell you this, but I did not put those flowers on your mom's grave."

"If you didn't, who did? And who put some in my dad's room at the nursing home?"

"That's a good question. Probably the same person who put those on my front porch, along with this note." Janna pulled the note from her pocket and handed it to Cade.

"What does it mean, 'Let Go'?"

"Beats me. I actually thought you might have had something to do with it." Janna raised an eyebrow, hoping she didn't sound too enthusiastic about the prospect.

"Me?" Cade drew his head back. If he did send those flowers, he was certainly doing a great job of playing dumb.

"You were the one who told me to let go of the rope swing at Hollow Creek and only you would know about that verse from the Dellingers' picture." Janna's tone sounded more accusatory than she'd meant.

"I told you, Janna, whoever you heard tell you to let go at the creek, it wasn't me. And I certainly didn't send you a note with that verse on it, either. I think someone is messing with us. I'm just not sure who it would be." Cade snapped his fingers. "Wait a minute, Janna. Your father was just leaving the nursing home when I went to visit Dad. Would he know peonies meant something to my mom?"

Janna shrugged, putting the mysterious note back into her pocket. "I don't know . . . maybe. My dad's not really the type to buy anyone flowers, though. Besides, how would he know about the verse on the Dellingers' photo?"

"I'm not sure." Cade glanced up at the clock above the kitchen sink. "It's only six o'clock. Let's call the nursing home and see if they know who made the delivery to Dad's room. Someone is usually at the front desk until around eight. Although, with today being a holiday, I don't know if we can count on that." He pulled out his cell phone, dialed, and then pressed the speakerphone button so Janna could hear.

"Shady Grove Senior Center. This is Mary. How can I help you?"

Janna remained quiet as Cade spoke. "Yes, is Kristin Smith still there, or has she gone home for the day?"

"Yes, sir. She's on until seven. May I ask who's calling?"

"Cade Thompson. I stopped by earlier to see my father, Bill."

"One moment please."

Cade looked up at Janna as they listened to whispering voices while the phone shuffled from the receptionist to Kristin.

"Cade." Her voice made his name sound like a long, sharp bird call. "Is everything okay? I saw on the visitation log that you were here earlier. Hate I missed you."

"I'll bet you do," Janna said under her breath.

"Everything's fine, Kristin. I'm hoping you can help me figure something out though."

"Anything for you, Cade."

The word *desperate* popped into Janna's head.

"There were some flowers in my dad's room earlier. I wondered if you knew who brought them to him."

"Let me check the visitor's log and see who came by to see your dad before you."

They could hear her shuffling some papers in the background. "Well, it looks like you and Calvin Petersen were the only two visitors this afternoon. I remember seeing Mr. Petersen, but he didn't have any flowers with him. There is one other place I could check. Hold on a minute."

Janna heard the phone tap the desk as Kristin set the receiver down, then the click of computer keys.

"Well . . ." Kristin returned to the phone. "I checked our delivery log, but it seems no one received flowers today or yesterday. Although, the receptionist is a temp, so she may have just let the delivery guy leave the flowers with her. Did the card have your dad's name on it?"

"Uh, I don't know. I'm not even sure if it had a card, but maybe the orderly who was in my dad's room saw it and thought it might be less confusing if he didn't know where the flowers came from. Maybe you could ask him. His name's Michael."

Kristin's end of the phone remained silent for a moment. It sounded like she was typing again. "I'm just looking at our time sheet for today in the computer and I don't see . . . was it Michael, you said?"

"Yeah, he was the same orderly who escorted my father back to his room this morning after his outburst. Mid- to late-twenties I would guess. Tall, dark-haired. He's kind of thin, but he looks strong, like a runner or something. He said he was new."

Janna was impressed Cade remembered so much about this guy, but she figured attention to detail was part of his police training.

"Cade, we don't have any orderlies who look like the man you described. Are you sure his name was Michael?"

Cade removed Kristin from speakerphone and pulled the cell phone to his ear. "Yes, I'm sure." He described the orderly in detail for Kristin again.

His voice became more agitated. "Kristin, how can you not remember this guy? You talked to him. You called him and another orderly over to help escort Dad back to his room. Yes. No, I don't remember the other guy's name, but he was blonde and a little shorter than Michael."

It was clear to Janna he didn't get the response he had hoped for when he finally told Kristin thanks for her help and punched the end call button in frustration. He put both hands on the top of the island and bent over, stretching his back.

"What'd she say?" Janna grimaced knowing the answer wouldn't be good.

Cade sighed and was quiet for a moment before returning Janna's gaze. "She said no one named Michael works there."

"What? That's ridiculous. Even I remember her calling two orderlies over to restrain your dad. One was blonde, right?"

"Yeah, but apparently Kristin has no recollection of that taking place." He sighed.

"But if Michael was new, would she even realize who you're talking about?"

"That's what I thought at first, but Kristin said she knows all the day shift staff and didn't know anyone named Michael. She didn't remember seeing the other guy either. Do you remember his name?"

"No, sorry." Janna shrugged. "I don't get it. If no one by that name works there, then who were those men who helped your dad this morning? And who did you talk to in your dad's room?"

Cade rested his forehead on his fist. "That's what I'd like to know."

~15~

"I don't understand what's going on." Janna massaged the headache out of her forehead as Cade drove them to Brian and Stacy's house. "First the peonies on your mom's grave, then the apparently invisible orderlies, the butterflies, and two more mystery bouquets. Either we've got a delivery-happy florist, insect problems, and a nurse with short-term memory loss, or we're both crazy!"

Cade laughed deeply. "I'm starting to think it may be the latter. Wait a minute— butterflies?"

"Oh yeah, I forgot to tell you about that." Janna adjusted her seatbelt so she could turn toward Cade. "I'm probably making a bigger deal out of the situation than necessary, but when we were upstairs getting cleaned up from our swim, I opened my windows to let in the breeze and a huge group of butterflies flew in and landed all over Grace.

Now that I think about it, it's not all that weird I suppose. I'm sure they were just attracted by the bright red and blue on her dress."

"Are you still as obsessed with butterflies as you were when we were kids?" Cade chuckled. "Remember the report you did in middle school? What was it, The Miraculous Monarch or something?"

"The Majestic Monarch, thank you very much. And no, although they are pretty, my obsession has dwindled appropriately with age." Janna chopped an imaginary end of discussion line in the air with her hands. "I can't believe you even remember that."

Cade put his hand on his chest and bowed forward. "I beg your pardon for butchering the name." He smiled. "I told you I remember a lot more about you than you probably think."

Janna shifted her position away from him and faced the windshield. "You know my mom thinks these things are all signs?"

"Signs?" Cade smiled again and raised an eyebrow. "Of what?"

"Oh, I don't know. She thinks God is trying to show us something."

"Did she say specifically what He might be trying to tell us? I'll take about anything we can get right now." He seemed a little too interested to hear her mother's theories on God's communicative tools. Were Cade and her mother in a conspiracy to make her tell him the truth about why she really came home?

"Who knows?" Janna threw her hands up in the air. She certainly wouldn't share what her mother had suggested in the kitchen before Cade had arrived. "So, what were you gonna tell me earlier at the church? Something before we got to Brian and Stacy's house?" She hoped he wouldn't notice she was beginning to make a habit of changing the subject.

"Oh yeah." Cade grimaced. "I didn't know if you knew where Brian and Stacy live."

Janna realized they were turning down a very familiar street. "Wait, isn't this near where we—" She stopped speaking as they pulled into the driveway and sat facing a small white house with blue shutters.

The house with the big picture window, wraparound porch, and spacious backyard, perfect for gardening. The house with built-in window boxes for all Janna's butterfly-attracting flowers. Their house.

Janna felt like someone knocked the wind out of her. She stared at the house and then looked at Cade.

He closed his eyes and scrunched up his nose. "I'm really sorry. I should have told you earlier and given you more time to prepare for this. It's just all this other stuff started happening and I—"

"No, it's okay." Janna's voice came out small and weak. "We've definitely been preoccupied today." She shrugged and let out a breath. "I guess I assumed you moved in there, you know, after everything happened."

Cade's face became solemn. "I thought about it. It just didn't feel right living there without—" He cleared his throat. "Anyway, Brian never told Stacy, so please don't mention it."

"Okay, I won't." Janna said meekly, swallowing the lump rising in her throat. She took a deep breath and readied herself to apologize to Cade for ruining all the plans he'd made for them. Before she could get a word out, Stacy opened the front door of the house and made her way down the porch steps.

Janna and Cade both climbed out of their seats, closing the car doors behind them.

"It's about time you two got here." Stacy's exuberant voice pulled them back from the past and into the present. "We thought maybe you changed your minds."

"Oh, sorry about that. We got caught up in some other things," Cade said.

Stacy smiled and greeted both of them more officially with a hug. "It's okay. I'm just glad the two of you made it. Where's the little girl Brian told me about?" She leaned to the side, peeking through the back window.

"Mom and Dad took her downtown to see the beginning of the Fourth of July festivities. By the way, Mom also asked if we'd be there later." Janna looked at Cade.

"Yeah, Stacy, aren't you and Brian heading out to that in a little while?"

"Actually, Brian doesn't have to ride in the parade this year, so we were planning on going down to Main Street a little later to visit all the vendors and watch the fireworks. We can all go down together after dinner if you'd like." Stacy winked at Janna.

Brian stepped out onto the front porch. "Honey, I'm gonna fire up the grill. You wanna come help me out back, Cade?" He nodded toward Janna. "Good to see you."

Cade nodded politely to Janna and Stacy, excusing himself. Stacy looped her arm through Janna's as they walked up the sidewalk and climbed the steps to the front porch.

"Why don't I give you the grand tour?" Stacy swept her arm dramatically across the air. "Those boys will be talking charcoal and muscle cars for the next thirty minutes. Which will give us the perfect amount of time to see the house. Plus, you can catch me up on all the juicy details about you and Cade."

"I'd love to see the house," Janna lied. "But I'm not sure how many juicy details I have to share about anything."

Stacy draped her arm casually over Janna's shoulder, like she used to in high school, and raised her eyebrows. "Humor me, girlfriend."

***

"So, if you'll step through here, we'll head to the kitchen." Stacy guided Janna down the hallway from the front door. The walls were lined with pictures of Stacy and Brian's wedding, family gatherings, and vacations. A visual history of their life together.

A wave of nausea hit Janna as they stepped into the kitchen. The appliances, curtains, and even the 1950's diner-style table she and Cade had picked out together stood staring back at her. Cade must have sold the house, furniture and all, to Brian after they broke up. What else would she have expected him to do? The plans were set, the house furnished, and they loved each other. All she had to do was follow the plan. Why couldn't she have just done that?

"Uh, may I use your bathroom before we finish the tour?" Janna swallowed hard, willing herself not to throw up.

"Sure." Stacy leaned toward her, concern spreading across her face. "Are you okay? You look as white as a sheet."

"Yeah, I'm fine. I probably just need to eat something. I'll just be a second."

"Well, the bathroom is—" Stacy pointed down the hall.

"I know," Janna interrupted. "I'll be right back."

Taking a few long strides down the hallway, she ducked into the bathroom, trying not to slam the door behind her. She bent down over the sink for a moment. Her face and neck felt hot and prickly. She splashed some water on her face and dabbed it off with a tissue. Closing the toilet lid, she sat down and tried to get rid of the dizziness in her head. She breathed in and out slowly until her nausea subsided. What would she say to Stacy? How could she go back out there and eat dinner with Cade at *their* table?

What was I thinking? This is too much history to deal with in one weekend. I never should have come back. I need to get out of here. Now!

She looked around the room, trying to come up with some way to get out of this situation. Standing up, she took a step to the small window directly across from the toilet. It was a little high, but if she stood on top of the toilet and stretched her arms, she could probably hoist herself up and out of the window. Then what would she do? Run home?

She unlocked the window and pushed it open. Fresh air blew in, helping to clear her head a little. Thankful the toilet lid was ceramic and could hold her weight, Janna climbed on top of it and leaned awkwardly to reach the windowsill. She was glad she worked out regularly once she became aware she'd have to hold most of her weight up on the window ledge. She pulled her head and torso through the small opening, but realized it wasn't wide enough for her hips to pass through completely.

A light knock at the door broke the silence in the bathroom, startling Janna and causing her to lose her grip on the windowsill outside. She slipped back through the window into the bathroom, bumping her head on the bottom of the open window frame and knocking over the laundry hamper by the shower as she fell back. She sat in the floor for a moment, surveying the damage.

"Janna, are you okay? Would you like a ginger ale or something?" Stacy slowly pushed the door open.

Janna remained sprawled out on the floor, holding her head, with a pile of dirty towels at her feet. The hamper lay on its side.

Stacy let out an uproarious laugh. "What in the world happened to you?" She looked at the open window. "Were you trying to escape?"

Janna rubbed her head and stood up. "I wanted to get some air."

"It looks like your plan worked out real well, Lady Houdini. Although, if you're planning to disappear, it might be easier to use the front door." Stacy smiled, closing the bathroom door behind her and placing a glass of ginger ale she'd brought by the sink. "Are you okay?"

"Yeah, I just bumped my head. I'll be fine."

"No, I mean about being here with Cade." Stacy pressed her lips together. "I know this must be pretty uncomfortable for you two, huh?"

Janna had forgotten what a caring friend Stacy was. They'd shared a few e-mails and occasional phone calls over the past few years, but Stacy was just another reminder of this town and Cade, so it had been easier for Janna to lose touch with her than deal with the emotions that always accompanied their conversations.

Stacy retrieved the glass of ginger ale from the sink and held it out to Janna. Guessing some sugar in her system might be a good thing, Janna sat back down on the closed toilet lid and took a sip. "Thanks, Stacy. I'm really fine now, I think. Just a flood of memories being around you guys, you know? I guess I thought I was prepared for this, but apparently I wasn't."

Stacy sat down across from Janna on the edge of the bathtub and patted her compassionately on the knee. "Janna, can I ask you something?"

Even though she felt sure she knew what the question would be, Janna nodded. She stared at the tile on the floor and ran her teeth across her upper lip. The tears welled up beneath her lashes as she lifted her eyes to meet Stacy's.

"I know Brian thinks I stick my nose into other people's business too much, but someone needs to say this. You and Cade. You still love each other, don't you? I mean, I know for sure he still loves you." Stacy's earrings jingled as she shook her head with certainty.

"How do you know that?" Janna's voice wavered.

"Because he's turned down every available girl in this town I have ever tried to set him up with. He even resisted Nurse Wiggles-When-She-Walks at the nursing home where his dad stays. Brian told me *all* about her." Stacy grinned saucily before getting up and sashaying across the floor, impersonating Kristin.

Janna laughed and wiped a drippy tear from her chin.

"And you, strangely enough, have never moved on to anything serious either from what I've gathered. So, what gives, Jan? Do you still love him?"

Fresh tears spilled down Janna's face, and she nodded again.

"Then, sweetie, why don't you speak up? Tell him how you feel."

"I can't." Janna looked to the floor again. "I hurt him so badly, Stace. How could he ever forgive me for what I did?"

"I think he forgave you a long time ago." Stacy pushed a lock of hair out of Janna's face. "Brian and I used to try to get Cade to talk about what happened between the two of you. He would never say an unkind word about you. He would just say some paths weren't for everyone, and your path led somewhere else. Maybe he understood why you had to go and figured if you came back, it would be some kind of sign you were supposed to be together."

"You're starting to sound like my mom." Janna sniffed and reached for more tissue behind her.

"I've always thought your mom was a very wise woman." Stacy raised an eyebrow and grinned. She put her hand on Janna's shoulder. "I just think you owe it to yourself and Cade to talk to him about this. My goodness, you owe it to me and Brian. Do you know how long we've been praying you'd come back and work things out with Cade?"

"You've been praying for us?" Janna dabbed the tissue under her nose. "Why?"

"Because you two are supposed to be together." Stacy grabbed a washcloth from the stand beside the bathtub.

A resurgence of guilt washed over Janna. Cade and her parents weren't the only ones she'd hurt when she left town. She didn't deserve Stacy's prayers. "Stacy, I'm sorry I haven't been as good a friend to you as I should have over the past few years. I didn't even come to your wedding."

"It's okay, Janna." Stacy wet the washcloth in the sink and wrung out the water. "I just figured you were too busy running away from Cade to turn around and see who else you were leaving behind." She handed the damp cloth to Janna and smiled. "Don't worry. You can pay your penance to me later. For now, let's get you cleaned up for dinner."

Janna molded the washcloth to her face before dabbing away at the blotchy red marks her crying had left on her cheeks and around her nose. She smoothed her hair into place and fanned her face with a clean tissue.

Brian called through the house, announcing dinner was ready.

"How do I look?" Janna turned to face Stacy.

Stacy scanned her friend's appearance and smirked. "Like a woman in love."

***

Dinner didn't take long, but Brian kept them entertained afterward, sharing stories from work.

"We were called to your dad's nursing home earlier this week, Cade. Someone had gotten hold of one of their family member's lighters during visitor hours and was burning all his socks in the trashcan. He said they made his feet hot."

They all laughed. Stacy stood and began to clear the table. Janna rose to help her, stacking Cade's plate on top of hers and pinching both their glasses between her fingers. Cade watched her as she carried them to the sink and stacked them beside the rest of the dishes.

"Anyway, he set off the alarm, so we were dispatched, but it didn't take much to put out the—" Brian made invisible quotation marks in the air. "Blaze. A couple of orderlies helped get him away from the trash can long enough for us to get our job done."

Cade sat up straighter in his chair and glanced over at Janna. "Do you happen to remember what those orderlies looked like?"

"Uh, one was older, like mid-forties," Brian took a sip of his soda. "And the other one looked like he was our age. Why?"

"The one who was our age. Did you get his name?" Cade's voice rose with excitement.

"I'm not sure. Gary or something?" Brian scrunched his eyebrows. "Why, are you friends with some of the orderlies there?"

"Not exactly. I just thought maybe I knew him." Cade slumped back down in his seat.

Stacy looked up at the clock on the wall. "Guys, we'd better go. The parade's already started, but I don't want to miss the fireworks. Brian and I figured we're so close to town, we'd just walk, if it's okay with you guys."

"Walking's fine," Janna said.

Cade followed the two women out the door and waited as Brian locked up. Brian and Stacy kept their stride quick as they trekked down the sidewalk toward town, giving

Janna and him a chance to comfortably linger behind. It seemed neither of them had anything to say.

Cade tried not to stare at Janna as they walked. He finally worked up the courage to say what was on his mind. "I meant to tell you earlier, you look really nice."

"Thanks." Janna's face reddened, but she avoided his gaze.

They walked in silence the rest of the way. Cade watched Brian take Stacy's hand and fought the temptation to reach for Janna's. He still wasn't sure what was going on in her head and didn't want to make her pull away from him again.

The foursome made it to the beginning of Main Street.

Janna pointed, stretching her arm out in exaggerated motion. "I think Mom's booth is way down on the other end."

"We'll catch up with you guys later," Brian said. "Stacy wants to stop by the animal shelter's booth and see if they have a puppy we can take home." Brian put his arm around his wife and gave her a squeeze. "I'm not enough of a handful for her."

Stacy leaned over to hug Janna and whispered something in her ear. Janna smiled and nodded to Stacy. Cade wondered what that conversation was about as Brian relayed to him where they would be sitting to view the fireworks.

Cade and Janna began to make their way through the crowd, navigating a sea of red, white, and blue. The path between the two rows of parallel booths became increasingly smaller the closer they got to the courthouse in the center of Main Street. As they neared the Shady Grove Memorial Hospital booth, Cade felt someone tap him on the shoulder.

"Excuse me, sir. I think you dropped this."

Cade stopped and turned around, unable to catch Janna's attention before she continued to make her way down the street. A young, blonde man stood before Cade, holding a small square of paper. Cade recognized him immediately. The blonde orderly from the Senior Center.

Cade took the piece of paper from the man without looking at it. "Hey, don't you work at the nursing home?"

"Yes, sir. I'm Gabe." He held out his hand for Cade to shake. "You're Cade, right?"

"You remember me?" Cade eyed him suspiciously, praying this guy wasn't a figment of his imagination like Michael seemed to have been.

The orderly nodded. "Yeah, you're Bill Thompson's son. Your father seemed to be doing much better when I left this evening. Have you seen him again today?"

"I stopped by earlier this evening to check on him, and he talked to me for quite a while. It was nice." Cade looked off into the crowd, hoping Janna finally noticed he wasn't behind her. He wanted someone to see him talking to this guy.

"Actually, I ran into your coworker, Michael, while I was there." Cade studied Gabe's reaction carefully, hoping he could shed some light on the mysterious orderly.

Gabe smiled. "Well, we usually do work the same shift."

"That's interesting because one of my dad's nurses, Kristin, seemed to think no one named Michael worked there or at least she had never met him. As a matter of fact, she didn't remember you either. I didn't have your name, but she didn't recognize you or Michael from the descriptions I gave her."

"I can't say I'm too surprised." Gabe seemed to ignore Cade's distrustful tone. "We often go unnoticed, but I assure you, both Michael and I have been attending to your father's needs for quite some time. We're taking very good care of him. It's been nice speaking with you, Cade, but I need to go." Gabe tapped the piece of paper he'd slipped into Cade's palm. "You hang onto that this time. Something tells me it's important."

257

Gabe turned and wandered off into the crowd as Janna came up beside Cade. "I'm sorry," she said. "I thought you were right behind me. Did you see someone you knew?"

"Yeah. That was Gabe, the orderly from Dad's nursing home. He assured me that both he and Michael were the ones who helped my dad this morning. Who knows why Kristin didn't have a record of them, but she tends to be a little preoccupied with herself most of the time."

Janna leaned over, pointing to the yellowed square of paper in Cade's hand. "What's that?"

"Oh. Gabe seemed to think I dropped it. I didn't even look to see what it was." Cade took a closer look at the piece of paper, noting it wasn't regular paper at all. It was a photograph. He flipped it over and looked at Janna, who shared his astonished expression. Laying in Cade's palm was the photograph of Moses and Eliza Dellinger.

~16~

The picture of the Dellingers had fluttered out of the window when they left Hollow Creek. *Hadn't it?* Janna thought, scratching her head. How did Gabe find it, and how did he know Cade was the last one to have it?

"Is this some kind of joke someone is playing on us?" Janna looked from the picture to Cade.

"No one knew about this picture but you and me. Unless, I don't know . . . maybe we just *thought* it flew out of the car." He shrugged.

"Cade, the picture slipped through my fingers and I watched it sail out of the window, remember?"

"Well, do you have any other reasonable explanation for how Gabe could have found it and known to give it to me?"

Janna tucked a wayward curl behind her ear and sighed. "Is it possible he was driving behind us and it got caught in his windshield wiper when it flew out of the window?"

"It's feasible but pretty unlikely." Cade pulled Janna away from the line of festival traffic as it picked up around them. "First of all, I don't remember anyone driving behind us this morning. But for argument's sake, let's say Gabe was. That would mean he would've had to see the picture fly out of the car, retrieve it from his windshield before it blew away, and track down my car at the Fourth of July Festival. How would he even know I would be here?"

"He didn't have to know you would be here." Janna tried to switch Cade's mind from cop mode to a simpler line of reasoning. "He may have just had the picture in his wallet or something, so he could give it back to you when he saw you at the Center. He wouldn't have needed your tag to know you're the one who drives a red Jeep Wrangler with a Shady Grove Police Department Annual Pancake Breakfast sticker on the bumper. I'm sure he sees your car parked at the Center all the time when you go to see your dad. He probably just spotted you walking around here and thought now would be a perfect time to give the picture back." Janna folded her arms, impressed with her own skills of deduction.

"And he recognized me from the back of my head?" Cade didn't sound convinced.

"Yeah, I'll admit that is a little creepy, but certainly no more than some of the other things that have been going on the past few days. Maybe Gabe's just a little socially inept, that's all."

A tap on Janna's back surprised her. She started and turned around.

It was Pam McClain. Two teenagers were with her. "Sorry, didn't mean to scare you two." Pam smiled and looked around at some of the tents behind them. "Where's Grace?"

"My mother decided to bring her to the festivities early." Janna peered down Main Street. "Actually, we were just looking for my mom. I'm assuming her booth is closer to the courthouse."

Pam nodded. "We just came from that area. She's in booth thirty-one, beside the 4-H petting zoo." She seemed to remember the teens standing on either side of her. "Oh, Janna, I'd like you to meet my daughter Adrienne, and my son Nick."

"It's nice to meet you both." Janna smiled.

"Hi," Adrienne said politely, smiling back at Janna. Nick, who appeared content to listen to his iPod instead of returning Janna's sentiment, didn't respond.

"You'll have to excuse him. He's forgotten his manners today." Pam shot her son a disappointed look.

Adrienne yanked gently on one of Nick's earbuds.

"Hey, let go!" Nick jerked away from his sister and repositioned the earbud.

Let Go. Janna thought of the note in her pocket from the jar of peonies. It referenced the same verse that appeared on the bottom of the Dellingers' picture. Maybe someone was playing a joke on them, but what was the punch line? She needed somewhere to sit down and figure out how all these things connected.

"Great seeing you, Pam, but we really should make our way to Mom's tent." Janna widened her eyes at Cade and raised her eyebrows to express a hidden agenda.

"Yeah, she's right." He seemed to pick up on her signals. "We've kept Grace waiting long enough. Pam, I'll see you on Monday."

"It was good seeing you two together again." Pam leaned over and whispered loud enough in Cade's ear for Janna to hear, "I'll expect a full report on Monday morning."

Janna suppressed a smile as Pam turned and continued down the street with her children. "C'mon." She grabbed Cade's arm by the wrist without thinking and pulled him toward the courthouse. "Let's go find Mom's booth. I need some space to work in."

Cade didn't pull his arm away as she skillfully and quickly maneuvered them through the dense crowd until they made it to the hospital's booth.

Her mother was busy talking to someone when they arrived, but they were greeted by Grace as they stepped behind the booth's front table. Janna let go of Cade's arm, and he scooped Grace up and gave her a hug. "We missed you, kiddo."

Grace smiled at him and then at Janna. Judging from the icing on her face, she'd chosen to show her patriotism by eating sugar cookies from the booth.

Janna's mother finished chatting and turned around. "Hey kids! You made it. I was beginning to wonder what happened to you two."

Janna swapped a look with Cade. "More than you could believe, Mom."

"Did I miss something?" Her mother looked confused.

Janna shook her head. "It's just been a weird day, Mom. Can I use one of those brochures for a minute?" She picked one up and turned it over to make sure she could write on it.

"Sure, honey. Why? Does someone need some information?" Her mother rearranged the other brochures on the table.

"You could say that." Janna picked up two trays of decorated sugar cookies and shoved them out of her way to the other side of the table.

Her mom gasped. "What are you doing?"

Janna could tell her mother was too concerned about her disorganizing the display to understand. "I just need some space to figure something out."

"Why don't you try the table behind the tent?" her mother rushed to the disheveled cookies and frantically began straightening each one on the tray.

Janna and Cade, with Grace in tow, walked around the side of the tent to find a table pushed up behind it. Janna's mother followed close on their heels, her curiosity overruling her earlier dismay.

The table behind the tent was filled with styrofoam cups in plastic sheaths. With one swing of her arm, Janna swept the stacks of cups onto the ground below. She ignored her mother's second horrified look.

"Desperate times call for desperate measures." Janna held out her hand. "Could I see that picture, please?"

Cade placed the picture in her hand, and she pulled the note from the jar of flowers from her pocket.

"Excuse me," a male voice called from the front of the tent.

"Oh, I'd better go see who that is." Janna's mother took a few steps and then turned back to her daughter. "You two have to promise to fill me in on what all this stuff is about when I get back."

"Okay, Mom. Just give me a minute to figure it out myself, and we'll catch you up to speed."

Janna placed the picture of the Dellingers beside the note she'd received with the peonies. The handwriting didn't look similar at all. The cursive on the Dellingers' wedding photo appeared to be written by a woman who used big loops in her letters. The note from the flowers was a little messier, and all the letters were slanted more to the right.

Cade placed Grace on the ground and bent over to study the writing more closely. "I've seen that kind of mark before." He pointed to the colon between the numbers, which looked more like tiny slashes than dots.

"Grace we'll find you," he said. "The handwriting on the note you received is the same handwriting I found scrawled on the door out at Moses Dellinger's old place."

"Are you sure?" Janna squinted, trying to remember what the handwriting on the door looked like.

"See?" Cade pulled out his phone and showed Janna the message on the bottom of the farmhouse door again.

It did look similar.

"So you think whoever wrote the warning on the wall for Grace is the same one who's been sending all those bouquets?" Janna tilted her head.

"I'm not sure. I'm just trying to understand how everything's tied together."

"Let's see." Janna dug a pen out of her purse and flipped the brochure over so she could write on the back side. She drew a straight line across the back of the brochure and started filling in the events from the past two days as best she could.

"So, you found Grace yesterday morning." Janna wrote as she spoke. "You saw the peonies on your mom's headstone yesterday too, right?"

"Mm, hm."

"Then you found the Dellingers' picture and the message on the door this morning."

266

Cade nodded at both events on the brochure.

"We went to see your dad, went swimming, lost the picture—we think—and then I got a note with the reference to the verse on the picture we'd already lost." Janna's hand began to ache from writing so fast. "Sometime during the past few days, your dad received a jar of peonies and then the orderly who no one remembers shows up and returns the picture. There." She stepped back from the piece of paper to take in the whole series of events. "I think that's about where we're at now."

"I do admire your attention to detail, but maybe we're overanalyzing this and it's all just a big set of coincidences." Cade pinched either side of his nose and squeezed his eyes shut. "I mean, okay, so someone put the peonies on Mom's grave and in Dad's room, but no note came with either of those bouquets. I'll admit the picture of the Dellingers showing back up is a little weird, but it probably just got caught in the door and then somehow got stuck to my clothing when I climbed out." He waved his hands around, acting out his theory. "I dropped it out here and Gabe happened to be around to give it back to me. Simple as that."

Janna blinked at him, her brain trying to catch up with the barrage of conclusions Cade had just arrived at.

A grin played around the corners of Cade's mouth. "Is there a chance you bought any of that theory?"

"Not really, but nice try." Janna patted him on the back for the good effort.

"Cade," Janna's mother called out as she stepped around to the back of the tent. "Someone dropped by to see you."

"Here?"

"Yes."

"When?"

"Just a second ago. I told him to wait and I'd come find you. He told me not to bother you, so I'm not sure he's even still out there, but he said he knew you. Young guy with dark hair. Said his name is Michael."

Cade's face lit up. He brushed past Janna's mom and stepped back into the booth. Janna picked up the brochure and took Grace's hand, following him. No one was out there.

"Was it him?" Janna asked.

"I don't know." Cade scanned the passing crowd. "I don't see him, do you?"

Both of them headed toward the front of the booth, scouring the area for a glimpse of him.

"He told me if you needed him, he'd be at the church. Is he a friend of yours, Cade?"

Cade and Janna exchanged looks again.

Janna's mom put her hands on her hips and huffed. "Are you two going to tell me what's going on or what?"

"It's a long story, Mrs. Petersen." Cade waved his hand through the air. "I'll explain it all to you later, but right now I feel a strong urge to pray." He lifted his eyebrow. "How about you, Janna?"

Janna nodded her agreement. "Let's head to the church."

***

They walked a few blocks over to the church where a spotlight shone on an American flag hanging under the stained glass windows on the front of the building. Janna carried Grace so they could keep up with Cade, whose pace quickened as they got closer to the church doors. He bounded up the steps and pulled the double doors open to the sanctuary.

"Hello?" he called out. "Michael?"

They scanned the sanctuary. Glass hurricane lanterns cast a soft glow over the empty pews, keeping the room just dark enough to provide a hiding place in its shadowy corners.

"Michael, are you here?" Cade's voice echoed through the vacant sanctuary.

He looked back at Janna and Grace. "I'm gonna go check the Sunday School rooms downstairs. You can wait here if you want. I'll be right back."

Janna lowered Grace to the ground and took her hand. She looked around the empty room. A row of stained glass windows decorated the plain white sanctuary walls on either side of the room, each displaying a different scene from the Bible. One of Adam and Eve in the Garden of Eden. One of Moses and the Ten Commandments. One of the angel appearing to Mary to tell her she would be the mother of Jesus. And several others portraying different events in Jesus' life. Janna sat down on one of the hard seats, running her hand over the dark wood on the pew in front of her. Grace crawled up in her lap. They sat in stillness for a few minutes.

Cade and Janna were supposed to be married here. Janna was supposed to walk down the burgundy runner in a white dress, peonies in hand, and say "I do" to the man she loved. It didn't seem like a difficult task when she thought of it now. Why had she decided instead to test what they had by running away?

Cade reappeared at the front of the church. "I checked everywhere in the building. No one's here." Sweat glistened on his forehead, and he sounded like he was out of breath. "If Michael was here, he left before we came. This is nuts." He ran his hand through his hair and laughed. "He asks for me and tells your mom he'll be here. It took us only a few minutes to walk over, and he's already gone. I'm starting to think you were right earlier when you said we're both crazy."

Janna pretended to be engrossed with Grace's braid. "My mom may have misunderstood him. Maybe he meant he'd see you here tomorrow morning or something." She met Cade's eyes and bit her lip.

"That's possible." Cade stepped closer to her. "Hey, are you okay? You look like you're gonna throw up or something."

"That's because I might." Janna's voice shook as she slid Grace off her lap and rose from the pew. "Cade, there's something I need to tell you." Stacy was right. Janna owed it to both of them to finally tell Cade the truth. If she didn't do it right now, while it weighed so heavily on her heart, it may go unsaid forever.

"About Michael?"

How would she even begin? "No, about us."

271

Cade walked over to the pew in front of her and sat down, turning in the seat to face her. "Okay." He put his hand on the top of the wooden bench. "What do you need to tell me?"

"I . . . I—" Janna tried to control her wobbly voice. Grace slipped her hand into Janna's and squeezed it, giving her the courage to go on. She took a deep breath. "I need you to understand why I left."

***

Cade studied the lines in his hands as he rested them on the back of the pew. "You've already told me why you had to leave, Janna."

"I know," she said. A tear rolled down her face. "But that wasn't the truth."

Cade cocked his head to the side. "What do you mean it wasn't the truth?"

"I didn't want to tell you the truth, so I said it was because we were too young and we hadn't experienced much. But that was only part of it. It wasn't the real reason." Her words spilled out so fast Cade barely had time to catch up before she continued. "I was scared, Cade. That's pretty much what it amounted to. I just had this overwhelming fear of—" Janna cupped her hands around her face and went silent.

"Fear of what, Jan?" Cade stood and slid out of the pew but made no move to get closer to her, hoping he provided the space she needed to get this off her chest.

A frustrated grunt escaped from Janna lips. "Of it not working out."

Cade took a deep breath. He wanted to grab her by the shoulders and shake her, but she might be more forthcoming if he stayed calm. "Why wouldn't it have worked out?"

"Because I wasn't good enough for you. I was afraid the second you realized it, you would regret marrying me, so I thought it would be easier if I made the decision for you and just left."

Cade clenched his jaw a few times and pressed his lips together. "Janna, why didn't you tell me this before?"

"Because I knew you. I knew you would talk me into going through with the wedding. I also knew if I didn't make you angry, if I didn't make you hate me a little, you would try to convince me to stay. I couldn't let you marry me out of obligation."

"Out of obligation!" The ridiculousness of her words made him forget to control the volume of his voice. "Janna, I

273

wanted to marry you because I loved you. I wanted to build a life together."

"Then why didn't you come after me?" Janna yelled back.

Cade closed his eyes for a moment and tried to suppress the anger he felt boiling up his spine and threatening to explode from his mouth. She had been playing with him, testing his devotion to her. *That was the real truth.* He'd let his anger and pride keep him from fighting for her before, but he wouldn't let her off the hook so easily this time.

"So it was really just a test?" His eyes narrowed as his voice ricocheted off the sanctuary walls. "That's the truth, Janna? You wanted to see how far you could push me away and how far I'd go to bring you back."

Janna looked down at her hands like a child who'd just broken something they weren't supposed to touch. "I just thought if you really loved me, you would have come for me. Then I would have known for sure I was enough for you, and I would never have to doubt it. You have to know I would never have hurt you in a million years if I had thought of any other way to prove to myself we really belonged together."

Cade stepped away from the side of the pew and walked up to the altar where the lanterns continued to burn.

Their flames mirrored the years of squelched resentment that had burned in him for the last several years.

He heard Janna slip out of the pew and take a few steps toward him.

"I was stupid, Cade, and what I did—it was childish and immature. You have no idea how hard it was for me to leave you."

"Hard for you?" Cade whirled around, cutting her off. "You want me to feel sorry for you, Janna? Is that it? You want me to say what you did was okay, and you're just allowed some do over now because you're older and wiser? I don't think so."

Janna held her hands up in surrender. "If you'd just let me finish explaining—"

"You've already said your piece, Janna. It's my turn."

Cade let the bitterness from the past few years swell up in his chest, giving him the courage to say everything he'd wanted to say to Janna since she left. "You're right. I should have come after you. I should have told you I'd do whatever you needed to make it work. I should have held onto you and never let you go. But that's not what happened, is it?" He paced back and forth in front of the altar. "I thought I was giving you space, like you needed. And what were you doing? Just sitting in Wilmington, waiting for me to come for you on a white stallion? In my defense, I was a tad busy, Janna. Mom died, dad got sick, and the whole world came crashing down on me. I needed you then. If I'd known this was all just some kind of game to you, I might not have felt so abandoned."

***

Sharp prickles of heat ran up the back of Janna's neck as she stepped forward obstinately. "Do you think it was easy for me to stay away? I loved your mother too, you know." She sniffed, wiping hot tears from her cheeks. "I didn't want you to have to deal with our issues while you were grieving. Believe it or not, I had your best interest at heart." She shook her head. "Don't you see? I had to wait until the time was right before I could come back and explain everything."

"Why is now the right time, Janna?" Cade stepped toward her and grabbed her by the shoulders.

Janna pulled away from his grasp and turned, walking a few steps away from him. She looked up at the stained glass window in front of her. It was a picture of Jesus praying to God before being betrayed by one of his disciples. Janna remembered the story Pastor Mabry told them during the sermon one Sunday about the picture. Jesus begged God to take his impending suffering away, but he remained willing to be used for God's purpose. Janna thought Cade's face looked like Jesus' in that picture. Begging her for answers. Asking her to end his suffering.

She stared at the picture of Jesus in front of her. "Somewhere between leaving you and Shady Grove behind me and trying to cope in the type of career I had chosen, I lost myself, Cade. I was sucked into a world I wasn't ready to handle, and I had no one to guide me but myself. After Molly Ann died on my watch, everything spun out of control. I realized that, despite my best efforts, I really couldn't help anyone when I was so lost myself. I tried to remember the last time my life made any sense to me. All I could think of was you."

Janna turned back to face Cade. "You don't know how badly I wish I hadn't been so reckless with your feelings. I should have just come clean and told you I felt insecure, but instead my flight response kicked in, and I did what I always do. I ran. And I ruined everything."

Cade didn't have a response this time. He walked to her and cupped her face in his hands. He studied her face, as if still unsure of what he was feeling as well.

"There's just one problem," he said, leaning in and moving closer to her face. "Your plan didn't work. Nothing you've done could make me hate you, Janna. Not even lying to me about why you had to go."

He leaned in further to kiss her, but before he reached her lips, a strong gust of wind flung the double doors of the church wide open, blowing out the candles and leaving them standing in total darkness.

~17~

A strange green light illuminated the sanctuary, accompanied by several loud pops. A blue light followed, then a red. This time the pops were not as loud, more like someone was making popcorn in the back of the church.

"The fireworks have started." Janna removed herself from Cade's embrace. "We told Brian and Stacy we'd meet them. They're probably wondering where we are."

It was too dark to see the expression on Cade's face, but even in the momentary blackness, it sounded like his earlier fervor had gone out like the candles. "First, we need some light in here," he said.

Cade waited until another smattering of colored light bathed the dark sanctuary in an amber hue. He picked up a long-stemmed lighter laying by the candles and walked over to relight their wicks. He lifted each glass hurricane and touched the flame to each candle on either side of the altar, brightening the room with their soft glow again.

The pent-up feelings that had just exploded all over the church's sanctuary left Janna feeling overwhelmed. Before everything went black, Cade had almost kissed her. She had wanted him to kiss her, but maybe it was okay they were interrupted before it actually happened. She needed some time to process what Cade said and how she felt about it. She wished she could just let go like the note on the jar of peonies encouraged her to do and just surrender herself to the feelings she had for Cade.

Cade seemed to sense her need for breathing room and followed her lead.

"I'm sure Grace would like to see the fireworks anyway, right?" he said.

Resting her knees on the pew, Grace sat facing them. Her hands gripped the back of the seat in front of her and her little body angled forward the way someone would sit at a sporting event, waiting for her team to score.

Grace hopped down from the pew and ran to Cade's side. Cade and Janna each grabbed one of her hands and walked her down the middle aisle of the church. Cade made sure the doors were securely closed this time.

"Let's not tell Brian that Pastor Mabry is burning candles in the church, okay? He'd flip out," Cade said.

"My lips are sealed." Janna swiped her fingers across the imaginary zipper on her lips.

They walked in silence to the community baseball field to view the rest of the fireworks. As they walked, both Cade and Janna pulled Grace up slightly by the arms, lifting her off the ground. She soon caught on and would let them take a step before swinging between them both as if she were on a trapeze.

Though neither of them spoke and Janna avoided Cade's glances all the way to the ball field, contented closure washed over her. As hard as that conversation had been to have after all this time, Janna was glad they finally talked it all out. It felt like a fresh start.

They finally reached the bleachers and located Brian and Stacy, who were sitting behind Janna's parents. Cade took a seat by Brian, while Janna sat on the other side of Stacy. Grace climbed down to the row where Janna's parents sat and plopped down into Janna's mother's lap.

"Is that Grace?" Stacy asked. "She's adorable. Hi Grace." Stacy waved.

Grace turned around and shot a gapped-toothed grin in Stacy's direction before turning back around to enjoy the fireworks display.

"So?" Stacy lowered her voice, letting the fireworks mask her words. "Did you guys finally get a chance to talk things over?"

Janna wasn't sure how much to divulge to her friend since things had been left up in the air at the church. "We each said what we needed to."

"I see." Another blue firework lit up Stacy's face. "And?"

"And," Janna snuck a peek at Cade. "I think we need to have a few more of those honest talks before anything definite is decided."

Stacy put her arm around Janna's shoulders and gave them a little shake. "Oh, it'll work out. I just know it. Just be open, Janna. Let go of the past and embrace your future." Stacy spoke a little louder, as the fireworks increased their frequency to complete the big finale. "You might be surprised how it turns out."

Once the fireworks display ended, the ball field emptied pretty quickly. Brian and Stacy bid them all goodnight.

"Good to see you, Mr. and Mrs. Petersen." Brian waved his hand to Janna's parents. "Cade, you walkin' home with us?"

Janna studied Cade's face. She'd been looking forward to walking back with him, hoping to have a few more minutes to talk, but it made more sense for her to ride back home with her mom and dad.

"Um, yeah, man. Can you give me a second?"

"Sure, I see Pastor Mabry over there. Stace, why don't we go talk to him for a few minutes? We'll come back for Cade." Brian gently pulled Stacy away from where she stood staring at Janna and Cade.

"So should I just plan to meet you all at church in the morning?" Cade's tone didn't indicate much about what he felt after their discussion in the sanctuary.

"Yeah, that would be good. Oh, and I'm sure Mom will make Sunday lunch if you want to come by after church to eat with us." Janna was thankful it was too dark for Cade to see her face flush.

"That would be nice." He leaned in a little so her parents, who were still standing close by, couldn't hear him. "I know it took us seven years, but I'm glad we finally talked."

"Me too." Janna smiled.

"See you tomorrow morning, then. Goodnight."

"Goodnight, Cade."

He turned and jogged over to Brian and Stacy, who were still talking to Pastor Mabry. Janna smiled as Stacy gave her a thumbs-up behind Cade's back. They must have finished their conversation with the pastor because Cade shook his hand and then turned, along with Brian and Stacy, to head back to their house. Watching Cade walk farther and farther away from her down Main Street, a familiar ache swept over Janna's body. She reminded herself tonight wouldn't be the last time they talked, especially since she didn't plan on going back to work in Wilmington.

"You ready, honey?" Her mother startled her.

"Oh, yeah, Mom. Sorry. We can head home now."

"Did Cade find his friend? What was his name? Michael?" Mom shifted a bag of leftover streamers to her other arm.

"No, we must have missed him. When we got to the church, it was empty. From what we could tell, it didn't appear anyone had been there recently."

"Oh, that's a shame. He seemed like he really wanted to speak to Cade about something. He said he had some sort of message to give him."

Lifting Grace onto her hip, Janna followed her parents back to their car. "He's an orderly at the Senior Center. At least that's what he's led Cade to believe. I'm sure if he really wants to speak with him, he'll find another way."

By the time they arrived home, it was ten o'clock.

Janna's mother unbuckled Grace from the backseat and scooped her up. "I'm gonna put this little one to bed. I'll bet she's exhausted after the day she's had. Would you mind bringing that bag of streamers in and leaving it on the kitchen table?"

"Sure, Mom." Janna grabbed the brown paper bag beside her on the seat, climbed out of the car, and followed her mother to the front door. "I think I'll get a shower before I go to bed, if that's alright. Will you be up a while, though? I'd like to talk to you after I finish."

"Okay, honey. I'll make us some hot tea after I put Grace to bed. Just meet me in the kitchen when you get through with your shower."

Janna dropped off the streamers and headed upstairs to grab some pajamas. Her mother settled into the rocking chair in the corner of Janna's bedroom, Grace resting snugly in the crook of her arm.

She heard her mom singing a familiar hymn to Grace as she grabbed a towel on her way to the bathroom. The song

285

she used to sing to Janna when she was a little girl and scared of thunderstorms. Her mother must have figured it would bring Grace comfort tonight, too. Although, for having been abandoned on the side of the road, Grace seemed to be coping remarkably well.

As she stepped into the shower and let the warm water wash over her like a cleansing rain, Janna softly sang the words of her mother's lullaby to herself.

***

Janna padded softly down the staircase to the kitchen, her hair still dripping from the shower. As promised, her mother sat at the island, along with two cups of hot tea.

She took a seat beside her mother. They each took a sip of tea before Janna spoke. "Mom, I've been meaning to tell you something." The words caught in her throat.

"What is it, honey?" Her mom rubbed her back like she was a small child.

"I just wanted to thank you for always supporting me, especially when I left. You and Dad always came to visit me. You didn't have to do that, but I truly appreciate you being willing to give me the time and space I needed to work everything out in my head. I realize now how hard it must have been on you for me to leave. I'm sorry for putting you through that."

"You're right, sweetheart," her mother said, stroking Janna's damp hair. "It was hard on us, but we also knew children need to find their own path in life. You have to let go and hope you raised them to make the right choices. You did what you felt was right for you, so out of respect for that, we chose not to press you when it came to visiting us here. There's a lot of history in this town for you. I know you wanted to avoid it for a while, but I'm thrilled you came back, even if it's just a short visit." Mom took another sip of her tea. "It seems like things are more comfortable between you and Cade now anyway, so maybe you'll end up staying longer than you planned."

Janna laughed and shook her head in disbelief. Her mother didn't plan to let this go.

"What? I didn't mean to suggest anything by that comment. I was simply making an observation." Her mom shrugged. "Besides, every mother wants her daughter to find true love. And I happen to believe Cade is yours." She tapped Janna on the end of the nose with her finger before taking a look at her watch. "You know, I think it's past my bedtime. I'll see you in the morning, honey. I love you."

"Love you too, Mom."

Janna stayed in the kitchen a few more minutes, finishing her tea. She was exhausted. There were too many things on her mind to sort through tonight, but there was someone else she needed to talk to before she joined Grace in bed upstairs.

She crossed her arms on the island and rested her head on her wrists. "Lord, I know I don't deserve half the things you've given me during this visit, especially after I've ignored you for all these months, but thanks for the chance to talk to Cade. Thanks for your patience with me, too. You know I've always been the last to learn the moral of the story." Janna chewed at her lower lip. "Anyway, I know I'm a lot to handle, but I guess what I'm trying to say is thanks for never giving up on me either."

Only a small night-light glowed in Janna's room, providing just enough illumination for her to make it to the bed without bumping into any of the furniture. She lifted the freshly laundered ivory spread and climbed underneath its softness. Her mother must have opened one of the windows to allow the cicadas and crickets outside to serenade them with a constant lullaby while they slept.

Grace had her back to Janna but shifted positions when Janna climbed into the bed, snuggling up in her arms.

Janna stroked Grace's hair until she drifted asleep, listening to the rhythms of God's creation outside the window.

***

Cade was starving by the time he got back from Brian and Stacy's house, so he made himself a ham and cheese sandwich before he went to bed. He carried his late night snack and a glass of orange juice into the living room and turned on the TV, letting its light fill the room with an artificial glow.

By the time he realized there was nothing good on that late at night, he'd finished his meal. He carried his plate and cup into the kitchen and put them in the sink. He switched off the kitchen light and walked down the hallway.

Pausing at the foot of the stairs to straighten the photograph of his parents that hung on the wall, he wondered if he'd have time to check on his dad again tomorrow after church. Maybe Dad would have two good days in a row for a change.

Cade continued upstairs to his room. His parents' room remained just the way it had been when they all lived there together. He'd never felt right about taking their room and still slept in the room he'd grown up in.

Walking to his bed in the dim light of the moon, Cade stubbed his toe on an old metal ammo box tucked underneath it. Janna had gotten it for him at the Army-Navy store when they were dating. It was usually pushed back far enough behind the bed skirt to stay out of his way, but tonight it seemed to have shifted, sticking out well past its normal parameters.

He sat down on the bed and rubbed his injured toe before bending over and pulling the box of items out from under the bed frame. Popping the latch on the front of the box, he lifted its lid and began sifting through the contents. He hadn't looked at some of this stuff in several years, but every item brought back a memory of Janna.

There was a picture of them at the county fair. Cade's arm was draped around Janna, and they were both smiling. Janna was showing off her new engagement ring. Stacy must have taken the picture.

Some old baseball cards, a deflated football, and a thin plastic catcher's mitt from little league were also stored within the box. His dad had tried desperately to get him into sports as a young boy, but there was always something more appealing about cops and robbers back then. Then it was girls. Well, just one girl in particular. Cade smiled at all the memories held in that one small box.

He'd almost closed the metal lid on the ammo box and returned it to its hiding spot, but a square, velvet-covered box in the corner, poking out from underneath some letters, caught his attention. He moved the letters—written in anger after Janna called off the engagement and never delivered—to retrieve the small blue box. He cracked it open, staring at the sparkling ring inside. Janna's engagement ring.

Cade ran his finger over the smooth band and admired the garnets on either side of the diamond. His mother had given him the diamond from her grandmother's old engagement ring to use in the new setting. He'd chosen Janna's birthstone for the accent stones.

He remembered how nervous he'd been carrying the ring in his pocket that day on the way to pick up Janna for the picnic he'd planned. When he got to her house, she was sitting on the porch swing waiting for him. He had been so excited that he got a little ahead of himself and dropped down on one knee in front of the swing, asking her to marry him.

When he remembered it now, Cade realized Janna hesitated before saying yes. At the time, he thought she was in shock, but now he wondered if that should have been his first sign she wasn't ready to make that commitment.

Placing all the items back into the ammo box and sliding it underneath his bed, Cade reminded himself it was too late for regrets. He needed to focus on the future.

He crawled underneath the covers. As his eyelids grew heavier, he made a mental note to look for Michael at church tomorrow. Janna was probably right when she said that's most likely what he'd meant when he told Mrs. Petersen where they could find him. Whatever the case may be, he was too tired to figure it out now. He closed his eyes and drifted out of consciousness into a sweet, peaceful sleep.

***

A few hours later, a loud clatter from downstairs woke Cade from a strange dream.

In the dream, he had been in the common area of his dad's nursing home. His dad was sitting in a chair across from him when Gabe and Michael, the orderlies, walked over and helped Cade's father to his feet. This time, instead of escorting him out of the room, they each took one of his arms and lifted him, swinging him back and forth the way Cade and Janna swung Grace on the way to the fireworks display. His dad's eyes were cleared of their usual haze, and a bright light had beamed from his face.

Cade sat up suddenly in bed, trying to figure out if the sound that woke him was part of his dream or reality. He tilted his head, listening carefully. The thumping intensified.

He had left his gun at work. As tame as life typically was in Shady Grove, he saw little need to carry a firearm. Other than target practice, Cade had never even used his gun while on duty.

With all the strange things that had been occurring lately, he wondered if keeping a weapon at home was such a bad idea. He climbed out of bed, grabbed his baseball bat from the closet, and said a quick prayer for safety as he snuck down the stairs. After checking out the living room and both closets in the guest bedroom downstairs, Cade listened again for the thumping noise. After a few seconds, he heard it again, coming from the kitchen.

He poised himself with the baseball bat before flipping on the light in the kitchen. The back door stood wide open. The breeze outside made it thump against the kitchen wall.

Cade peeked outside to make sure no one was out there and stepped back inside, closing the door and flipping the deadbolt this time. In his hurry to get to bed, he must have forgotten to lock up. That door had always been a little loose on the frame anyway. The wind could have easily blown it open if he hadn't locked it.

He propped the baseball bat against the kitchen table and shuffled back to the light switch. Turning around, he shot one last glance around the kitchen to make sure everything was in its place. Something on the back of the door caught his eye. He blinked the drowsiness from his eyes and took a step forward.

Grace we'll find you was scrawled across the bottom of the kitchen door.

~18~

"Do you have any idea what time it is, Cade?" Brian slurred, when he finally answered the door. Cade had pressed the doorbell rapidly several times before he heard voices and someone clanging around. Brian seemed relieved to see his best friend standing on the front porch and lowered the golf club in his hand, propping it beside the door and motioning for Cade to come inside.

He called up the stairs, "Stacy, it's just Cade. You can go back to sleep."

"I'm really sorry I woke you guys up, but I have to show you something." Cade walked with Brian into the living room.

Brian rubbed the back of his head and yawned. "And it couldn't have waited until tomorrow morning?"

"Well technically, it is tomorrow morning, and no, it couldn't wait. Does this look familiar?" Cade held out his phone for Brian to see the message painted on the bottom of his back door.

Brian squeezed his eyes shut and blinked himself awake, looking over the picture. "Um, yeah. That's the door at the old Dellinger place. Please tell me you didn't wake me up to show me *that*."

"Look more closely at the door."

Brian took the phone from Cade. Cade hoped he would notice this door was painted white and had curtains, not like the old rickety one at the Dellingers'.

Brian's eyes grew wide. "Dude, is that in your kitchen?" He seemed awake now

Cade nodded. "About thirty minutes ago, a loud thump coming from downstairs woke me up. I went to the kitchen and the back door was wide open, banging in the breeze. I found the message when I closed the door."

"You think someone was in your house?"

"I'm not sure." Cade scratched his head. "If they were, they would've had to wait until they were sure I was asleep to leave the message. I was in the kitchen getting a snack right before I went to bed and nothing was there, so whoever it was snuck in between about ten and one this morning. I can't really remember if I locked the back door or not, so they could have easily opened the door, written the message, and left without me hearing anything. They probably counted on me finding the message in the morning on my way out. I think the only reason the door was open is because the wind caught it."

"You don't lock your doors?" Brian sounded more appalled by that than the idea of an intruder in Cade's house.

"Did you hear a word I just said?"

"It just seems unfathomable to me that a member of the police force would sleep with his doors unlocked."

"Well, I don't always. I just forgot this one—oh, never mind." Cade slapped his hand through the air the way he felt like slapping Brian. "We don't have time to waste arguing over my home security procedures."

"What are you guys looking at?" Stacy yawned from behind them.

Both men flinched and almost bumped their heads together.

Brian let out a deep breath and placed his hand over his chest. "Good grief, Stace. You scared me to death. You should warn a man before you come sneaking up on him like that. You're lucky I left my golf club at the door. I could have killed you."

"I'm sorry." Stacy hid a smile behind her hand. "I didn't realize you two were on some secret mission down here." She pointed to the picture on the phone. "What's that?"

"We found that message out at Moses Dellinger's old farmhouse yesterday morning, and now someone has written the same thing on Cade's door. Did you know he doesn't lock his doors?"

Cade snapped his fingers in Brian's face. "Could you focus, please?"

"What does it have to do with Grace?" Stacy shook her head.

"It's a long story, Stacy, but we think, or at least we thought, someone left Grace at the old farmhouse, and the message was warning her to stay there until they came back for her. Now that someone has written the same thing on my door, I'm not sure what's going on."

"You know what might help us straighten all this out at two o'clock in the morning?" Brian asked.

Cade and Stacy looked at him and shrugged.

"Some coffee. Shall we take this little powwow into the kitchen and brew up some properly caffeinated theories?" Brian directed them with his hands.

Cade and Stacy smiled at each other. Stacy patted her husband on the back. "Okay, Brian, I'll make you some coffee while Cade fills me in on what's been happening around here."

***

Brian and Stacy listened intently as Cade shared every detail of the events of the past few days, from the strange flower deliveries to the picture he found at the Dellingers' blowing away and then mysteriously reappearing. He concluded his account by telling them about Michael showing up at the festival, looking for him.

"It sounds like someone is trying to send you a message." Stacy said. "Do you think 'Grace we'll find you' could mean something different than you think? Like maybe Grace wasn't dropped off in the cornfield. It could be she ran away and hid for a time in the farmhouse. Whomever she was running from may have left the message on the door to let her know she wouldn't get away so easily."

"I think someone has been watching too many mystery movies on cable." Brian patted Stacy on the head insolently.

"It's just a hunch, honey." Stacy sipped her coffee. "I'm not saying I'm right."

Cade tilted his head. "That thought did cross my mind a few times, but nothing that's happened seems to connect Grace to anyone who would want to harm her. Besides, if someone knew where she was, why would they leave the message on my door instead of Janna's?"

No one at the table had an answer.

"I've got an even better question," Brian said, breaking the silence. "I understand why they're leaving these notes and flowers on or by the door: because that way someone is sure to see them. What I can't figure out is why they write their message on the bottom of the door? It seems like if you wanted to leave something a person couldn't miss, you'd put it at eye level."

"You're right. That does seem unusual." Cade ran his index finger across the top of his lip. "You know, what I really need to do is go back out to the old house and look around one more time. We were so distracted by raccoons making noises upstairs and weird messages on the door before, maybe we missed something the first time."

"You mean right now?" Brian's eyebrows crumpled together. "While it's still dark out?"

"Yeah. Whoever wrote the message could be staying there at night or something." Cade stood up from the table. "Do you guys have a flashlight I could borrow?" He looked at Stacy.

"Sure. Actually, we have a few flashlights. One for each of us." Stacy elbowed Brian gently in the arm.

"We don't really need to get involved in something that's not our business, do we?" Brian laughed nervously. "We should just wait here. Cade can call us if he finds anything or runs into trouble. Right, bud?"

Cade pressed his lips together to prevent a smirk from appearing on his face. "It would be helpful to have two more sets of eyes out there, but it's okay. I can just call you guys if I find anything."

"See." Brian laughed uncomfortably. "He doesn't need us."

"I really appreciate your willingness to go, Stacy. But, I mean, if Brian is scared, I totally understand. He doesn't have to come." Cade hoped he'd hit a nerve.

Stacy caught on to Cade's reverse psychology. "You're not scared, are you, Brian?" She broke a doe-eyed stare out of her arsenal, which Cade knew Brian could never resist.

"Who me?" Brian pointed to himself as if the accusation was completely unfounded. "Nah!" He swatted his hand at them both. "Why would I be scared to go poking around in an old, rundown farmhouse? At night. In the pitch black darkness. With the ghost of Old Man Dellinger lurking around—" His voice trailed off.

Cade could see they were losing him. He hoped Stacy had another trick up her sleeve.

"Just think how great we'll feel when we've helped this little girl, honey." She put her hand on his arm. "She doesn't have anyone else. We may be her only hope." Her chin quivered.

Cade had to hand it to her. Appealing to his sense of duty. Classic. "Yeah, Brian," he said. "Are you going to put your own fears ahead of a defenseless child? What about the oath you promised to uphold as a firefighter to protect the weak?"

Brian closed his eyes and shook his head slowly. "That's just a . . . suggestion."

Stacy pleaded one more time. "I just can't believe the man I married would be so selfish and put himself before a child. I thought I knew you better than that, Brian." She put her hand to her face and turned away from him, shaking her head in disgust. She looked up at Cade and raised her eyebrows.

Brian took a deep breath and sighed. It seemed she'd found his Achilles' heel. Cade knew Brian couldn't stand for Stacy to be disappointed in him.

"Oh, alright." Brian gritted his teeth together. "I'll go. But I'm telling you right now if I hear any weird noises or even so much as a spider web touches me—" He threw up his hands.

"We are on our own. Got it." Cade pulled the keys out of his pocket. "I'll go start the car."

"I'll go change and get the flashlights." Stacy rose from the kitchen chair.

Brian's shoulders slumped. "I'll get my golf club."

***

Cade parked his car across from the field where the old house stood. They all climbed out and clicked on their flashlights before they cut across the road to the perimeter fence.

Brian held one line of barbed wire down with his foot and pulled the other one up so Stacy could slide through

303

without getting scratched. He offered the same courtesy to Cade before trying to squeeze through himself.

"Let me help you there, buddy." Cade turned to lift the wire up on either side of the fence. "You're gonna have to cut back on the cake if we keep crawling through tight spaces like these." Cade laughed, hoping the jab at Brian's weight would get his mind off the imminent danger he imagined.

The three of them shone their flashlights on the front entrance to the house. Cade made the first move, stepping up to the front door. He turned and put his finger to his lips. They nodded obediently. Stacy walked up to the front door and stood beside Cade. They both looked back at Brian expectantly. Not to be outdone by his own wife, Brian, who still held tightly to his golf club, took the steps up to the front porch.

"Now, I'm gonna crack open the door," Cade whispered. "And we're gonna stay together this time. We'll check out each room and clear it before we move on to the next. We'll start upstairs and work our way down, okay?"

Stacy nodded her consent, but Brian turned around at every little creak the old porch made.

"Okay Brian?"

No answer.

"Brian!" Cade growled and slapped his friend on the shoulder.

Brian let his paranoia overrule his common sense. "What?" he yelled.

"Shhh!" Cade and Stacy hissed in unison.

Brian lowered his voice and nodded wildly. "Yeah, yeah I heard you. Upstairs first, downstairs last. Stay together. Got it."

Cade turned the knob as quietly as he could and carefully pushed the front door open. The hinges on the decrepit door moaned as it swung open. Cade hoped if anyone dangerous was here, the sound did not alert them of their presence. The three of them moved together to the foot of the stairs.

Pointing the flashlight up the stairs, Cade ran it across the banister of the upper level, checking to see if anyone was there. "Watch out for the top step."

Cade and Stacy got to the top of the stairs ahead of Brian. The moon shone through the window at the top of the staircase, giving the upper level an eerie glow. They both reached for Brian and pulled him in between the two of them.

Brian lifted the golf club in his left hand, ready to take a swing at whoever was up there. The floorboards settled as the three of them took a few more steps ahead, making the house moan again.

Brian jumped back at the noise, dropping his flashlight and swinging his golf club back and forth at the shadows on the wall. He lost his grip, sending the club flying through the window behind him. The sound of shattering glass filled the hallway.

"Whoops." He laughed nervously and grimaced. "I thought we could use a little more light up here." Brian bent down and retrieved his flashlight.

Cade dropped his face into his hand. Stacy took her fearful husband's hand and led him back to where Cade stood.

Brian glanced back at the broken window. "That was my favorite golf club." After seeing the frustration in Cade's face, he put his head down like a scolded puppy. "I'm sorry."

Cade signaled with his flashlight to the room where he'd found the Dellingers' wedding picture. They would start there. Stacy led Brian into the room first. Cade closed the door behind them. The last thing they needed was for someone to sneak up on them.

"I didn't have a chance to check the closet very thoroughly yesterday. How about you guys open the bureau drawers and see if anyone left anything in there?"

"C'mon, Brian." Stacy pulled him by the arm to the bureau.

Cade held his flashlight in his mouth, freeing his hands to pull both closet doors open. No raccoons this time. He slid the shelves to the side of the closet with his foot and ran his flashlight over the entire space, looking for any kind of message or sign someone had been there. When he determined nothing was to be found, he turned to Brian and Stacy, hoping they'd had more luck with the bureau.

Stacy, who sat in front of the old dresser, looked up at him, shaking her head. "There's nothing in the top three drawers. We can't get the bottom drawer open. I'm not sure, but maybe someone locked something in there."

"Wanna help me a sec, Brian?" Cade laid his flashlight on the floor and motioned for Stacy to stand back.

Brian handed Stacy his flashlight and sat down in front of the stubborn drawer. He and Cade both braced one of their feet on the wood beside the drawer and each took the large handles on either side with both hands.

Cade mouthed, one, two, three, and they pulled on the drawer handles with all their might. It didn't budge.

"There's something stuck in the top, holding the drawer back." Stacy waved both flashlights on something poking out of the top of the drawer. "Here, you guys pull on the handles again. I'll try to wiggle whatever it is out of there."

Cade and Brian braced their feet and pulled back on the handles again. Stacy grabbed part of the thing holding back the drawer and moved it back and forth to loosen it.

"It's really in there, guys, but I think if we try one more time I can get it." Stacy squinted at the lodged object and wedged her fingers in the space between the drawers again.

Cade looked at Brian. "Last time."

With one final exertion, they pulled on the handles. Stacy had a firmer grip on the item this time and gave it a forceful tug, ripping it out of the drawer and falling backward.

Brian looked at his wife, "You okay, babe?"

"Yeah, I'm fine." Stacy stood and dusted herself off. "Look, it's some kind of cloth."

Cade and Brian got up from the floor. Cade grabbed his flashlight and held it up to the piece of purple cloth in Stacy's hand.

"That's from Grace's dress. The one she was wearing when I found her." He tapped his flashlight in his hand. "So, she was here."

He took the piece of cloth from Stacy and put it in his pocket. He walked back to the drawer and pulled it open. Nothing else was in there.

Stacy asked the question they were all thinking. "How would she have gotten her dress caught in the bottom of the bureau?"

"Maybe someone was chasing her and the drawer was open." Brian shrugged. "She got caught on the edge, and it ripped her dress. Then maybe the person she was with slammed the drawer shut and the piece of dress got stuck."

Stacy and Cade both raised their eyebrows at each other and stared at Brian a moment.

"That is the smartest thing you've said all night." Cade grinned and patted his friend on the back. "Let's go check the other rooms up here. Then we can look around the lower level."

The remaining rooms upstairs were empty.

Brian and Stacy followed Cade back down the stairs. They all quickly surveyed the living room and downstairs bathroom together before heading for the kitchen.

"We should probably check all the cabinets in here, just so we can say we officially ruled out any other clues at this location." Cade kept his voice low. "I'll check the walk-in pantry over here."

Stacy began checking the cabinets above and below the sink and directed Brian to do the same with the cabinets across the room.

Cade inched into the pantry. It would be a perfect place for someone to hide. Only empty shelves greeted him as he let the beam of his flashlight bounce over the walls. He left the pantry and entered the kitchen again, a little disappointed. "Did you guys find anything?"

Stacy shined her light in Cade's direction. "Nope. All the cabinets on this side are empty. What about you, honey?" She and Cade looked at Brian.

"I checked all the lower cabinets. They were empty. I just need to check these up here, and we'll have cleared the kitchen." Brian clucked a sound from his throat and gave them a thumbs-up.

He pulled open the first two cabinet doors in front of him. "I really don't think there's anything else to see in this place, guys." He closed the cabinets and walked to the last set of doors in the row, holding his flashlight in his mouth. As he opened the cabinet doors, his flashlight revealed a pair of glowing eyes staring down at them from the upper shelf. A huge field rat scampered out of the cabinet, screeching its disdain for having been discovered in the cozy kitchen hideout, and jumped down onto Brian's head.

Brian screamed and dropped the flashlight, sending it rolling across the floor, where it highlighted the bottom of the kitchen door. "Get it off me! Get it off me!" Brian danced around wildly.

Stacy ran over to her husband. "It's off, Brian. It's off of you. It jumped to the floor and ran into that hole over there." She mapped the rat's path with her flashlight.

Cade was too preoccupied with what he had seen when the flashlight lit up the back door to be worried about Brian. He walked over to the kitchen door and pointed his flashlight at the bottom.

Brian picked up his flashlight and brushed himself off. He and Stacy walked up on either side of Cade and aimed their lights at the same spot Cade beamed his.

"What is it?" Brian asked.

"The message that was here before —Grace we'll find you—" Cade took a step back. "It's gone."

~19~

A peculiar noise woke Janna from her tranquil, dreamless sleep. She rolled over and squinted at the clock on her bedside table. Two o'clock.

She had always been a light sleeper, hearing every creak or pop the house made throughout the night, but this noise was something else. She shifted onto her back and titled her head to listen.

Plink. Plink.

Janna sat upright in bed and glanced over at Grace, who was still sleeping, undisturbed by the noise. She lifted the covers, placed her feet onto the carpet, and angled forward on the mattress, straining to hear the noise again. It was difficult to tell where it came from. She climbed out of bed and closed the windows, hoping she would eliminate the now cacophonous sound of the cicadas outside.

Plink. Plink.

Grace rolled over in the bed but didn't wake.

Plink. Plink.

The noise had to come from the bathroom.

She didn't want to wake Grace by flipping on the bedroom light to get to the bathroom, so she pulled open the top drawer of her bedside table and removed the small flashlight her mother kept stored to use if the power went off during storms. She grabbed her glasses from the top of the bedside table.

Janna lit a path for herself on the carpet and moved quietly as she slipped into the bathroom. She closed the door behind her and reached for the light switch. Nothing happened. She tried the switch again, flipping it up and down. The light never came on.

They must have had a storm overnight, and it knocked out the power. She shone the flashlight around the room, trying to locate the mysterious sound.

Plink. Plink.

Janna aimed the light at the faucet above the bathtub. She watched as two tiny drops of water chased each other out of the bottom of the faucet head and fell into the claw-foot tub.

Plink. Plink.

Seven years later and her parents still hadn't fixed the leak. Janna adjusted her glasses, thinking about the sound two drops in an empty tub would make. Instead of hearing the light tap she would have expected, she heard the sound water makes only when it drops into another liquid. She moved closer to the tub, tilting her flashlight down so she could see what the dripping water hit. The bathtub was full of water.

"What in the world?"

Was it possible that she'd accidentally stopped up the drain during her shower earlier? The drain stopper attached to a chain that usually hung over the faucet. Occasionally, it would slip off and drop down into the drain when she showered, but she'd simply pull it out and drape it back over the faucet head again.

That was the best conclusion Janna could come up with in the middle of the night. Or, morning, she guessed. Either way, she hadn't had enough sleep to understand how it happened, so she'd just have to figure it out in the morning.

She bent over the tub and unplugged the drain. A slight buzz above her head announced the power had returned. The light flickered and came on in the bathroom.

Janna was thankful for the ability to see more clearly around the room now. She looped the chain of the stopper around the faucet twice, just to make sure it didn't stop the tub up again. She shook the water from her arm as best she could before turning around to grab a hand towel from the bar beside the sink. As she reached for the towel, she caught a glimpse of the mirror. The words *Grace we'll find you* were written in red across the reflection of her face.

Janna dropped the hand towel and backed away from the mirror, accidentally bumping into the side of the tub. Her mouth felt like sandpaper. She swallowed a couple of times to get control of her voice before she screamed the only word she could think of. "Dad!"

***

Cade, Brian, and Stacy stared at the now blank door in front of them in the Dellingers' kitchen.

"What happened to the message?" Stacy asked.

"It was Moses Dellinger." Brian cupped his hand around his mouth and lowered his voice to a horrified whisper. "He doesn't like us in his house."

Cade sighed and shook his head. "I think a more realistic explanation would be that whoever wrote the message didn't want anyone else to find it. I take it they don't know we got a picture of it the first time we were here. I mean, why bother hiding something if someone's got photographic proof of it?"

"I'm sorry guys," Stacy interrupted, "Before I try to come up with any more guesses as to what's going on, I need to go home and wash this filth off of me." She pulled a spider web from the sleeve of her shirt. "Ugh."

As much as Cade wanted to stay or maybe even go over the old house a third time, the fact that someone took the time to come back and get rid of the message on the door worried him. "Okay, Stace. I'll take you and Brian back home. I should probably head over to Janna's to check on things there soon anyway."

***

Once they stepped through the front door to Brian's house, Stacy headed upstairs to get a shower. Brian pointed to the kitchen. "C'mon, I need some more caffeine."

He brewed another pot of coffee and sat at the kitchen table, drinking his second cup.

Cade paced back and forth across the linoleum. "I thought about this the whole drive back, and I've come up with only one lead." He raised his index finger.

"Oh, yeah, what is it?" Brian sat up straighter in his chair.

"That this whole thing . . ." Cade waved his hand around, "is absolutely crazy."

"Wow. Excellent skills of deduction there, bud." Brian sipped his coffee.

"Think about it, Brian. If someone is trying to send me some sort of message, why don't they just come out and threaten me or something? Why leave weird messages that I wouldn't understand anyway?"

"Here's a thought." Brian scratched his eyelid and propped his chin on his fist. "What if the message on your door wasn't for you? What if it was for Grace? Maybe someone saw you pick Grace up in the cornfield and tracked down where you live. They may have just assumed you were bringing her back home with you and snuck in to leave her another warning."

Cade rolled his head in a circle, stretching the aching muscles in his neck. "I suppose it's possible they could have followed me home after seeing me drop Grace off with Janna and thought I might be bringing her back later."

"Hey!" Brian snapped his fingers and perked up. "Let me see your phone for a sec."

317

Cade pulled his cell phone out of his pocket and tossed it to Brian. He leaned over Brian's shoulder while he swiped through several pictures.

"Wait . . . did you erase the pictures you took at the Dellingers'?"

Cade jerked the phone from Brian's hand. "No, let me see that." He cycled through the photos again. The message on the door wasn't among them.

"This is what happens when you don't lock your doors at night." Brian's voice sang in an uneven pattern. "The guy who snuck in your house must've erased it, dude."

"Wait a minute, what about the picture of my door? It was just in the phone a minute ago."

Brian made a wry face. "Oh, I might've accidentally hit delete before I closed it."

Cade hung his head. "Great."

"It's fine man. I don't need the picture to share my brilliant theory." Brian pulled the phone from Cade's hand and laid it on the table. "Both messages were written too low to be eye level for us, right?"

Cade nodded.

"Maybe that's because they were intended to be at Grace's eye level. Granted, writing them in bright red is a little too obvious for us to miss, but it doesn't seem like this guy is playing with a full deck of cards if you know what I mean." Brian tapped his temple.

Brian's humor always took the edge off Cade's mood. He relaxed his shoulders. "If that's true, why would they waste time sneaking into my house to write the message? Why not just come back and take her?"

"They've probably seen you at the police station," Brian said. "They'd be stupid to try to take her if they thought she was with a deputy sheriff. Besides, they're probably afraid Grace told you something about them, so they're most likely just lying low until they can get her alone. In the meantime, they're using these messages to keep her in fear."

Cade smiled. "You really do think better when you've got some caffeine in your system."

"No doubt." Brian raised his mug to Cade before gulping down another mouthful of coffee. "I guess it's too bad for them she wasn't with you when they decided to sneak in and desecrate your back door. It kinda defeats the purpose if the person you're trying to scare isn't around to get the message."

Cade's phone vibrated on the kitchen table. Brian was so startled he knocked over his coffee cup. He picked up the phone and passed it to Cade as he scrambled to soak up the

319

spilled coffee with some napkins from the table. "Who in the world would be calling you right now, man?"

"Maybe it's Moses Dellinger. He's probably calling to tell us he doesn't like us poking around in his creepy, dilapidated house like you said. Should I tell him it was all your idea?" Cade laughed and looked at the caller ID. "It's Janna. Hello?"

Janna ran her words together into one long high-pitched sentence.

"What? Janna, calm down, I can't understand a word you're saying. Take a breath and tell me again."

"Someone was in my parents' house, Cade." He heard her take a deep breath. "I heard a noise coming from the bathroom. I went to check it out, and the message from the old Dellinger place was written on the mirror."

"On the mirror? Okay." Cade frowned. "I don't want to alarm you any further, Janna, but I received the same message a few hours ago on the bottom of my kitchen door."

"What time did you find it?"

Cade rubbed his forehead. "I got to Brian's house around two, I guess, so maybe around one thirty, one forty-five. Why?"

"I don't know." Janna slurred her words. "When I got up to investigate the noise, it was around the same time. Not sure that means anything, though. I'm sorry, I really can't think straight right now."

"It's okay, Janna. Did you tell your parents?"

"Yeah, my dad's upstairs checking things out."

"Good." Cade motioned to Brian, who carried a pile of coffee-soaked napkins to the trash can, that he would let himself out. "Listen, you guys just stay put. I'm going to call a few friends of mine from the station and have them come check out the house. I'll be over as quickly as I can. Everything's gonna be okay Janna, I promise."

***

After discovering the message on the mirror, Janna had scurried to her bed, scooped Grace up while she was still sleeping, and raced downstairs to her parents' bedroom.

Her dad had come out of their room and calmly listened as Janna explained what happened upstairs. He instructed them to stay put until he checked everything out. Janna passed Grace to her mother and called Cade while they were waiting for him to return. She hung up the phone and looked at her frightened mother and Grace.

"It's okay. Cade's sending some deputies over here to check things out. He's over at Brian and Stacy's, so he may beat them here."

Her mother nodded without speaking, probably still in shock from waking to her daughter's screams. Grace seemed unfazed, rubbing her sleepy eyes.

Janna's father returned from the upper level a few minutes later. "I checked all the rooms and closets upstairs and didn't see anything or anyone. Do you remember if any of the windows upstairs were unlocked when you went to bed?"

"Only my bedroom windows were opened, Dad. Everything else was closed tight."

"I know everything down here was locked up, and there don't appear to be any signs that someone was able to get in through the windows or doors."

The doorbell chimed through the house. Janna followed her parents to answer it. It was Cade.

Worry coated his face the way concern filled his voice. "Mr. and Mrs. Petersen, Janna, are you guys okay?"

"We're all fine, Cade." Janna's dad said. "Come on in."

Cade turned as a deputy sheriff's car pulled into the driveway. Two plain-clothes officers emerged from the car carrying flashlights and walked up to meet him on the front porch.

"Thanks for coming out on such short notice, guys. I know this is your weekend off, but I needed professionals on this one. I'll make sure to note your loyalty to your duty in your next evaluations." Cade pointed at Janna and her parents. "Officer Blevins and Officer Myers, these are the Petersens. And that's Grace."

Both men nodded and shook their hands firmly, assuring them they were glad to help.

"I want you two to secure the perimeter for me first. Check for broken glass in the windows or any sign of forced entry around the doors. When you're finished, search every inch of the interior of the house. I'm talking the laundry room, linen closets, storage space in the basement, everywhere. If someone broke in here, I need some hard, strong evidence of it. Document anything you see. Then report back to me. I'll be upstairs taking a look at the message on the mirror first. I'll join you to search the house if necessary."

"Yes, sir," the officers said in unison.

Janna stared at Cade, impressed by his take-charge attitude. She almost forgot someone broke into her parents' home while they were all sleeping. *Where was all that fortitude seven years ago?*

Cade turned to her after delivering final orders to his men to take pictures of anything strange they found. "Janna, can you show me where the upstairs bathroom is? Grace, you stay down here with Mr. and Mrs. Petersen, okay?"

Grace nodded her understanding.

"Don't let her out of your sight for even a second," he said to Janna's parents.

Cade followed Janna up the staircase and through her bedroom to the bathroom. "I need you to explain to me what happened one more time. Sometimes people will remember something important when they refresh their memory of an incident like this. Start from the beginning. Don't leave anything out, no matter how insignificant it seemed at the time."

Janna repeated what she'd told him on the phone and walked to the tub. "I discovered the noise was coming from the faucet on the bathtub. When I walked over, I noticed the tub was full of water, like someone had just run a bath for themselves."

"Did you hear anything else at this time, like someone scurrying around or scratching noises? Close your eyes and think for a second." Cade's tone let Janna know he was in full investigative mode.

She closed her eyes but shook her head. "All I could hear was the dripping water. I unplugged the drain, and the water went down right away. I stood up, shook off my hand, and reached for a towel. That's when I saw this." She opened her eyes and pointed to the message written on the mirror.

"There's no way to be completely sure, but it looks like the handwriting from all the messages is similar enough to assume the same person wrote all three." Cade snapped a photo on his phone.

Janna ran her finger above the Ls. "See how loopy the letters are? Looks like a woman's writing to me."

Cade stepped closer to the mirror and stretched his hands between it and the floor. "Well, I guess that blows Brian's theory out of the water. He thought someone left the messages for Grace to find, but there's no way she would be able to see the mirror unless she was standing on something or someone held her up. I suppose she could have pulled up the little stool over here." He pointed to a small step stool by the tub that Janna's mother used to hold extra washcloths. "How could anyone assume she would use that stool to get up and look in the mirror? Unless," Cade's voice trailed off.

"Unless, what?" Janna was more intrigued than scared now.

"Unless Grace is the one writing the messages." Cade walked to the other side of the bathroom and squinted at the mirror. "Brian, Stacy, and I went back out to the Dellingers' old farmhouse tonight before you called, and the message on the door was gone. We also found a piece of Grace's dress in an upstairs bedroom, so now I'm certain she was there before I discovered her walking the cornfields."

Janna didn't seem as convinced. "What five-year-old do you know who writes in cursive?"

"What five-year-old can draw something from memory the way she did earlier? Weirder things have happened."

"So you think Grace wrote the message at the Dellingers' before you found her and then snuck out last night to wipe it away? She found your house somehow and wrote the same message on your door? And then she snuck back in here, wrote it on my mirror, and crawled back into bed like it was nothing?"

"I know. It sounds insane." Cade smiled. "I'm just grasping for straws here, Jan. It seems like the more we find out the less things make sense."

That marked the third time Cade shortened Janna's name, like when they were teenagers. She wished all these strange things weren't going on so they could focus more on mending their relationship, but that would have to wait. There were more pressing issues at hand.

A soft knock on the door interrupted them. Officer Blevins and Officer Myers stepped into the room. Janna's parents and Grace were right behind them.

"No sign of forced entry anywhere around the perimeter, sir," Officer Blevins said. "We've cleared all the rooms downstairs. It appears no one other than the residents of the house have been inside the home tonight."

"Good work, guys. I'll need you to monitor outside the rest of the night. I trust that will not be a problem."

"No, sir." They nodded.

Janna's mother butted her way in between the two officers. "Since you're both giving up the rest of your night to make sure we're all safe and sound, why don't I warm up some homemade cinnamon rolls for you sweet boys and make some coffee. I don't think any of us will be able to go back to sleep after all of this anyway."

"Thanks, ma'am. We'd appreciate your kindness," said Officer Myers.

"Just follow me downstairs. I'll get some coffee started." Janna's mother motioned for them to come with her and looked at Grace in her arms. "I'll bet you're starved, too. Let's go see what we can round up for you as well."

Janna's dad nodded at Cade before joining the officers downstairs for an early morning snack.

Cade smiled warmly at Janna. "I guess I'll head home and grab a shower and a change of clothes, but I'll be back in half an hour. You should try to get some rest if you can. We don't have to be at the church until ten thirty, so you've got some time to get a few more hours of sleep."

Janna's brows tightened with worry. "You still think it's okay to go to church today after all that's gone on?"

"I figure that's probably the safest place to be right now. Don't you think?"

"Yeah, you're right. Besides, I wouldn't mind asking Pastor Mabry what he thinks about that First Peter verse. Someone wanted me to understand what it means, and the pastor probably has a hundred commentaries on different verses. Maybe he can shed a little more light on the note I found with the peonies."

"I'm sure it wouldn't hurt." Cade stood awkwardly in the bathroom doorway for a moment, staring at Janna. "Well,

I guess I'll be going, but I won't be gone long. Will you be alright?"

"Yeah, I think so. It's just a little disturbing to know someone snuck in here while we were all sleeping and wrote that in the room right next to us." Janna crossed her arms around her torso and shivered, wrapping herself in the embrace she wished she would receive from Cade. "Do you think I could wipe the message off the mirror now?"

"Sure. Three officers have seen it and we have pictures, so you can clean it off if that will make you more comfortable." Cade lifted his hand in a small wave before he left Janna standing in the bathroom alone.

She sighed and opened the cabinet door under the sink, extracting some glass cleaner and paper towels. It looked like the message had been written in lipstick, so she sprayed plenty of cleaning fluid onto the paper towel. She stood back looking at the cursive on the mirror and noticed it was very similar to the handwriting on her fourth grade butterfly report. She tilted her head to the side and squinted. The e in *we'll* looked more like a loopy i to her, and the apostrophe looked more like the dot that should've been positioned above it.

Janna smudged the loop out of what they had all assumed was an e with her thumb and stood back to review

329

the message again. *Grace will find you* was now emblazoned across the mirror.

~20~

Janna laid down on her bed and tried unsuccessfully to go back to sleep for a few hours. She couldn't turn her mind off. If it did say Grace *will* find you, what did that mean? Who would have written it at the farmhouse, at Cade's, and at her parents'?

She sat up and clicked on the lamp by her bed. She opened the drawer in the top of the nightstand and retrieved the brochure she'd taken from her mother's booth. Flipping it over to review what she'd documented so far, she added Michael showing up at the hospital's booth and saying he'd be at the church to the list. Then she wrote *Grace we'll/ will find you*, showing up at Cade's house and on her mirror. She wasn't sure why, but she had a strong feeling whoever wrote the message in her bathroom was also the person who clogged the drain and let the bathtub fill with water.

331

She was more alert to think it through now and realized there was no way for the tub to fill up so high from the few drops that would have escaped from a leaky faucet. Someone had to have turned the faucet on and let it run for a few minutes before it could rise up that high inside the tub. The faucet was pretty squeaky, so why wouldn't she have heard that?

The officers said there was no forced entry, meaning whoever left the note on the mirror didn't sneak in after they had all gone to bed. They were already inside the house. If that were the case, when would they have had a chance to sneak in before she locked up on their way to Brian and Stacy's?

Janna gasped. "The peonies at the front door."

She had been so preoccupied with trying to see who had rung the doorbell yesterday afternoon that she hadn't thought twice about leaving Grace standing there with the door wide open. Her dad always kept the screen door oiled so it didn't squeak, and she'd scanned the street for at least a minute or two before she headed back to the porch. Had someone rung the doorbell and placed the peonies by the door to distract her so they could sneak into the house and hide?

Grabbing the brochure, Janna headed to the kitchen. It was too soon for Cade to have returned, but she wished she could share her ideas with someone. Her dad was sitting alone at the island, reading the paper.

"Hey, Dad. Where's Mom?" Janna grabbed a glass from the cabinet and poured herself some of orange juice. She sat down on a stool next to her father.

"She wore herself out trying to entertain those officers and went to lie back down for a few hours with Grace in our bedroom." He turned the page on the newspaper. "The officers stepped outside onto the porch for a little while. I'm thankful Cade sent them over here to watch out for us for a while, although, I'm pretty sure if someone were here earlier, they will have no intentions of coming back once they see a police car parked outside."

Janna sipped her juice. "It was nice of them to come on such short notice and on their day off, too. Talk about dedication to the profession, huh?"

Janna's father laid the paper down and looked up at his daughter. "Janna, you realize they did that out of respect for Cade, don't you? You can tell from the way they followed his orders without questioning him that he's an extremely revered member of the police department. And the way he looks out for his parents' house and has taken care of his father's needs since his mom's passing takes some initiative. He's really an extraordinary young man."

Janna laughed. "Dad, I don't think I've heard you have so much to say about one subject before. I think you've been spending too much time around Mom."

Her dad picked up the paper again. "Well, we all know I don't always have a chance to get in a word edgewise when your mother is around, but we both want the best for you. It seems to me that you've overlooked an obvious choice."

"If it makes you feel any better, I haven't totally overlooked him." Janna tilted her glass, watching the orange juice "waves" splash up on either side. "I've just been running away from him for so long, I haven't given him time to catch up."

"Well, maybe you should run back and let him tag you this time." Janna's father smiled. "I think God brought you back here to realize what you left behind, Janna."

The words Cade's father had spouted before they left the nursing home yesterday popped back into Janna's head. *He brought her here for you.*

"Have you spoken with Mr. Thompson recently?" She wondered if maybe her father might be the elusive peony bestower.

"Yes, as a matter of fact, I stopped by the Center yesterday. I ran into Cade on my way out. I'm surprised he didn't mention it to you." Dad closed the newspaper again, folding it over. "He told me his father had some sort of episode while you were there."

Janna nodded. "Mr. Thompson started screaming for Cade's mother while we were there and had to be escorted back to his room by some orderlies." Janna tipped back her glass and swallowed the rest of her juice. "By the way, did you happen to notice a tall, dark-haired orderly hanging around Mr. Thompson's room when you were there?"

Her dad shrugged. "I can't say I've ever paid attention to the orderlies when I've been over there. Why?"

"No reason," Janna said. "It's just this guy—the one who says he's an orderly at the Center—well, he keeps showing up everywhere, but no one seems to have seen him except for me and Cade." She tilted her head to the side. "Well, now that I think of it, I guess Mom saw him too."

"Hmm, that is strange," Dad replied, unruffled as usual.

"Oh and someone, maybe this orderly guy, has been randomly leaving bouquets of peonies for us to find everywhere. In Mr. Thompson's room at the Center. On Mrs. Thompson's grave. They even left one on our front porch yesterday afternoon. You wouldn't know anything about that, would you?" Janna tipped her head, reading her father's reaction to her less-than-subtle accusation.

Her father laughed. "I don't know anything about flowers. It sounds like someone is trying to send you a message though. Maybe the flowers are some sort of sign."

"Now I'm sure you've been hanging out with Mom too long." Janna playfully bumped her shoulder into her dad's, like she would have with an old friend. "Who knows what it means, but thanks for the advice about Cade. And thanks for always supporting me."

"What are parents for?" He patted her on the back before he got up and walked out of the kitchen.

Janna's stomach growled as she watched her dad leave. It was time for some breakfast.

***

A soft knock on the back door pulled Janna away from studying the events chronicled on the brochure she'd laid across the island.

Cade opened the back door and poked his head through. "It's just me."

336

"Come in," Janna said in between bites of the French toast she'd made herself for breakfast. "I was just looking over everything trying to come up with something that made any kind of sense."

She noticed Cade still wore the same clothes he had on last night. Bits of spiderweb clung to his shoulder, and there were dirty handprints on the leg of his jeans.

"Sorry it took me so long to get back over here." Cade shook his head. "I wanted to check my place one more time. I sat down on the couch for just a minute to rest my eyes and ended up falling asleep. I wouldn't even be here right now if the sun didn't shine so brightly through my front window. As soon as I saw what time it was, I figured I'd better head back over here and make sure everything was okay."

"Take a look at this." Janna held up the brochure, eager to bounce her ideas off Cade. "I added everything that happened last night, and look. Do you notice a trend?"

Cade pored over the timeline Janna had created. He looked up at her and shrugged.

"A lot of this has happened in threes. See." She dragged her fingers along the page, connecting events. "Three jars of peonies, three messages, three times you've seen

337

Michael. There is a definite pattern. I just don't have a clue what it signifies."

"What about Gabe? I've only seen him twice."

"I was thinking about that. I figure last night wasn't the last time we'll run into him. It's pretty obvious, to me at least, that Michael and Gabe are connected somehow. It just seems like anytime something weird happens, one of them is around."

"That's pretty good detective work." Cade looked amused. "I'm not sure I would have noticed a pattern like that on my own. Hey, since you're looking for a new job, maybe you should consider a move into law enforcement."

Janna laughed. "Well, if it makes you feel better, I've been looking at this thing for the past two hours, so I was bound to strike it rich with one of my theories."

Cade put his hands behind his head and stretched. "It's closer to an actual lead than anything I've come up with."

"Oh, I almost forgot to tell you," Janna said, her mouth still a little too full. "I don't think the message says 'Grace we'll find you.'" Cade stared at her as she took a couple seconds to swallow the large bite in her mouth. "I think it's actually 'Grace *will* find you.' Of course, I have no idea what that means either, but doesn't it sound like

338

something a parent would tell a kid to say during hide and seek? You know, like 'Grace will find you.'" Janna shuffled her hands back and forth and made her voice wiggle in singsong fashion.

"Your guess is as good as mine." Cade's laughter was interrupted when his stomach growled loudly.

"Did you eat breakfast yet?"

"No, I was going to stop by Mac's on the way over, but I forgot they're closed on Sundays."

Janna popped up from her stool. "How about I make you some coffee and French toast then?"

"That'd be great." Cade raised his eyebrows enthusiastically. "Can I help you?"

"Sure. I'll get the ingredients," she said, retrieving the eggs and milk from the refrigerator and the cinnamon from the spice rack on the counter. "You want to grab a mug from the cabinet to the right of the stove and pour yourself a cup of coffee?"

Cade did as instructed and sat back down at the island. Janna whipped the eggs, milk, and cinnamon together and dipped the bread into the mixture before placing it onto the skillet. A comforting sizzling noise filled the room, accompanied by the sweet, warm smells of cinnamon and butter.

Janna flipped the toast over in the skillet and turned around in time to catch Cade smiling at her. She could smell the toast as it browned and forced herself to turn back to the stove before she had a chance to reciprocate.

As she pulled a plate from the cabinet to transfer the French toast to, she heard Cade slide his stool back and walk toward her. She kept her back to him for a moment, listening to the sounds of his nervous, rapid breathing. He came closer to her. She reached over and flipped the burner on top of the stove to OFF before she turned around to face him.

He was only inches from her face. He looked into her eyes as if asking permission to kiss her. She blinked and nodded numbly as she leaned forward to accept his request. Cade put his hands gently on either side of her face, like he had at the church the night before. Their lips were only inches away from meeting when Janna's mother barged in, sniffing the air and brushing past Janna and Cade to check the stove.

"Is something burning?" Her mother opened the oven door and surveyed all the switches to make sure they were turned off. "Oh, Cade, you're back."

Cade stepped away from Janna and moved to stand beside the refrigerator. Janna shot her mother a meaningful stare.

Her mother quickly realized that she'd intruded during an intimate moment. "I'm so sorry. Did I interrupt something?" Her eyes looked at Cade and then darted back to Janna, who could feel the red creeping up into her cheeks.

Cade laughed boisterously. "No, Mrs. Petersen. I'm the one who can't get the timing right on this one." He grinned at Janna and pointed behind himself. "I think I'll go see if Officer Blevins or Officer Myers noticed anything suspicious during their watch. I'll be back for the French toast."

Janna and her mother watched him exit the kitchen and head down the hallway for the front door.

"Unbelievable." Janna put her face in her hands and laughed.

"I am really sorry, honey. I didn't know you two were in here or I would have . . . I don't know, coughed or something to announce my presence." Janna could see the smile tugging at the corners of her mother's mouth. "Hopefully, that won't be the last time he tries to kiss you."

Never let it be said that Julia Petersen lacks perception, Janna thought. It was somewhat amusing to her, but she didn't want her mother to know, so she rolled her eyes in mock irritation and tried not to smile. "Mom, seriously."

Her mother threw her hands up. "Okay, I'll stop. I just have one more question for you and then I'll leave you alone."

"Okay, one last question." Janna sighed, not sure if she wanted to provide an answer for whatever her mother planned to ask her. "What is it?"

Mom looked disdainfully over the T-shirt and jeans Janna had changed into after the incident in the bathroom. "You're not wearing that to church, are you?"

***

Janna pulled a simple black dress over her head and put in her pearl earrings before pinning her hair up on either side. She pulled a few tendrils loose to hang around her face and stepped back to check her appearance in the mirror behind her bedroom door.

"Janna. Are you ready to go?" her mother called up the stairs.

"Yeah, Mom. I'll be right down." She slipped on her black heels.

Cade met her at the bottom of the stairs, dressed in a familiar-looking shirt and oversized pants.

"In my hurry to get back over here, I forgot to bring a change of clothes," he said, placing his folded jeans and T-shirt on the bench by the front door. "Your dad let me borrow one of his dress shirts and a pair of pants."

Janna stifled a laugh and sniffed the air. "Did you get a bath today, too?"

"As a matter of fact, smarty pants, I did. Along with providing me this handsome getup, your mother graciously let me take a shower in the master bath." He pulled on the belt loop of his pants to show her how loose they were. "Your dad went to get me a belt."

"I'm sure a belt will bring the whole ensemble together nicely." Janna waved her hand like a magic wand.

Cade shook his head and held up one end of an unknotted striped tie. "I can't seem to figure this tie out, though. I'm used to clip-ons."

"Here, let me show you." Janna pulled him over to the mirror in the entryway.

She could feel him watching her as she looped the skinny end of the tie around the thicker part. She folded it over and pushed the tie back through the hole she'd created. Her arm rested on the front of his shoulder as she tightened the tie. She turned him around by the shoulders to face her.

"There, looks perfect." She patted the front of the tie.

Cade turned back to the mirror and pretended to be fascinated with his reflection. "Are we still talking about the tie?"

Janna swatted him playfully. "Pride goeth before the fall."

Cade laughed. "Where'd you learn how to do that?"

"My dad showed me when I was a little girl. I don't really know why. Maybe he thought I'd marry a state senator one day and I'd need to know how to help him with his tie or something."

They shared a laugh at the unlikelihood of that scenario as Janna's mother emerged with Grace from the back bedroom. "Well, she's all ready for church. Aren't you Grace?"

Grace shot them a toothy grin.

Janna's mother had dressed her in the purple sundress she was wearing when Cade found her wandering the cornfield; except now, even after being doused in the muddy water of Hollow Creek, it was stain-free. A matching purple ribbon held Grace's hair back. Janna was surprised her mother let Grace wear the purple flip-flops Cade had purchased for her.

"You look very nice, Grace." Janna smiled and nodded to the little girl.

"Wait a minute," Cade said, bending down to look at the hem of Grace's dress. "Mrs. Petersen, did you sew up a hole in this dress?"

Her mother shook her head. "No, I just laundered it and ironed out the wrinkles after your little swim."

"Do you remember seeing any kind of tear in the fabric anywhere?"

"No." Janna's mom shrugged. "It was just dirty. I did look over the fabric to make sure I'd gotten all the stains out, so I think I would've remembered seeing a hole. Why?"

"It's just that I found a piece of this dress sticking out of a drawer in the Dellingers' old farmhouse. Here, I'll show you."

He walked over to the pair of dirt-streaked jeans he'd just laid on the bench and extracted a piece of purple cloth from the pocket. He brought it over for Janna and her mother to inspect. The fabric was identical to the dress Grace wore now.

Janna squatted down to Grace's level and examined her dress. She looked over the hem and even behind the neck, where the tag would normally be. The dress appeared to be in perfect condition.

"Maybe it came from her shoes, Cade," said Janna's mom. "You can make little fabric-covered shoes for girls, and you said you found her barefoot, right? She was probably running around and snagged her shoe on the drawer."

Cade scratched the back of his head and blew out a strong breath. "You're probably right, Mrs. Petersen. It's probably something as simple as that. Everything that's been going on lately has been so strange. I guess I'm starting to become a little paranoid."

Janna's father returned from the master bedroom with a belt. "Here you go, Cade. See if they fit a little better now."

Cade slipped the belt around his waist and buckled it as tightly as he could.

Janna's mother looked over each of them. "We all look like we're ready to go. I just need to grab the desserts for the potluck after service."

"We're not coming back here for lunch?" Janna tried to contain her disappointment.

She had hoped lunch at home would provide a more relaxed atmosphere for her and Cade to sort out what was going on between them.

"Janna, it's the first Sunday of the month. We always have potluck on the first Sunday so everyone can catch up with one another." Her mother pushed a stray hair away from

Janna's forehead. "I'm sure there are a ton of people who'd like to know what you've been up to the past several years."

"That's what I'm afraid of," Janna said under her breath.

If they had lunch at the church, a hundred people would come up to her and tell her they were so glad she was back in town. The idea of playing "twenty questions" with the well-meaning ladies at church didn't appeal to her either.

"It'll be okay," Cade leaned over and whispered in her ear, "We can find Brian and Stacy and sit with them. It won't be so bad. Then later, you and I can find a quiet place to talk."

Janna bit her lip to stifle the huge smile threatening to give her away. "Okay, Mom. Lunch at the church will be fine."

Her mother walked back to the kitchen to retrieve her desserts. Janna watched as her dad began patting his pockets.

"Did you lose something, Dad?" Janna asked.

"Actually, I just remembered I'm supposed to give you something, Cade."

"You were supposed to give *me* something?" Cade pointed to himself.

"Yes." Her father continued, still patting his pockets. "I ran into a friend of yours when I was out picking up a

Sunday paper earlier. He wanted me to give you a letter, if I could just find it."

"A friend of mine?" Cade's forehead wrinkled. "You mean Brian?"

"No, this was a young man I've never seen before, so I thought maybe he was mistaken when he said he knew you. Then he told me he worked with your dad at the Center, so I figured he recognized me from visiting your father and assumed I knew you too."

"Did you get his name?"

"I did, but it's escaping me right now. If I could just find the letter he wanted me to give you. He probably signed his name to it."

"What did he look like? About Cade's height, with dark hair?" Janna glanced at Cade who seemed to be thinking the same thing.

"No." Janna's dad shook his head slowly. "Very clean cut-young man with kind eyes. Here it is." He placed a small white envelope into Cade's palm. "He asked me to give you this if I saw you."

As Cade tore the top of the envelope open, Janna stepped closer to see what it said. They both stared at each other in silence after they read it.

The words were printed this time, so there would be no confusion in the message.

"I was right," Janna said. "It was an i."

"Grace will find you," Cade read aloud.

Janna's dad clapped his hands together. "I just remembered the young man's name. Gabe."

~21~

Janna stood stunned for a moment, staring at the message in Cade's hand. "Gabe wrote all those messages?"

"You're sure he said his name was Gabe?" Cade looked at Janna's father.

He nodded. "I'm certain. He had blonde hair and was about Janna's height. He told me to give you that envelope and let you know he'd be at the church this morning if you needed to speak with him."

"Calvin, can you come help me with these pies?" Janna's mother called from the kitchen.

"Cade, do you have all the information you need from me?"

"Yes, thank you Mr. Petersen." Cade smiled politely and turned to Janna. "I guess that makes the third appearance for Gabe, huh? Maybe you were onto something with the pattern you noticed earlier."

"Michael told you he'd be at the church, too. Do you think they are playing some kind of trick on us?"

"That would explain how someone made it to my house and your parents' at the same time to leave those messages. There were two of them." Cade rubbed his forehead.

Janna sighed. "If they're trying to tell us something, they're making their motives very unclear. What would two orderlies have to do with her?"

Cade knelt down so that he was eye level with Grace. "Do you know two men named Michael and Gabe?"

Grace nodded her head.

Janna gaped at her.

Cade's tone remained calm and steady. "How do you know them, Grace?"

She turned and pointed to a family picture of Janna and her parents behind them on the wall.

"Are those men your family?" Cade placed his hands on Grace's shoulders. "Is that what you're trying to tell us?"

Grace nodded again.

"Well, neither one of them is old enough to be her father. At least I don't think so." Cade stood and exhaled sharply. "Maybe they're her brothers."

"Why would they leave her out in an old farmhouse?" Janna crossed her arms. "If they're working at the Center, they have the means to take care of her. Why wouldn't they have told us they were related to her when we came to see your dad?"

"Good point."

Janna looked at Grace. "Honey, why didn't you tell us you knew those men?"

The little girl's face was hard to read. Janna wondered what else Grace knew that she hadn't shared with them.

Cade cocked his head like he remembered something. "At the Fourth of July Festival, Gabe told me they often go unnoticed. Maybe, in some strange way, leaving all these creepy messages is their way of getting attention. You said it yourself—children who have been through trauma express themselves in different ways. Maybe they're all foster kids and no one paid attention to them, so Grace stopped talking, Michael started telling people to come find him, and Gabe just followed people around returning things they thought they'd lost."

It all sounded so far-fetched, a burst of laughter escaped from Janna's pursed lips.

Cade laughed too. "I know. It sounds ludicrous!"

Janna's parents returned from the kitchen with several pies in tow. "What's so funny?" Mom asked.

"Nothing, Mom." Janna shook her head, grabbed Cade by the arm, and pulled him away from Grace to the foot of the stairs and out of her mother's earshot. "I think the best thing we can do right now is head to the church and see if Michael or Gabe is there. Then we can confront them about Grace and find out why they've been doing all these crazy things."

"You're probably right." Cade kept his voice low. "We're not accomplishing anything by standing here talking about all this anyway."

"Are you two ready to go?" Mom stood by the door holding Grace's hand.

"Yeah, Mom." Janna raised her eyebrows at Cade. "We're ready."

***

Cade wanted Grace to be with them when they spotted Michael and Gabe, so he'd suggested they follow Janna's parents to the church in his car.

"I still don't understand what any of this has to do with us? Other than the fact you're the one who picked up Grace, why would they even bother with us?" Janna asked.

"At first I didn't think all this had anything to do with us, but they made a point to find employment at the nursing home where Dad is staying, and those peonies were placed on Mom's grave the day after you came home. It's like they knew you'd be here or something, Janna. Everything seems too well orchestrated to just be a coincidence anymore." He glanced back in the rearview mirror at Grace, who stared out the window.

Janna turned in her seat to face Cade. "What about the verse on the Dellingers' wedding picture? How would they have known you took the picture with you or that I had even seen it, much less have known to put that verse on the jar of peonies on my porch?"

"I'm not sure." Cade shook his head. "You know, it makes me really angry that they used my dad in all of this. They must have told him to say all those things to us at the nursing home. When I went back to check on him, I heard Michael tell him his days would become easier. We all know

354

that's not going to happen." Cade's voice grew louder. "Not to mention the fact, one or both of them broke into my house and your parents'. That's what makes me angrier than anything." He pounded the steering wheel with his fist. "They were in your bedroom while you and Grace slept."

"It's okay, Cade." Janna placed her hand on his wrist as they neared the church. "Grace and I are both fine."

"I know, but I'll just feel better when we can challenge them face-to-face and make them explain why they've been doing all these weird things to us." He pulled into a parking space close to the church's entrance.

Cade removed Grace from the backseat and took her hand as they walked behind Janna's parents into the sanctuary.

Mrs. Petersen turned back to them. "Since we're a little early, your father and I are going to take these desserts back to the kitchen in the fellowship hall and see if they need help setting up. We'll be back in a few minutes."

"Okay, Mom." Janna pointed to a row of pews near the front and looked back at Cade and Grace. "Do you want to sit up close or be a back-row Baptist?" She smiled.

Cade was too distracted to appreciate her joke. "Close to the front is fine, but we'll have to keep a watch on the door to make sure we don't miss Michael or Gabe."

One of the side doors at the front of the church swung open. Cade and Janna spun around to see if it was one of the orderlies. It was Pastor Mabry.

"Good mornin' Cade, Janna. How are you little Grace?" Pastor Mabry bent down and shook her hand before standing and offering the same greeting to Cade and Janna. "You two are early. Did you come to help set up for the potluck?"

"My mom and dad did, but we were just tagging along."

"Well, it's good to see you both. Would Grace like to go to Children's Church this morning? I'm sure Mrs. Keever is already here setting up. They're doing a great series on Daniel right now."

"Um." Cade lowered his eyebrows. "I'm not sure I want her to be away from us."

"It's probably okay, Cade," Janna said. "Besides, I'm not sure she'll understand the sermon if she stays out here. Who knows, maybe being around some other kids will bring out her social side, and she'll become more willing to talk to us."

Cade thought it best to follow Janna's instincts on this one. "Grace, do you want to go see Mrs. Keever in Children's Church?"

A smile lit up Grace's face.

"It's settled then." Pastor Mabry turned and began walking out of the sanctuary. "If you'll just follow me downstairs."

***

The entire basement of the church had been renovated since Janna had been there last. They passed two rooms before stepping into the brightly colored Children's Church room. Sunlight streamed in through the basement windows, making the lime green walls, covered with pictures the kids had drawn of different Bible stories, look even brighter. Janna recognized Zacchaeus, the wee little man, who climbed up into a sycamore tree to see Jesus, and a smile spread across her face as she recalled the song they'd been taught in Children's Church long ago.

Mrs. Keever was preparing snacks in the corner. She turned at the sound of their conversation in the doorway.

"Oh, Cade, Janna, it's so good to see you." She left her snacks and walked over to give them both a hug. "Oh, and you brought Grace. I hoped I'd see you again, sweetheart." She patted Grace on the head.

"Mrs. Keever, would it be alright if we left Grace here with you for Children's Church?" Cade looked around nervously, like someone might pop out from behind one of the tiny tables in the corner of the room.

Janna knew he didn't want to let Grace out of his sight, but it was sweet of him to put her comfort above his own.

"I'm sure she would love to participate in the Bible lesson today, wouldn't you Grace? The other children should be here any minute." Mrs. Keever looked at the clock above the child-sized hand washing station. "Do you want to stay for a few minutes and see how she interacts with them before you leave for the service?"

"That'd be great." Cade's voice dripped with relief.

"I need to step back into my office for a moment before the service starts," Pastor Mabry said. "I trust you'll both be at the potluck after service."

"Yes." Janna answered for both of them. "Actually, Pastor Mabry, would you have a moment or two to speak with me about a particular verse I've been studying recently?" She shot a sideways glance at Cade. "Maybe after the potluck has started, and you've had a chance to eat lunch?"

Pastor Mabry took a few steps backward toward the door. "Sure, Janna. Just come find me after lunch is finished.

We can all step into my office and pull out a few commentaries. Would that help?"

"Definitely."

A collection of small voices filled the hall as time neared for the service to begin. Several kids raced into the room and ran to Mrs. Keever for their snack. Grace released Cade's hand. Janna and Cade both watched as Grace made her way to some blank paper and colored pencils on a table at the back of the room.

They studied her for a moment to make sure she'd be okay alone with the other children. One by one, as the other children retrieved their juice boxes and cups filled with colorful fish-shaped crackers, they flocked to Grace, taking their seats around her. A few of them stood up and gathered around her more closely, encircling her. They seemed engrossed by whatever she was drawing, but their close proximity didn't seem to bother Grace.

"See, she's making friends already." Janna patted Cade on the back. "We should probably head up to the service ourselves. Cade?"

"Ok, we can head upstairs," he replied, but still seemed uneasy. "Thank you, Mrs. Keever."

Cade and Janna took the stairs back up to the sanctuary.

Janna's mother waved at them as they entered through the front of the church. Janna moved slowly to the pew where her parents sat, scanning the growing crowd for Michael or Gabe.

Cade whispered, "I'm gonna make a quick pass around the sanctuary and head up to the balcony before the service starts."

She nodded and took a seat beside her mother.

Janna's mother turned sharply to face her daughter. "Where's Cade going?"

"He'll be right back." Janna followed him with her eyes. "He went to check on something."

***

Cade finished his loop around the sanctuary and took the stairs two at a time to the balcony. He would be able to see everything from up there. He scanned over pew after pew, looking for anyone he didn't recognize from years of attending this church. As far as he could tell, there was no sign of the orderlies.

The choir stepped out in their burgundy robes and everyone stood for the first hymn. Cade thought it would be best to ease back into the crowd before everyone sat down again. He quietly crept back down the balcony stairs and edged his way along the side of the sanctuary. Several people turned to look at him. Offering them a rueful smile, he hoped they'd forgive the visual distraction he caused. He made it to the pew where Janna stood singing with her parents and scooted in beside her.

Janna offered him the other half of the hymnal she held. He pretended to sing while his eyes darted to every corner of the room for signs of Michael or Gabe.

Brian and Stacy both waved from a few rows behind them. Brian mouthed *You okay?*

Janna elbowed Cade's arm. "People are going to start noticing you're looking for someone if you don't stop that," she whispered through tight lips.

Cade adjusted his posture and made himself stare at the hymnal he shared with Janna. She was right. No need to draw attention to himself. That would just defeat the purpose. He needed to be aware of his surroundings without causing others to be aware of him.

Pastor Mabry left his seat in the front pew and made his way to the stage as the first hymn concluded. He welcomed everyone and instructed the parishioners to greet those around them before they took their seats.

Janna couldn't help herself and looked around anxiously during the announcements. The sun beaming through the stained glass windows caused her to notice the pictures contained within them again. One in particular—the one of the Virgin Mary's visit from the angel, Gabriel—looked very familiar.

Everyone rose for another hymn, but Janna couldn't take her eyes off the picture in the window. She studied Mary's face for a moment, trying to understand why the picture unnerved her. She moved her eyes to the angel floating above Mary. Something in Janna's brain clicked and put together the pieces of the puzzle surrounding all the strange events of the past three days.

She gasped. Several people around her looked up. She clamped her hand over her mouth, thankful everyone's singing muffled her reaction from the rest of the congregation.

Cade leaned over and whispered, "What is it, Janna? Are you okay?"

Janna nodded but kept her hand over her mouth. *It couldn't be.* She studied the stained glass picture one last time.

The face of the angel hovering above Mary was Gabe's, the orderly from the nursing home.

The hymn concluded and everyone sat down. Janna wanted to signal to Cade somehow to look at the picture, but instead she sat somberly in the pew, trying to tell herself this couldn't be right. She had seen Gabe's face only once at the nursing home when he and Michael escorted Cade's father off to his room. She'd briefly seen the back of his head as he left Cade at the Fourth of July Festival, but she was sure it was his face that stared back at her now from the stained glass window.

Pastor Mabry's voice broke her train of thought as he prayed before the sermon. Janna closed her eyes and tried to ignore all the ideas pouring into her head. She was just stressed and sleep-deprived. Besides, what she was thinking couldn't be reality. She listened carefully to the pastor's words.

"Father, we come to you today to take part in your holy Sabbath day. We ask that you give us an understanding of your Word and your will as we gather today. Remove any stumbling blocks from our path. Make your message clear to us, Lord. In your holy name, Amen."

"Amen," Janna echoed with the rest of the congregation.

This was ridiculous. Her imagination was running wild because of all the strange things that had been happening. *Focus, Janna. Listen to what Pastor Mabry is saying.*

"Today we will wrap up our study of First Peter," the pastor began. "We know from the past couple of weeks that First Peter was written to encourage the Christians living in Asia Minor to hold steadfast to their faith despite any suffering they may be incurring because of it. When we look to put the same message into practice today, we see it is still very applicable in our lives."

Janna looked at Cade, thinking about the suffering he had incurred over the past few years with losing her, losing his mom, and losing his dad now to a debilitating disease.

"Let's take a look at what the Scripture says." Pastor Mabry opened his Bible and held it above the lectern he stood behind. "Turn with me in your Bibles to First Peter, chapter five, verse ten."

Cade and Janna exchanged looks before turning to the familiar verse.

"'And after you have suffered a little while, the God of all grace, who has called you to his eternal glory in Christ, will himself restore, confirm, strengthen, and establish you,'" Pastor Mabry read.

His version was a little different than the verse from the Dellingers' wedding photograph, but it shared the same overall theme.

"So you see, dear brothers and sisters, Peter is trying to let Christians know their lives won't be perfect simply because they believe. There will be suffering. There will be misunderstandings that damage relationships, and there will be things we don't understand no matter how hard we try. But this verse reminds us of another important fact. Look with me at what happens after the hard times are over and our suffering is finished.

"He will restore us, support us, and strengthen us in his kindness is what the Word says. With his grace, God has provided us a way to become restored after our suffering and stronger after our hardships, supported by His love."

Molly Ann Brenner's face popped into Janna's head. *Where was God's grace then?* That little girl suffered through abuse for years and didn't even live long enough to know something better awaited her in the future.

Pastor Mabry closed his Bible. "How can we apply this to our circumstances today in the modern world?"

Janna wondered if her thoughts had passed through her lips accidentally.

"We are no longer being thrown in prison for our beliefs. We aren't persecuted for worshipping the one true God. In fact, we have the freedom today to share his Gospel with the world. Now, we suffer in more discreet, yet just as detrimental, ways. Absorbing unkind words. Letting forgiveness be withheld when it should be released. Not saying what we need to say to those we love."

All Janna could hear in the still sanctuary were a few sniffs from the ladies around them.

Without warning, Cade reached over and took Janna's hand. Instead of pulling away this time, like she always did, she looked deep into Cade's eyes and saw that Stacy had been right. He had forgiven her. He loved her. And she loved him. She was tired of running. She was tired of always being in control, and she was tired of fighting against what she felt for him.

The heat from their hands seemed to dissolve the miscommunication, misunderstandings, and unrequited longings of the past seven years. A peace she hadn't felt in years washed over Janna as she turned her attention back to Pastor Mabry's words.

"Be mindful of Peter's parting words to the Christians in Asia Minor when you suffer here on earth. Look at verse twelve after he thanks Silas for delivering the letter to them.

'I have written briefly to you, exhorting and declaring that this is the true grace of God. Stand firm in it.'

So remember when you experience suffering, you are really experiencing grace as well. Let's bow our heads and take a moment to thank God for His grace and the hope we have in Him to get past our suffering and experience joy again."

Janna bowed her head and prayed silently. *Lord, I do thank you for your grace and for the forgiveness Cade has shown me over the past few days. I still love him, Lord. I know now you brought me back here to show me that. In my suffering over losing Molly Ann Brenner, you brought me another little girl to help Cade and me mend our wounds. You gave us something to work on that would bring us back together. Even though all these other things have been distracting us, please give us time to sort out our feelings. Please give us another chance to make things work.*

Janna opened her eyes as the choir began to sing a closing hymn and the offering plate made the rounds. Pastor Mabry offered a final prayer, asking the blessing for the food they were about to eat, before he dismissed everyone to lunch.

Cade and Janna continued to hold hands after they stood up, both forgetting for a moment they were supposed to be looking for Michael and Gabe.

"We should probably go pick up Grace," Cade said to Janna's parents.

"Okay, kids. We'll see you at lunch." Her mother smiled and seemed to focus her attention on their joined hands. "Take as long as you need."

Cade laughed as Janna rolled her eyes. He squeezed her hand before they headed downstairs to pick up Grace.

Mrs. Keever met them at the front of the room. "Grace had a wonderful time today. The other children just love her."

Janna exchanged a smile with Cade.

"Today the kids learned about Daniel's vision from the messenger and how the archangel helped the messenger get into Persia," Mrs. Keever continued. "After I told them the story, all the kids drew a picture. Would you like to see Grace's?"

Cade and Janna nodded and followed Mrs. Keever to where the rest of the children sat coloring their pictures. Grace wasn't there.

"Grace, where are you, dear? Maybe, she's in the restroom." Mrs. Keever walked to a door beside the tables

368

and knocked softly. "Grace? Janna and Cade are here to take you upstairs for lunch."

The doorknob turned and a little girl with bouncy auburn curls emerged. "Holly, have you seen Grace?" Mrs. Keever asked her.

Holly shook her head.

"Well, she was just right there drawing a moment ago." Mrs. Keever didn't sound especially concerned. "It's okay. She's probably just playing a game or something. You know, hiding from us."

Cade traded a concerned look with Janna. "Mrs. Keever, Grace isn't the type of child who plays games."

"Grace?" Janna looked over all the children. "Have you guys seen Grace?"

One of the boys pointed to the basement window. Janna bent down, gently grabbing the young boy by the shoulders.

"This is very important, okay?" Janna calmed her tone. She didn't want to frighten the little boy. "What's your name, sweetheart?" She looked at the name tag hanging around his neck. *Ryan.*

"Wy-an." He sucked on his lower lip.

"Okay, Ryan. I need you to listen very carefully to me. The little girl, Grace, who played down here with you guys earlier, did you see her climb out the window?"

Ryan nodded, taking a bite of one of the crackers from a cup in his hand. "She went out they-ull." He pointed again.

Janna cocked her head, unsure if she understood the boy correctly. "She climbed out the window all by herself? How did she get up so high?"

"No." Ryan's face became serious. "The men came to the window, and she went up."

"The men?" Cade shot Janna a bewildered look. "What men, Ryan?"

"The men from the pick-chull." The little boy motioned back to where Grace had been sitting when they'd left the room earlier.

Janna, Cade, and Mrs. Keever walked to the end of the small table where some crayons were scattered, along with Grace's drawing of the Bible story.

They all stared at the picture, trying to decipher what men the little boy meant.

In the picture, a man bowed down on his face and two men stood in front of him.

"The man bowing is Daniel," Mrs. Keever said, "and the two other men are the messenger and the archangel who helped him. Grace drew it very well."

"I'll say." Janna bent down even closer to the picture.

Standing in front of a bowing Daniel was Gabe, the messenger, and by his side, the archangel, Michael. The orderlies who often went unnoticed did not escape their attention this time.

~22~

"I'm so sorry, Cade." Mrs. Keever wrung her hands. "I don't know how I didn't see anything. There are just so many little ones running around down here. I should have noticed she was gone. If something happens to her, I'll never forgive myself."

Cade didn't respond to Mrs. Keever. Instead he picked up the picture of Gabe and Michael that Grace had drawn. He turned away from Mrs. Keever and Janna and took several steps to the window from where the boy told them the two men from the picture had lifted Grace out of the room.

"It's okay, Mrs. Keever. It's not your fault." Janna patted her on the arm and looked at Cade. "What do we do?"

Turning around, he shook his head slowly and looked at her helplessly. "I don't know."

372

Remembering the discovery she'd made in the sanctuary just minutes before, Janna's memory cycled through the events that led to this moment.

How had Gabe and Michael always known where to find them? They knew Janna would be home when they left the peonies. They knew when Cade would be at his dad's nursing home. They knew to come find them at the Fourth of July Festival. They knew when he would go back out to the farmhouse with Brian and Stacy and see that the message on the door was gone. They knew where to find Janna's dad, and they even knew Grace would be alone without them during the church service. Had they been following them around this whole weekend, or was it something else?

If they were really what Janna thought, how could that be? Encounters like that happened only in the Bible.

"Well, we can't just stand here and do nothing. C'mon, there's something I need to show you upstairs." She grabbed Cade's hand and pulled him toward the door. "Mrs. Keever, can you stay here for a while to see if Grace comes back? My mother has my cell phone number if you need to reach us."

"Absolutely," Mrs. Keever said.

The parents of the other children in the room arrived in a thick herd. Janna pulled Cade through the crowd, and they raced up the stairs into the sanctuary, bursting through one of the side doors.

"Slow down, Janna." Cade caught his breath. "What did you want to show me?"

Janna shook her head. "I thought I was crazy at first—I don't know, maybe I still am, but look." Janna pulled him to the stained glass picture of Mary and the angel Gabriel and let go of his hand.

Cade's eyebrows wrinkled in confusion as he stared at the window. "I'm not sure I'm following you here."

"Look at the angel's face, Cade. His hair is different, but it's his face! It's Gabe's face!" As soon as the words escaped her mouth, Janna realized how insane she sounded.

Cade didn't seem to be catching the resemblance. He turned back to her. "What exactly are you saying, Janna?"

"Just hear me out, okay?" Janna bit her upper lip and looked around the sanctuary. "If my memory serves me right, the angel Gabriel appeared to Daniel, Zachariah, and Mary. The archangel Michael shows up several times in the Bible too. Angels even appeared to the shepherds at Jesus's birth."

Cade only blinked. "Yeah."

"Well, think about it, Cade."

"Okay." Cade ran his fingers down his chin and looked back to the window. "Are you saying you think the orderlies, Michael and Gabe are—" He stopped and stared back at Janna.

"Yes," Janna dragged out as she gave him one long nod. "That's what I'm saying."

Cade licked his lips and sighed. "That's a pretty, um, dramatic conclusion to arrive at, Janna. Aren't we throwing the whole 'they're her brothers' idea out the window a little quickly?"

"Haven't you heard a word I just said?"

"Yes, Janna. I heard everything you said, but—"

"The message 'Grace will find you' is true, Cade." Now that it was all coming together in Janna's mind, it didn't matter to her if Cade thought she was crazy. "Grace found you. Or technically, I guess you found her, but it doesn't matter. My mom was right. These were signs. The peonies, the messages in red, the strange visits from men nobody else can see. God is trying to tell us something."

"Now that's not entirely true, Janna. I know Kristin and Mrs. Keever didn't see Michael and Gabe, but that little boy Ryan did. Even your parents did."

Janna began pacing in front of the window, trying to come up with something to make Cade see that her theory was right. "I know, but children sometimes see what we choose to ignore. They don't need rational explanations to believe in the impossible. Maybe my parents could see them because they believe in signs from God, too," Janna said. "I don't know that I can explain this to you, Cade. But I know. I *know* I'm right."

Cade shook his head. "I'm not doubting your feeling here, Janna, but you do realize that you're starting to sound like my father, right?"

Janna turned back to the picture of Gabe in the stained glass window. "Maybe so, but you have to admit what he said was right. I *was* lost, and I came here looking for myself again," Janna's voice quivered. "I did come back for you. Just like he said."

She watched as Cade clenched his jaw a few times. He seemed to still be processing everything Janna had said.

"Pastor Mabry even said it this morning, Cade." Janna didn't take her eyes off the window. "After we suffer, we'll be restored. That's why God led me back here. That's why he led me back to you. I suffered because of what happened to Molly Ann Brenner. You've suffered tremendous loss over the past seven years. Your mom and now your dad, too." A tear splashed onto Janna's wrist as she looked down at the burgundy carpet. "And we suffered without each other. At least I know I did."

Cade walked to her and picked up her trembling hands. "I did suffer without you, Janna. And I don't ever want to lose you again."

He released her hands and caressed her face with his fingers for the third time, except this time he bent forward slightly. Janna could taste the salt from her tears as their lips met. They kissed only for a moment before Janna pulled back gently from Cade's face. She threw her arms around his waist as he encircled his arms around her protectively. They held each other for a few minutes before Cade pulled away from their tender embrace.

"Listen, Janna. Let's say you're right about all this. Maybe all the messages and flowers were signs, but I just know I won't feel right about anything until we've heard that from Michael and Gabe themselves. Where do you think we could find them?"

"The messages all said Grace will find you, right? Think back to when you first saw her. To where she found you, Cade. Where would she be?" Janna's eyes widened.

"The cornfield."

***

377

Cade and Janna peeled out of the parking lot, and made it to the cornfield in about ten minutes. Cade pulled the car over to the side of the road where he'd told Janna he'd found Grace walking along the stalks.

Shielding their eyes with their hands as the midday sun beat down above their heads, they scanned the cornfields for signs of anyone.

Their only companions were the crows picking up loose corn kernels from the ground.

Janna sighed. "I really thought she'd be here."

"I know, me too." Cade cupped his hands around his mouth, calling out, "Grace? Grace, are you out here? Please show us where you are."

"Grace, please come out and tell us what we're supposed to understand about all of this," Janna added.

Only the corn stalks answered them as the wind breezed through the field.

"What if she's gone? What if we never see her again?" Tears welled up in Janna's eyes.

How can this be it, God? What were you trying to tell us? What were you trying to teach us in all of this?

Janna looked up expecting to see Grace standing in front of them. She and Cade were still the only ones besides the crows in the cornfield.

"Where else would they have taken her?" Janna asked.

"I don't know, Janna. Maybe we should head back to the church and see if they left any more messages for us."

They walked back to the Cade's car, defeated. Janna feared the little girl they'd come to love might be gone forever. Why would God send her if he was going to take her back without an explanation? It wasn't fair.

The crows in the field squawked loudly before taking off for another field of corn. A loud rustling behind Cade and Janna caught their attention. They turned from the vehicle to see Grace step out of a row of stalks and turn her back to them, walking in the opposite direction. She ran her fingertips over each stalk, just like Cade said she had been doing when he found her.

"Grace, wait!" Janna called out, running to the girl and dropping to her knees at Grace's feet. "How did you get back here? Please tell us what's going on."

Grace stared deeply into Janna's eyes, exactly the way she had when Janna had met her a couple days ago. The little girl remained silent.

The stalks rustled a little as Gabe stepped into view behind Cade. "Don't you know by now?"

Cade stepped protectively to Janna's side as she stood. Grace turned and walked to Gabe, taking his hand.

"Then you are—" Janna pointed slowly to Gabe.

Michael stepped into view and took Grace's free hand. "Yes, we are."

"You finally read the message correctly, Janna," Gabe said, exchanging a smile with Grace. "Grace *will* find you."

A strange laugh bubbled up from Janna's chest. "Uh—forgive me, Gabe, but I don't understand." Janna looked to Cade's confused face. "We don't understand."

"You were never supposed to understand it. You were just supposed to believe."

"Believe what?" Janna had hoped that once they found either Michael or Gabe, they'd be able to clear up the confusion, but it was becoming more confusing by the second.

"When you're lost, the only way you find your way back is through grace," Gabe said matter-of-factly.

"Why didn't you tell us that from the beginning, then? Why go to the trouble of sending us all those cryptic messages and signs?"

"Would you have believed us if we'd just told you the truth?" Gabe smiled again but didn't wait for her to answer him. "He had to get your attention before he shared the message with you, Janna. If he hadn't used unusual means, you wouldn't have noticed it."

ALLISON GREEN MARTIN

For once in her life, no words came to Janna's lips. Gabe was right. Janna was always too consumed with being in control, being the one in charge. Somewhere along the way, she'd forgotten that she didn't have to do life alone.

Janna jumped as Cade cleared his throat. "Lots of people are suffering in this world. Lots of them begging God for an answer, begging him for grace," he said. "Why would he choose us?"

Gabe didn't miss a beat. "Because he was asked."

Janna thought about Stacy saying she and Brian had been praying for Janna's return. For her to reconcile with Cade. Janna knew her parents had been praying the same thing.

"So, you're saying that just because someone asked God to show us grace, He did it?" Janna was still missing something. She just wasn't sure what.

Gabe nodded and looked at Grace. "It's time for us to go."

"Wait. That's it?" Janna took a step forward. "That's all the answer we get?"

"What else do you need to know, Janna?"

Janna thought for a minute about Gabe's question. She had come home to find herself again, and in the meantime, she'd also found a fresh start with Cade. What more *could* she ask God for?

"Nothing, I guess." Tears began to form behind Janna's eyes. "It's just—we don't want Grace to leave us."

"Grace is all around you, Janna. Even when you can't see it. It finds you in small ways every day—in the beauty of bright pink peonies, in the majesty of a swarm of butterflies, or in a single act of forgiveness." Gabe nodded at Cade, who stepped closer to Janna and put his arm around her. "Grace is never far from either of you."

Janna watched as Grace removed the silver charm bracelet from her tiny wrist and walked to her. The small, silent girl, whom Janna had loved from the first moment she saw her, fastened the bracelet around Janna's wrist.

Janna ran her thumb over the word *Grace* engraved upon the bracelet. "Thank you," were the only two words she could muster.

Cade pulled Janna close to him again as they watched Gabe and Michael lead Grace back toward the field from where she'd emerged. Before Grace disappeared behind the waxy, green stalks for the last time, she turned back and smiled.

Shock set in as Janna and Cade walked back to the car and climbed in. Neither of them spoke as Cade started the engine. Janna felt like she was trapped in a strange dream again as Cade drove them back to the church.

Cade held the door to the fellowship hall open for Janna. They both walked numbly into the open room where everyone sat chatting and eating. Pastor Mabry approached them from a side table.

"Whenever you two want to look through those commentaries, we can head to my office as soon as you'd like."

Janna looked at Cade, who answered for her. "We appreciate that, sir. But I think we figured it out."

"Okay, great." Pastor Mabry smiled. "Well, if you change your mind, just let me know."

Cade and Janna nodded before making their way to the table where Brian, Stacy, and Janna's parents sat together.

"Oh, honey," Janna's mom said. "Mrs. Keever said you had to look for something—she couldn't remember what though. Did you find whatever it was?"

Janna smiled as she glanced around the table at her friends, her family, and the only man who'd ever held her heart. "Yes," Janna said, running her fingers over the word *Grace* etched into the silver bracelet she hid under the table. She reached for Cade's hand. "I found it."

ACKNOWLEDGEMENTS

A very special thank you to:

My first readers, Jane Green, Holly Hamrick, Pamela Lynch, Cathy Baker, and Tim Knopp for your honest feedback.

Every member of The Writer's Den and the Catawba Valley Christian Writers for your enthusiasm for the story and for helping me hone the details.

Naomi Bivins for telling me to "just do it."

Elizabeth Proctor for understanding the vision behind the cover and making it happen.

Calvin O. Ware for taking the time to read a very rough first draft and offering thoughtful encouragement.

Ryan, Finn, and Lydia for being the best of everything in my life.

"…with God all things are possible." ~ Matthew 19:26

www.ingramcontent.com/pod-product-compliance
Lightning Source LLC
Chambersburg PA
CBHW030806260626
47169CB00001B/213